# THE BARGAIN OF A BARONESS

LINDA RAE SANDE

Twisted Teacup
PUBLISHING

The Conundrum of a Clerk

The Charity of a Viscount

***The Cousins of the Aristocracy***

The Promise of a Gentleman

The Pride of a Gentleman

***The Holidays of the Aristocracy***

The Christmas of a Countess

The Knot of a Knight

***The Heirs of the Aristocracy***

The Angel of an Astronomer

The Puzzle of a Bastard

The Choice of a Cavalier

The Bargain of a Baroness

The Jewel of an Earl's Heir

The Vixen of a Viscount

***Beyond the Aristocracy***

The Pleasure of a Pirate

***Stella of Akrotiri***

Origins

Deminon

Diana

# PROLOGUE

*S*ummer 1815, Cherrywood Estate, Derbyshire, England

Under a canopy of blue sky, Hannah Simpson lay on the freshly scythed lawn and stared up. The sun had long ago burned away the morning dew, but it hadn't yet made it high enough to blind her as she watched the white clouds float overhead.

Hannah had a thought her mother would be cross if she knew she didn't have a blanket beneath her. A maid would be forced to remove grass stains from her gown if she wasn't careful. Her thoughts turned to more pleasant subjects, such as the elephant that had formed from a single cloud and was now chasing—very slowly—a turtle.

She recalled how the day before, Graham had, for the very first time in his eleven years, lifted her hand to his lips and kissed the back of it. He and his parents, Thomas and Emma Wellingham, had just arrived at Cherrywood, the Burroughs' family country estate in Derbyshire, for a rare holiday away from town.

Hannah lifted that very hand so it hovered above her

eyes, blocking out the golden ball of light that threatened to blind her.

Had Graham noticed how her hand had trembled in his? How her pulse quickened with his touch? How a pink blush colored her face and every bit of skin above the neckline of her sprigged muslin gown?

"It's good to see you again, Miss Hannah," he had said before he stepped back and bowed.

"And you. It's been far too long," she had responded, only a hint of a scold in her voice.

They both lived on the same street in London, after all, although Graham and his parents sometimes made the trip to their real home, Woodscastle, in Chiswick. The townhouse in King Street had been his mother's before her marriage to Thomas Wellingham, and they used it when travel to Chiswick proved difficult.

The Simpson townhouse—practically a mansion—was directly across the street.

"School," Graham had replied, in answer to her scold. "When it's done, I promise I shall see more of you." All at once, his face had reddened, his eyes darting sideways as he realized what he had said.

Hannah had giggled at the thought of what he might be thinking. "If we're to be married, then I expect that will be true," she countered, hoping to assuage his embarrassment.

*H*annah had often wondered what life with Graham Wellingham would be like when they did finally marry. Their parents had frequently spoken of a day when the two would wed. Talked as if a marriage had already been arranged in some formal sense.

The Wellinghams—Thomas and Emma—were good friends with her parents, Sophia and James Simpson. Emma had acted as midwife when Hannah was born. Hannah's older twin brother, Henry, had been too impatient to await Emma's arrival that fateful night when four babies had been born to three mothers.

Graham, nine months younger than those babes, had probably been conceived that night.

The sunlight that warmed Hannah's face suddenly disappeared. "You look like an angel."

Hannah blinked as she dropped her hand to her midriff. Although the one who interrupted her reverie was cast in shadow, she knew immediately it was Graham. She grinned. "You say that as if you've actually seen one," she chided.

Graham lowered his gangly body to the grass and stretched out next to her. "Every time I see you," he said with a wink. His gaze moved to take in the clouds above them, and he allowed a guffaw. "I thought you might be napping, but now I know you are deciding who will win the race."

Hannah giggled. "The race?" she repeated.

"There's an elephant chasing a turtle," he said as he pointed to the clouds directly above them, "and a race horse, too."

Continuing to giggle as she followed his finger, her eyes widened when she saw exactly what he described.

"So, are you betting on the turtle? Or the race horse?" he asked, his gaze turning to her.

Hannah allowed a brilliant smile as her hand once again shielded her eyes. "I don't see a finish line."

"If I was the turtle?"

Hannah turned her head in the grass to regard him, sobering at his question. "I would bet on the turtle, of course. But why ever would you cast yourself as the turtle rather than the horse?" she asked in a whisper.

"Because a turtle will live far longer than the horse," he replied, his hand reaching for hers.

Closing her eyes to concentrate on the warmth of her hand in his, Hannah grinned and allowed a long sigh. "Promise?"

Graham turned his head in the grass. "And if I do?"

Hannah's eyes fluttered open, and she angled her head to regard him through blades of grass that had escaped the edge of the scythe. "Then I suppose I shall have to marry you," she said with a prim grim.

"Promise?" he countered.

Her brows furrowing at the seriousness in his expression, Hannah said, "Of course."

"And if the horse wins the race?"

Hannah lifted herself onto an elbow and stared down at Graham. "Are you asking me to place a wager on this race?"

Graham inhaled as his gaze once again went skyward to see that the elephant was no longer, its shape pulled apart into a series of wispy clouds. Only the shapes of a horse and a turtle remained above them. "Only to agree to a bargain," he finally replied.

Inhaling sharply, Hannah directed her attention to the clouds and allowed a sound of disappointment. "He's gone," she whispered.

"The turtle is still there," Graham countered.

"As I suspect he always will be," Hannah murmured. "I'll make you a bargain, Graham Wellingham. No matter what happens—no matter who wins the race—I will be your wife one day," she vowed.

Graham allowed a brilliant smile. "Quite a bargain, considering I have not yet proposed marriage," he teased. An 'oof' escaped his lips when Hannah pounded a fist onto his midsection. "As if we have any say in the matter," she said in complaint.

He inhaled slowly and lifted one of her hands to his lips. "We do, and we shall. Miss Hannah Simpson, I accept the terms of your bargain."

Settling back onto the grass with a grin of victory, Hannah's attention was once again captured by the clouds.

The horse had won this particular race, although his shape had shifted with the slight breeze, his legs breaking away into wisps and his head separating from his body. A moment later, there was no sign of the horse.

The turtle, however, continued its slow crawl across the sky.

# CHAPTER 1

## A GENTLEMAN AWAKENS
## WITH A START

*onday, March 25, 1839*

The sky was barely gray when Henry Simpson's eyes opened with a start. His gaze swept past the ornate blue fabric canopy above his bed and to the window. Thinking that whatever woke him was behind the drapes and beyond the glass, he stepped out of the bed and hurried to the window.

The air surrounding him was chilly. Henry was sure he saw his breath when he exhaled. The last chunk of coal in the fireplace was barely a burning ember, and it was far too early for his valet to arrive with more.

Pulling the drapes apart, he quickly discovered the source of the sound that had awakened him.

Neighing horses. Two of them. From the looks of their coats and their size, Henry was sure they were shires.

Almost directly across the street, a glossy black town coach hitched to those shires had stopped in front of the townhouse located at 3 King Street. Their heads bobbing, the horses stomped their impatience at having been halted.

He watched as the driver stepped down from his perch and opened the coach door, moving aside to allow the equipage's lone occupant to emerge.

Having paid witness to this scene at least two other times —both Monday mornings at dawn—Henry knew exactly what, or rather whom, to expect to step down from the coach.

A rather comely young woman.

She was always garbed in a fine wool redingote and a stylish, warm hat. She always carried a valise, and she always gave the driver a curtsy before she hurried to the red door. Then she would use a key to gain entrance and disappear behind the door.

For the brief moment after she stepped over the threshold, but just before she shut the door, she glanced up and down the street as she removed her fashionable hat and gave the driver a final wave before he set the horses into motion.

That's when Henry had the chance to see her crown of blonde curly hair. A moment to take in her pleasant expression, as if she was glad to have arrived at the townhouse of Emma and Thomas Wellingham. A second to determine she possessed a porcelain complexion and cheeks blushed pink from the cold. And another to watch as she turned and shut the red door against the morning chill.

This morning, she afforded him a longer look. For after she stepped down from the coach, she rushed to stand in front of the two horses, one gloved hand raised so she could shake her forefinger at them.

The two horses immediately quieted, and their heads dropped. Then the young woman pulled a couple of apples from her reticule. She held first one and then the other to each horse and watched as they downed them. Next, she dipped a curtsy and displayed a brilliant smile.

Henry blinked, sure the horses bowed their heads to her curtsy. He blinked again when he was sure she had briefly directed her attention on him, giving him as large a smile as she had afforded the horses.

A moment later, and the young woman and her valise disappeared behind the red door.

Henry allowed a long sigh of disappointment as he let the drape settle back into place. Given it was too early to be rising for the day—he usually had his valet wake him at seven o'clock so he would be ready for breakfast with his parents before he departed for the Bank of England—he crawled back into his still-warm bed and replayed the young woman's arrival in his mind's eye.

He imagined what it would be like to meet her at the curb. What he might say in response to learning who she was and why she always arrived so early at the Wellingham townhouse on Monday mornings.

Was she related to the Wellinghams? Or was she a servant of some sort? Her clothing certainly suggested she was a woman of some means, but Henry had long ago learned appearances could be deceiving.

Maids were often given their mistress' cast-offs, both clothing and shoes.

He had thought it might be easy to gain an introduction, but with the Wellinghams leaving so early for their positions at Wellingham Imports every morning but Sunday, and usually returning well after dark, Henry found he couldn't invent an excuse that would have him paying a call on them whilst the young woman was in residence.

Staring at the dark blue velvet above him and then the matching counterpane that covered most of the bed and a few of the pillows, Henry imagined what she might look like with the velvet wrapped around her body. From his brief sightings of her, he was sure she had a pleasant figure beneath the broad skirt of her otherwise fitted redingote.

He imagined what it might be like to unwrap the soft blue fabric from her body. What she might do as he peeled back the velvet and revealed her nakedness. What it might be like to smooth his hands over her silky soft skin.

How would she react if his hands were cold? Would her skin pebble with goosebumps much like his mistress' had? Back when he employed a mistress? Letitia always squealed and scolded him when he attempted to warm his hands on her.

Or would she welcome his touch? Lean into it and cover his hands with her own to guide them over the places she wanted cooled?

Henry closed his eyes and imagined what it might be like to have a lover he didn't have to pay for the privilege of a shared evening. What it might be like to have a lover who looked forward to spending time with him as much as he looked forward to spending time with her. A lover who sometimes made the first overture.

His eyes shot open as he considered his father had such a lover.

His mother!

The two were hopelessly in love. Hopelessly devoted to one another.

And so happy.

Was it too much to ask for the same for himself?

His thoughts went back to the young woman he had spied from his window.

Only by accident had he discovered the young woman took her leave on Saturday afternoons, and then only because he happened to be in the front parlor for tea with his mother when the same black coach and driver stopped and waited for a time until she appeared from behind the red door and stepped up and into the coach.

Of course his mother had noticed his attention on the window rather than on his cake or cup of tea. The twinkle in her eye had him giving her a quelling glance, until he thought she might know the identity of the young woman.

"Who is she?" he had asked, thinking she of all people would know.

"Would you like me to find out for you?"

The enthusiasm in her query had him immediately shaking his head. "No," he had replied before he quickly turned the conversation to the upcoming theatre season offerings.

Now he wished he had expressed more interest.

Then he thought of what he feared she might be.

A housemaid.

He wasn't sure why a housemaid seemed unacceptable. His father had been in service at one time. He had been a butler—the head butler of the large estate home of Merriweather Manor near Chiswick.

That had been long before Henry was born, though. Long before his parents were known as reputable landlords of a string of townhouses in King Street.

Long after his widowed mother's disappearance from Merriweather Manor had set the *ton's* tongues to wagging as to what might have happened to her.

No one would have guessed Sophia, Lady Grandby, youngest daughter of a duke and aunt to the current Duke of Ariley, had married the butler.

Sometimes love made for some hard choices. And sometime it resulted in the best decisions.

If the comely young woman was indeed a housemaid, Henry decided he could at least give her the benefit of a doubt. Discover more about her.

Who knew? She could already be married.

But he doubted it.

As he nodded off to sleep, his mind filled with images of her naked body tucked against him, Henry vowed he would discover who she was.

And whoever she was, he vowed he would not be *too* disappointed.

# CHAPTER 2

## PREPARING TO PAINT

*eanwhile, across the street at 3 King Street*
The sensation of being watched was so powerful, Miss Laura Overby nearly glanced over her shoulder as she let herself into the Wellingham residence.

It wasn't the first time she had sensed someone watching her. The hairs on the back of her neck prickled only the Saturday before when she was leaving the Wellingham residence to return to her parents' townhouse. Then there was the Monday prior when the sky was still gray at the time of her arrival in King Street.

On that particular morn, she had spotted a young boy in front of a nearby townhouse. Still dressed in his sleeping gown, he had no doubt escaped the nursery and hadn't yet been missed by his nursemaid. He stared at her as if he thought she might thwart his attempt to run away. Even before she was past the Wellingham's threshold, though, a servant captured the urchin and returned him to the residence.

Laura grinned at the memory, but a quick glance at that

particular townhouse proved the boy hadn't repeated his attempt at an escape.

She allowed her gaze to sweep up and down the side of the street, acting as if she might be looking for the source of a particular sound, but there was no one nearby.

Laura knew it wasn't the driver of the Overby coach. He had already bounded up onto the box and was about to set the horses in motion. Horses she had just calmed with some apples she had pilfered from the pantry at her parents' townhouse in Curzon Street.

So that left the other side of the street, including the window to which she had directed her attention ever so briefly just a few moments ago.

Lifting her valise and pausing a moment on the threshold to once again glance up and down King Street, Laura was struck by how little traffic there was on a street that had at one time been far busier. The addition of nearby Regency Street had relieved the congestion on King as well as replaced the part of King that had at one time connected its northernmost end directly to Oxford Street.

Seeing only a few passersby, none of whom seemed the least bit interested in her, Laura was closing the door when she once again caught sight of the face in a third-story window across the street. Pretending not to notice, she continued to shut the door until she heard the latch click into place. Then she hurried into the front salon and peeked around the closed drapes just in time to see the face move in the window.

Move and then disappear.

A rather handsome face, she thought. Angular in a strong sort of way, with high cheekbones. Although she couldn't make out his eyes from her brief glance, she knew his head was topped with light-colored hair.

Perhaps he was the husband she had learned about from

the lady of that house. If so, he appeared on the younger side, but then Laura hadn't yet learned the woman's age. Lady Simpson had the good fortune of possessing ageless beauty. She could have been forty or eighty years of age for all Laura knew.

"Is something the matter?"

Laura whirled around to discover Emma Fitzsimmons Wellingham regarding her from the salon's doorway. The subject of her current painting, Emma was resplendent in a teal dinner gown, her hair caught up in a simple but elegant bun atop her head. "No, ma'am. I was checking on the morning light," she replied as she dipped a curtsy. "In a few minutes, there should be enough of it."

"I so appreciate you coming this early on a Monday morn," Emma said as she moved to the fireplace. "Mrs. Larsen will bring tea in a few minutes. I trust you had a good visit with your family yesterday?"

"I did. Thank you for asking."

"How is the baby?"

Laura allowed a smile as she moved to the valise and opened it. "Todd is not so little any longer," she replied, referring to her youngest brother. "He's just started walking. Emily is excited for her come-out this week, and Stephen and William have a new tutor, although Father believes he might hire another given the difference in my brothers' ages."

"I'm surprised Mr. Overby hasn't sent your oldest brother to Eton," Emma remarked. William Overby Sr. was one of Wellingham Imports' most valued employees, a broker for imported goods from the Far East.

William had begun his tenure as a caddy to her husband when he was still a street urchin. Upon the death of his mother, the warehouse manager, Stephen Bingham, had adopted William and his sister, Kate, and had raised them as his own.

Given such humble beginnings and his status as a commoner, it was a surprise when Lady Lily, the illegitimate sister of the Earl of Trenton, chose William to be her husband. But she had at one time been a housemaid and then a lady's maid to Emma's half-sister, Samantha.

"I know he has considered sending him off to school," Laura said, pulling several tubes of paint from a satchel, "but I think Mother would miss him too much. She might be an earl's sister, but I think she favors the life of a commoner. For all of us."

For a moment, Emma considered the comment. Lady Lily could have chosen a life of privilege. A husband who was an aristocrat—she'd had at least four suitors besides William who were—but instead she had set her cap on William.

That had been over twenty years ago. Their children's births had been spread out over that time. Laura was the oldest followed by her sister, Emily.

"Besides, Mother has heard too many stories of what the boys do to get into trouble at Eton," Laura went on as she pulled several brushes from the valise. "But I think she'll be glad when he goes to university. Less chaos in the house."

"Todd will be three by then," Emma said, her eyes twinkling in delight. She remembered very well how her only child, Graham, had behaved at that age.

"If you're implying there will be *more* chaos, then you catch her meaning perfectly," Laura said with a giggle. "Father has offered to hire a nursemaid with every birth, but Mother insists on seeing to the babes herself."

"So... you don't miss living there when you're staying here?" Emma asked carefully.

A blush colored Laura's face. "Would you think me a terrible person if I said I do not?"

Emma allowed a chuckle. "I was an only child, so I am not familiar with having brothers and sisters," she replied. "I do wish I had grown up with my half-sister, though." Her gaze went to a painting of a Yorkshire landscape on the wall above the settee. "Samantha, my half-sister, painted that during the first year of her marriage to Ethan, Marquess of Plymouth," she explained. She didn't add that it had been the same year Samantha learned Emma was her sister. Emma had known far longer, but only because she had discovered letters her late father had received from Samantha's mother, Caroline, Viscountess Chamberlain.

"I wondered if it was a Fitzsimmons," Laura said in awe, her attention going to the painting of a castle on the moors near the sea. "My mother has a Fitzsimmons in her salon. It was a gift from her brother," she added, referring to the Earl of Trenton. "I've heard there are others here in London."

"I have one in my office," Emma said as her brow quirked. "It was painted during the spring, and the greens depicted in the pasture are exactly as they appear in Derbyshire during that time of the year." She paused as she watched Laura strip a Dutch cloth from a canvas that was mounted on a wooden easel. "Have you given a thought to painting landscapes?"

Laura shook her head. "I have not, but that is only because I have lived here in London my entire life. I hardly think the squares can be considered landscapes. Perhaps I will find a good landscape should I ever travel outside of London."

"I rather imagine you would be as skilled at landscapes as you are at portraits," Emma replied, her gaze going to the back of the canvas. Although she could have peeked at what lay beneath the Dutch cloth at any time the day before, she had resisted the urge, deciding to wait until she was invited to do so by the artist. "Let me know when you'd like me to resume my pose."

"I'll be but a minute," Laura replied as she turned to

regard the canvas on the easel. The painting, very close to completion, displayed Emma as a well-to-do gentlewoman. Dressed in an elegant dinner gown of deep teal and accessorized with jewels that included aquamarines and sapphires at her ears, around her neck and one wrist, a quick glance would have the viewer believing Emma was an aristocrat.

Given her relationship to so many, it was an easy assumption to make. Her late father's brother was Viscount Chamberlain, the head of the Foreign Office. His cousin, Temperance, was the Countess of Mayfield. Emma's half-sister, Samantha, was the Marchioness of Plymouth. And Emma was married to Thomas Wellingham, whose cousin, Gabriel, was the Earl of Trenton.

For the last few weeks, Emma had been sitting—or standing, rather—for a portrait her husband had insisted on having painted. "For my office," he had explained. "So I can look at you whenever I wish."

"My office is directly behind yours," she had argued, thinking his reason a folly. Reminded he was far too inundated with paperwork to rise from his desk and make his way to hers, Emma had acquiesced and arranged for Laura to do the painting along with another to be kept secret from Thomas.

Laura had agreed with the proviso that she be allowed to live with the Wellinghams—except on Sundays—until such time as the paintings were complete.

Emma was happy to grant Laura the use of the guest bedchamber and have Laura join her and Thomas at the dinner table every evening. Their London home had grown far too quiet over the intervening years since their son's departure for Boston, and they rarely made the trip to Chiswick to spend time at Woodscastle.

. . .

oving to the window, Emma opened the drapes and arranged the gathers in the sheers that covered the glass until they were even. As she did so, she noticed a face in a window across the street. Recognizing Henry Simpson, she gave a wave and grinned when he acknowledged her with a salute.

"Mr. Simpson is certainly up early this morning," she remarked as she made her way to where she had stood for an hour every day for the past fortnight.

"Mr. Simpson?" Laura repeated. "Do you mean Lady Simpson's husband?"

Emma grinned. "Her son, actually. He's a clerk at the Bank of England. I noticed him in a window across the street," she explained. "Probably his bedchamber window given its height."

Laura's eyes widened, and she wondered if he had been the one watching her. "Lady Simpson has been ever so kind to share her tea with me," she said as she carefully moved the easel closer to the window and angled it so the filtered light illuminated it.

As if her words were a cue, Mrs. Larsen, the housekeeper, appeared at the door carrying the tea tray.

"Oh, please do the honors, Mrs. Larsen. We're just getting started," Emma said from where she stood in front of the fireplace.

The housekeeper dipped a curtsy and went about preparing the cups of tea. She placed one on the table next to Emma and gave the other to a grateful Laura before she took her leave.

Laura drank deeply before she set aside the cup. A surreptitious glance out the window confirmed she could see the first two stories of windows across the street, which meant she could be seen from them.

The thought had her wondering if Lady Simpson's son was watching. Could he see her through the sheers as she mixed paints into a flesh color? Watch as she began applying them to the part of the painting where one of Emma's hands was resting on a plinth? There was no plinth in the parlor, but Laura had fashioned one from a stack of books on a side table. Behind her subject, the fireplace was acting as the edge of a Greek temple.

Had his mother made mention of her to him?

"I'm so happy you and Lady Simpson met. I should have introduced you the first week you were here."

"I was happy to make her acquaintance," Laura replied. "I think she is lonely in that large townhouse," she added, not taking her attention from the canvas.

"She'd like another grandchild or two," Emma remarked.

Laura paused her brush mid-stroke. "Doesn't she already have... *eleven*, I think she said?"

Emma tittered. "Indeed, but she has only the one by way of her daughter, Hannah, and now that Lady Harrington is widowed, I suppose Lady Simpson thinks it's time her son marry."

"Past time," Laura confirmed as she continued her work on Emma's fingers. "Apparently he hasn't courted anyone, but he grows longer in the tooth every day."

"I've often wondered why he hasn't taken a wife," Emma murmured. "When he was a young buck, the young ladies flocked to him at balls and such. He was so amiable."

"And handsome," Laura put in. She cleared her throat. "At least, according to his mother." The face she had seen in the window had to have been him, she decided.

Once again, Emma struggled to keep from laughing. "He *was* handsome. He's *still* handsome, and given how his father has managed to remain so despite his age, I rather expect Henry will keep his handsome appearance as well."

"So his mother does not exaggerate?" Laura murmured, changing brushes.

"She does not," Emma replied. After a pause, she asked, "Has she offered to introduce you?"

Laura paused in mid-stroke. "Pardon?"

"Has she offered to introduce you to her son?" Emma clarified.

Resuming her work, Laura considered how to respond. "She has not. But I rather imagine she wants him wed to the daughter of a peer."

Emma frowned. "I've never had that impression from her," she argued.

Pausing her work again, Laura glanced back out the window, almost letting out a yelp when she realized Henry was watching her.

Dressed in a fashionable great coat and having just donned a top hat, he disappeared from view when a town coach pulled up and stopped. Before it continued down the street, she was sure he was gazing at her out the coach window.

A frisson passed through her entire body, for the way he stared at her was most disconcerting. Most disarming. Alarming, really.

For she had seen that look in her father's eyes every time he returned from Wellingham Imports and took her mother's hand in hers to kiss it. Every time he leaned forward and kissed her on the cheek. Every time he rose from the dinner table and suggested it was time for bed.

Laura was old enough to know what such a look meant. In the case of her father, it was most certainly love, for he professed it every morning and every night to her mother, even when all the children were present.

But she knew there was more to it.

Lust.

Even before she had formed the thought in her head, her nipples tightened and a blush covered her face. She inhaled sharply and held the breath a moment.

"Laura?"

She gave a start, careful to pull the brush away from the canvas lest she make an errant stroke. "Yes?"

A slow smile spread over Emma's face. "It was *him*, was it not?"

Realizing she'd been caught staring out the window, Laura gave a slight shrug. "I... I really can't say. Just someone getting into a coach." She resumed her work, humming softly.

Emma's smile settled into a grin of satisfaction, but she said nothing.

## CHAPTER 3

## COUSINS REUNITE

*M*arch 29, 1839, at Grandby & Son, 300 Oxford Street, London

Graham Wellingham stepped from a worn hansom cab and regarded the front of his cousin's place of business a moment. He let out a low whistle before he made his way to the front door on legs still adapting to dry land.

A secretary watched from behind an elegant marble-topped counter as he made his way along the corridor, his expression betraying his initial revulsion at seeing who he thought might be a beggar invading the premises. Then his eyes widened in recognition. "Mr. Wellingham?"

"How do, Mr. Adams? Is Thomas about?" Graham had barely finished his query when he turned to discover the subject of his search hurrying from behind a mahogany desk.

"Graham?" Tom Grandby halted on the threshold of his office and regarded his cousin with a look of shock. Not only was Graham several years older than when he'd last seen him, he was sporting a short, thick beard and clothes suggesting he had taken up farming in the country. "How are you here?"

Graham gripped Tom's proffered hand and shook it

before he said, "I stowed away on the *Alanzaar*. We arrived in Wapping early this morning. Thought I'd stop here first to discover if I still have a home to go to."

Tom grinned and indicated he should join him in his office. Graham followed him into the elegant room, his attention diverted to the artifacts on display at one end of the carpeted and wood-paneled office. "I see you've made your fortune," he muttered as he admired an Ancient Greek vase, a globe made entirely of Brazilian lapis lazuli, and a marble statue of Dionysus.

"With a good deal of Father's help," Tom admitted. "He's pretending to be retired now and rarely comes into the office."

"Got tired of funding railway lines?" Graham guessed.

Tom chuckled. "I think he grew tired of the travel required," he countered, "although these days he takes Mother with him. They're in Yorkshire at the moment. A pleasure trip, he claims." He paused as he moved to the credenza behind his desk. "Now that I have married, I'm of the same mind." He waited for Graham's reaction and wasn't surprised at seeing his cousin's look of shock.

"*Married?*" Graham repeated. He stared at Tom as if he'd been shot. Then he glanced back toward the office door before turning his attention back to Tom. "Who are you, and what have you done with Thomas Grandby?"

"It happens to the best of us," Tom said with a sheepish expression.

"Do I know her?"

Tom indicated the chair in front of his desk, and Graham settled himself into the soft leather. "Lady Victoria," Tom said as he poured brandy into two crystal rummers.

Graham furrowed a brow. "Somerset's daughter?" he finally guessed, referring to Jeremy Statton, Duke of Somerset. His eyes widened. "*You* married a duke's daughter?"

Grinning, Tom nodded. "We live at Fairmont Park, an estate just north of London. She trains horses. And of course me, at times." He offered a glass to Graham, who took it with an appreciative nod.

"I cannot believe you went off and got married," Graham whispered, his expression having sobered.

"I wasn't looking to marry when I took her as a client," Tom said in a quiet voice. "But now I cannot imagine..." He allowed the sentence to trail off. "Well, let's just say I was smitten, and now I'm in love."

"Children?"

Tom shook his head. "Not yet. We've only been married a couple of months, but..." He gave a shrug. "I expect to be a father before Christmas," he whispered hoarsely.

"You'll make an excellent father. All that experience from having so many brothers and sisters," Graham remarked. He knew because he had grown up in the same household at Woodscastle.

Graham had nine other cousins besides Tom.

"I appreciate the sentiment."

"What about your uncle, Henry?" Graham asked, referring to Henry Simpson. "Has he finally been caught in the parson's mousetrap?"

"Henry?" Tom repeated as he grinned. "No. And he's not courting anyone, either, which has both my grandmother and Aunt Hannah vexed beyond measure." He noted how Graham jerked at the mention of Hannah. Henry's twin sister and Graham had been close growing up. Most thought the two would be a married couple before they reached their majorities. Instead, a whirlwind courtship had Hannah accepting an offer of marriage from someone else.

"And you?"

Graham settled back in his chair and finally took a deep breath. "No wife. No child. Despite the Boston matrons who insisted their daughters would be perfect for me," he claimed with a roll of his eyes.

"I hear there is a good deal of wealth in Boston," Tom said, his brows waggling as if he referred to young ladies' dowries.

"That I can attest to," Graham agreed. "Given how much I've brought back with me. In fact, is your older brother still a banker?"

Tom nodded. "Roger is at Barclay's, yes, but you'd be better off leaving it with Burroughs at the Bank of England."

"Lord Andrew is still a banker?" Graham asked in surprise. "He must be—"

"Retired now, yes, but his son, James, has taken his place." When Graham gave a start, he added, "He just returned to London at the end of December and married Emily in January."

Graham blinked. "Cousin Em?"

Allowing a chuckle, Tom said, "She's four-and-twenty, and Mother was over the moon happy she didn't have to do anything for the wedding."

When suspicion clouded Graham's expression, Tom added, "She *wanted* a quick wedding. Once she set her cap on poor James, there was nothing to be done for him."

"She didn't marry for affection?" Graham asked, his brows furrowed with concern for his youngest female cousin.

"Oh, she did. James adores her," Tom replied. "Has since she was a child, I think. They are like two peas in a pod. Practically live in the library of their townhouse in Curzon Street."

Graham's expression softened. "I am glad for her. I shall have to pay a call once I've finished with all the immediate requirements of my return."

Frowning, Tom put forth the next logical question. "Pray tell, what brought you back from Boston?"

Not yet ready to admit the real reason for his return to British shores, Graham said, "It was time. I've got a trustworthy partner—and part owner—seeing to the business there, and I'm thinking from his recent letters that Father wants me to take over the business here. Which I'm happy to do."

His father, Thomas Wellingham, had inherited an import and export concern from Graham's grandfather and then proceeded to build Wellingham Imports into a thriving business. Graham's mother, Emma, was the head accomptant and had been overseeing a room full of clerks since before she had married his father back in 1802.

"Have you been out to Woodscastle yet?" Tom asked, referring to their childhood home in Chiswick.

"Haven't made it that far."

"I don't think your parents have been there in months. They spend their nights in the townhouse in King Street," Tom explained. "But I'm sure your bedchamber at Woodscastle is still the way you left it."

Graham sighed. "At the moment, I would be happy sleeping on a floor," he murmured. "Been sleeping in a hammock on the ship these past few weeks."

"No need to do that," Tom countered, his brows furrowing. "Do you need a ride? In fact..." He glanced over the papers on his desk. "I will take you there. I have my phaeton, and there are still some things in my bedchamber there I haven't yet moved to Fairmont Park."

Not about to turn down the offer of a ride, Graham said, "Much appreciated. Father isn't expecting me—or the shipment I came with—until tomorrow, so I think it best I take a shower bath, shave, and get some sleep. Maybe go to Brooks's later tonight in the event Father is there."

"Long night?"

"Long month," Graham replied. "I'm not much for sea

travel. I never would have made it in the navy," he added before sipping the brandy. He allowed a sigh of satisfaction. "This is heavenly. Do you get it from a French smuggler?"

Tom grinned as he shook his head. "The same shop in Jermyn Street from which we all get the stuff," he replied, referring to Berry Bros. His manner sobered as he leaned forward. "Is there perhaps another reason for your return to British shores?"

Graham jerked upright, pretending surprise at hearing the query, but then he remembered who sat across from him. "Mother wrote to me."

"I rather imagine Aunt Emma writes to you frequently," Tom hedged. With ships contracted by Wellingham Imports making the trip back and forth across the Atlantic at regular intervals, it was likely correspondence was included with the goods.

"She does," Graham admitted. He dipped his head and then drank more of the brandy.

"So she told you about my Uncle Charlie's death."

Glowering, Graham said, "He might have been your uncle, but he was my Achilles' heel."

Tom winced. "He didn't know you held a candle for Aunt Hannah—"

"I know. And I didn't fight him for her back when I had the chance."

The words settled like a stone between them, and Tom leaned back into his chair, as if he feared his cousin would take a swing at him. "I often wondered about that," he prompted.

Graham took a steadying breath. "We were both so young," he murmured, referring to Tom's aunt, Hannah Simpson. "And I needed the chance to make my way in life. A few years to prove myself at the business. Make some blunt. Buy a townhouse in Westminster or Mayfair."

Tom nodded his understanding. "Hannah always had a steady stream of admirers," he countered. His father's half-sister, Hannah, had been born in 1803 and was two years older than Tom and almost a year older than Graham. As the daughter of a duke's daughter and her second husband—a man who at one time had been a butler—Hannah had straddled two worlds. She had embraced her aristocratic relatives as much as she did those of the working class.

From the time they were children, Graham had been raised to believe Hannah would one day be his wife.

He had counted on it.

So when Baron Charles Harrington, heir to the Mayfield earldom, announced he would be taking Hannah as his wife and future countess at the third ball of the Little Season of 1821, Graham thought it was some sort of sick joke.

A visit from Hannah two days later confirmed what the gossip rags had printed.

She had accepted the baron's offer.

Despite the bargain she had struck when they were younger, she had agreed to marry another. Graham was on a ship bound for Boston the following week.

Nearly eighteen years later, his mother's letter with word of Hannah's year of mourning nearly at an end had Graham turning over his duties to his partner, Benton Sinclair, at Wellingham Imports in Boston and returning to England on the next ship.

"Will you fight for her now?" Tom asked in a whisper.

Graham drained the brandy. "I shouldn't have to," he replied in a hoarse whisper.

Tom gave him a quelling glance. "There are as many men anxious to wed her—or bed her—now as there were when she agreed to marry Harrington," he warned.

Wincing, Graham said, "But she made a bargain with *me*. And this turtle intends to collect."

# CHAPTER 4

## AN HEIR APPARENT RETURNS

*eanwhile, at Harrington House in Park Lane, Mayfair*

The black town coach might have been glossy when it departed from Eton, but it was covered with splatters of mud and a little layer of dust by the time it covered the three-and-twenty miles to the Earl of Mayfield's mansion in Park Lane.

Baron Edward Harrington, son of the late Charles Harrington and now heir-apparent to the Mayfield earldom, stepped down from the coach and regarded the stucco-covered brick pile that stood before him.

Until he had left for Windsor when he was twelve years old, Harrington House had been his home. At some point in the future, Stanley Harrington, Earl of Mayfield, would die of what would most assuredly be old age, and Edward would inherit not only the earldom, but also the house.

When he had left Eton that morning, he thought he couldn't wait.

Now he was having second thoughts.

Apparently, his grandfather was still spending his blunt on horses and stables rather than on the upkeep of the house. The gardener obviously hadn't paid a call since the autumn before, and soot stained the stucco. At least the green wrought iron fence looked as if it were still in good repair, and the pavement in front had recently been swept clean.

Edward gave a nod to the liveried footman who was seeing to his trunk as he took a deep breath and headed for the front door.

The dark blue door opened even before he had a chance to use the lion head brass knocker. Potter, as ancient as he had been when Edward was but a tot, stood, stooped nearly in half, and actually displayed an almost toothless grin at seeing him.

"Potter, you haven't aged a day," Edward said with a brilliant smile.

"You lie like a rug, sir," the butler responded, his aged laugh sending him into spasms of a cough that had been with the servant for over a decade.

"Oh, that's one I'll have to remember," Edward said as he entered the vestibule. He blinked as he surveyed the interior. "Let me guess. Mother finally convinced her ladyship a renovation was required."

"Truth be told, I don't think she asked," Potter replied in a hoarse whisper.

"Is she in residence?"

"She is. I'll let her know—"

"I'll surprise her," Edward said, knowing it would take the butler at least ten minutes to make his way up the stairs to the first floor parlor. "Any idea where I might find her?"

"Right here, actually," Hannah Simpson Harrington said, stepping from somewhere beyond the vestibule to regard her son with a mixture of surprise, happiness, and annoyance. "Did you... did you get expelled from school?"

Edward's jaw dropped at the same time his brows arched.

"Mother! Easter is this Sunday. I have the week to attend the entertainments before classes resume," he replied.

Hannah let out a gasp of relief and hurried to pull her son into a hug. "I'm so sorry. I have lost track of time and of the calendar," she claimed, right before she kissed his cheek and then stepped back to regard him. "Are you getting enough to eat?"

"Yes, Mother. But I could always do with more," he replied as he patted his flat mid-section.

Turning to Potter, Hannah said, "Tea in the parlor, as soon as it can be arranged. Just a couple of cakes. And let's do have a luncheon in the breakfast parlor."

"A cold collation has already been arranged, my lady," Potter replied.

Blinking, Hannah regarded the butler a moment before she turned her attention to her son.

"Don't look at me. I didn't order it," Edward said with a grin.

"Potter, you're not allowed to retire," Hannah stated before she grabbed her son's arm and pulled him into the hall. "Tell me everything," she ordered as she led him to the curved staircase.

Edward furrowed his brows, his gaze taking in his mother's gown. "You're still wearing lavender," he said, censure apparent in his voice.

"I haven't yet paid a call on my modiste," Hannah replied defensively.

"I'll take you on the morrow."

Hannah paused on the stair landing. "I rather doubt you'll wish to spend your limited days in London at a modiste's shop," she said.

"I'll be spending time with you," he argued. "Have you accepted all the invitations for this week's entertainments?"

Dipping her head, Hannah resumed her climb up the

stairs. "It's not as if I receive very many these days. I am a mere baroness, after all. A widowed baroness, barely out of mourning," she added in a quieter voice.

Edward pulled several missives from his waistcoat pocket. "You might not have received many for this week, but I certainly have," he countered. "I've responded to every one saying I will be in attendance. I expect to escort you to all of them."

Hannah's eyes widened at seeing the folded notes. "You're only sixteen. And just how long will you *be* in London?"

"Just the week, Mother. Before I leave, I want you to have invitations to ride in the park from no less than four gentlemen or a proposal from one."

"What?"

"Father has been dead for a year," he said. "It's past time you find another husband. I won't have you acquiring the reputation of a Merry Widow through no fault of your own."

Hannah regarded her son with a combination of shock and awe. "A Merry Widow?" she repeated in alarm. "Where is my son, and what have you done with him?"

Only this past Christmas, Edward had put voice to a complaint that she might become a Merry Widow, flirting with younger men and possibly entertaining them in her bed. The mere idea of spending time in another man's company had sickened her. *How dare you? I loved your father*, she had said in response, her voice filled with enough rebuke to silence her son.

Silence him, perhaps, but Edward wasn't deterred from his mission to see to it his mother remarried.

He had been doing some research.

"I've grown up, Mother," Edward stated, bringing Hannah's attention back to the present. "I feel awful about what I said at Christmas. I only did so because one of my classmates claimed he would bed you should he ever have the chance."

Hannah had never fainted in her entire life, but at that moment, she understood how it could happen. "Edward!" she admonished him.

"He is sixteen, and I think he has tupped every serving wench at The George Inn," he said as they entered the parlor. He paused as he took in his surroundings. "Well, this is different," he whispered, his gaze darting to the new furnishings that filled the parlor.

Sure her face was bright red at hearing her son's cavalier comments about one of his classmates, Hannah decided it was best not to dwell on the subject. "Your grandmother had it redone just after Christmas," Hannah said, referring to Temperance Fitzsimmons Harrington, Countess of Mayfield. "It would have been done months ago, but the Chippendale furnishings took so long to be crafted."

"I like it," he murmured. "Where *is* Grandmother, by the way?"

"At the office of *The Tattler*," she replied with an arched brow, the way she always responded to queries about London's premiere gossip newspaper.

Edward frowned. "Is she editing that rag now?" he asked in surprise.

"Not exactly, but I expect she'll be assisting the Countess of Aimsley in choosing the stories to feature until the day she dies, which won't be for several decades," Hannah claimed. "So be warned. Familial ties do not exempt you from a mention if you've done something scandalous. Such as being kicked out of school."

"Noted, but I was not expelled, nor will I ever do anything to earn that demerit." Edward waited until his mother was seated on the room's only settee. He took the chair opposite.

A maid delivered the tea tray, the salver in the middle loaded with slices of cake as well as several flavors of biscuits.

"Don't fill up on sweets, darling," Hannah warned as she poured him a cup of tea and watched as he helped himself to a slice of cake and two biscuits. "Potter is seeing to a cold collation for us."

"Eat dessert first, Mother," Edward countered. "You're always too full from luncheon to enjoy the best part of a meal."

Hannah giggled and then placed a hand on her chest. "I think that might be the first time I've done that since..." She allowed the sentence to trail off as she suddenly sobered, her eyes brightening with tears.

"Oh, Mother," Edward sighed.

"I cannot help it. I loved your father."

Edward grimaced. Although he had lived at Harrington House long enough to know his parents felt affection for one another, he had always had the impression his mother felt trapped, as if she didn't truly wish to be there. As if she had accepted his father's suit when she would have preferred to accept someone else's. That she would continue to claim a deep and abiding love for her late husband seemed odd to him.

"And this son appreciates having had parents who weren't diddling with others, but—"

"Edward!" she admonished him, her mouth left open in shock.

Her son ignored her scold. "But there must be another man on this planet you could love just as much," he said, his brows arched. "It's time you allowed suitors."

Hannah sucked in a breath, wondering how her son could know there had been another. A man she had known her entire life. A man she would have gladly married if he had ever bothered to propose. "He had his chance," she whispered defensively.

Not much of one, but then, she hadn't exactly had much of a choice, either. At least they had seen to an amiable parting and a reminder of their bargain.

Her bargain.

Although she was tempted to replay their last night together in her mind's eye, she forced herself to remain in the present. "He was a good man," she murmured. "*Is* a good man." She hadn't meant to make it sound as if *he* had died.

Edward's eyes widened. "So... I guessed right?" he half-asked as he straightened in his chair.

Immediately regretting her words, Hannah shook her head. "I didn't mean it like that, Ed. Honestly, I—"

"Who? Who had your heart? Who *has* your heart?"

She recoiled from the query and then turned her attention to pouring herself a cup of tea. Two lumps of sugar plopped into the steaming liquid before tears dripped from her eyes.

"Oh, damn, but I'm a dunderhead," Edward said as he pulled a handkerchief from his waistcoat pocket and passed it to her. "I'm so sorry, Mother. Please, forget I asked."

Hannah sniffled as she wiped the tears from her cheeks. "I'm crying because I miss your father," she claimed between soft sobs. "Every morning and every night."

Edward dipped his head. He resisted the urge to ask about the time in between morning and night. "Be that as it may, you have my blessing if you wish to remarry, Mother," he whispered.

Her dark blonde brows furrowing, Hannah regarded her son and allowed a sigh. "I appreciate your words, I do. Even if they are entirely unexpected. But I rather doubt there will be another husband for me."

"Well, I can see I am the last to know when my heir is in residence," a gruff voice sounded from the threshold.

Hannah and Edward turned to see Stanley Harrington, Earl of Mayfield, regarding them with a quirk.

Edward quickly stood and gave his grandfather a deep bow. "My lord, it's so good to see you again."

"Must be almost Easter," Mayfield said as he moved to embrace his grandson.

"Today is Good Friday, in fact," Edward replied. "I only just arrived a few moments ago. Can you afford time for some tea? Or would you like me to pour you a brandy?"

Mayfield glanced at Hannah and frowned. "A few minutes home, and you've already reduced your mother to tears?" he chided.

"Guilty as charged," Edward replied with a shrug, his eyes downcast.

"It's not you," Mayfield whispered, patting Edward on the back. "Yes, I'll take some tea," he said loudly. "But only because it looks as if every cake in the house is on that tray."

Despite her depressed disposition, Hannah grinned. "All except for one, which your grandson has managed to eat in all of three bites."

"I would have said two," Mayfield murmured in delight.

"I think cook must have known Edward was coming home today," she added as she poured a cup for the earl. "I do hope we didn't wake you from your nap?"

Mayfield scoffed. "Haven't been back to bed yet. Not that I plan to. Not when Edward is home. We'll have to play a round of billiards so I can learn what new shenanigans are happening at Eton."

Hannah rolled her eyes. "I'm not certain I wish to know what my son might be doing to get himself expelled," she murmured.

"Mother, I'm not like that," Edward assured her. "Not

since..." He stopped and swallowed. "Well, ever since I became the heir-apparent. Wouldn't be seemly to be caught dressing the statues in ladies' gowns or acquiring white tickets."

Hannah took a breath and let it out all at once. "Thank you," she said in a quiet voice. "I know it must be terribly tempting."

Edward screwed up his face in a grimace. "Mayhap when I was fourteen," he replied. "Not now. I'll be seventeen in a fortnight."

"I recall painting the statue of Henry the Sixth in white wash when I was nearly seventeen," Mayfield commented. "Wasn't caught doing it, but I was still expelled for a month."

Boggling at this bit of news, Edward didn't know if he should laugh or look shocked. He managed a bit of both.

"Mayfield!" Hannah scolded, although a grin lifted the corners of her mouth. "White wash?"

"Now there's the Lady Harrington I know," Mayfield said with a hint of mischief.

Hannah was glad he hadn't referred to her as the Dowager Baroness Harrington. She didn't wish to be known as such until her son married and had a son of his own. And even then, she knew she would wince every time she heard the word 'dowager.'

The earl and his countess had always been so welcoming. Even though she was merely the granddaughter of a duke, Hannah couldn't help but think the Mayfields had wanted their Charles to marry a woman with closer ties to an aristocrat. An earl's daughter. Or a marquess' daughter. Even a duke's daughter. Their son had deserved the very best.

Instead, Charles had courted her in earnest, claiming he had fallen in love with her at first sight. That even if she'd been a pauper's daughter, he would have been honored to make her his baroness. His future countess.

Although Hannah hadn't believed him at first, she soon learned his words were truth. He had proposed seven times over the course of seven days, each event a bit more elaborate than the one before, each ring featuring a unique and more expensive gemstone. Although she never wore all of them at the same time, she tried hard to wear one of them at least once a week.

It was the least she could do in memory of a man who had been near and dear, a friend and confidante, even if he hadn't been much of a lover.

Perhaps Charlie had sensed she felt affection for another.

"Will you join us for luncheon?" Hannah asked of her father-in-law.

"Wild horses couldn't keep me away," Mayfield replied, responding to the invitation to luncheon. "Which reminds me. There are six new horses you'll have to meet while you're here, Edward. Comber has managed quite an interesting mix of lineages with this year's colts."

"Six?" Edward repeated in surprise. "You have room in the stables for that many new racers?"

Mayfield nodded. "Had Comber expand the stables at the country estate. The pasture is good there, and he's got a crack groom seeing to their training," the earl responded, referring to his son-in-law, Alistair Comber. Lady Julia, Mayfield's only daughter and Edward's aunt, had married the second son of the Earl of Aimsley over two decades ago.

"Speaking of Comber, I hear I missed a wedding," Edward said, his manner suggesting he didn't appreciate being left out of a cousin's nuptials.

"Juliet went and got herself an earl," Mayfield said with a guffaw. "Married Christopher, Earl of Haddon. He's Morganfield's whelp, which means she'll be a marchioness before too long." His words were filled with pride as well as amusement. "Poor man apparently hit his head. Knocked some sense into him, and Juliet took advantage."

Hannah inhaled sharply. "It wasn't like that at all," she argued, her eyes wide.

Edward couldn't help but chuckle at hearing his grandfather's words. From the letter he had received from Juliet, he had thought the marriage was more Haddon's idea than his cousin's. Apparently they suited one another, though. Her missive implied she was quite happy ensconced in a large townhouse at the corner of South Audley Street and Curzon Street. With any luck, he would see her at Lord Weatherstone's ball—the first ball of the Season—this week.

"And what's this I hear of Cousin Tom?"

A brilliant smile appeared on his mother's face. "He managed to convince a duke's daughter to marry him."

"One of my classmates claims she's a Somerset daughter," Edward replied. "Can that be true?"

"Lady Victoria is now Lady Grandby," Mayfield put in, one brow arched with admiration. "The duke's youngest daughter. She trains race horses and is best friends with Juliet, so I'll have competition at the races this year," he added as he rolled his eyes. "I've always claimed I would never beat a woman, but..." he shook his head. "Comber has some of mine matching race course records," he claimed. "So I'm not too worried."

"A race course is a good location for a fair fight, Grandfather," Edward replied.

Potter appeared on the parlor's threshold. "Luncheon is served in the breakfast parlor," he announced in a voice that wheezed.

Edward was quick to stand and offer an arm to his mother. "I shall pay a call on my Cousin Tom this very afternoon and give him my congratulations," he said with a grin. "Seems I've missed much these past few months."

"Such is the way of life sometimes," Hannah murmured, taking his arm and allowing him to escort her to the breakfast parlor. When she was alongside the earl, he offered his arm and she gladly accepted.

Ensconced between the two men, Hannah had the impression the coming week would be full of surprises.

This day had certainly brought one.

# CHAPTER 5

# A BARGAIN REVEALED

*eanwhile, back in Tom's office*

His brows furrowing with curiosity, Tom finished his brandy and called out to his secretary. "Mr. Adams, have the phaeton brought 'round. I'm off to Woodscastle and then to Fairmont Park, and I won't return until the morning."

Jasper Adams, secretary to both Gregory and Tom Grandby since Tom's start at Grandby & Son, hurried to the door and said, "Right away, sir."

He disappeared while Tom stared at his cousin. "I trust you'll tell me about this bargain whilst we're on the road?"

Graham's green eyes narrowed a moment before he gave a nod. "Of course. And then you'll tell me where I might find the baroness on the morrow."

"That's easy," Tom replied as he stood up and gathered a few papers into a leather satchel. "Harrington House in Park Lane." From his cousin's reaction, Tom wondered what he had expected to hear.

"What's she doing there?" Graham asked as his eyes widened. "Did Mayfield die, too?" he added, thinking perhaps Charles had inherited the earldom before his untimely death.

"No, but Uncle Charlie never acquired a house for them to move into. Their apartments were spacious enough, so they simply lived at Harrington House," Tom explained. He pulled on his great coat. "As for your other question, Mayfield will probably live to be a hundred," he stated, referring to Charles Harrington's father. "Or at least as long as his countess is alive. He has no intention of allowing another man to get his hands on her."

Graham stood, his body listing a bit before he managed to steady himself, the sensation of vertigo quickly passing. Despite having departed the ship at first light earlier that morning, his body still felt as if it were moving. "Still the horny bastard he was?"

"Only for his wife, apparently. Besides, Lady Mayfield still secretly edits *The Tattler,* and he knows if he does anything gossip-worthy, he'll end up on the front page."

Graham allowed a guffaw as he tucked his top hat beneath his arm. "Who inherits when he finally dies?"

Tom blinked. "Charlie's son, of course."

Graham wavered as another round of vertigo had him struggling to stay upright.

"You all right?"

A grimace appeared on Graham's face. "I'm still getting my land legs back," he complained, but his brows furrowed deeper. "Hannah... Hannah has a son?"

His cousin took a deep breath and finally allowed a nod. "Just the one. Edward. He's... sixteen. Nearly seventeen, I think. Has a good head on his shoulders, though," Tom added as he led them down the main corridor toward the front door. He placed his top hat on his head once they were outside, his gaze sweeping busy Oxford Street in search of his phaeton and the large black shire that pulled it. "They didn't have any daughters."

"Here, sir," Bobby, the boy from the mews in back called out from the curb.

"Ah, here's our ride," Tom said as he hurried to the phaeton and gave the stableboy a coin.

But Graham didn't make a move to climb onto the equipage, instead moving to stand in front of the largest horse he had ever seen. "Damnation," he muttered.

"Actually, his name is Jake," Tom said as he joined Graham to admire his horse. "Alistair Comber put me onto him. He couldn't find another large enough to make a matched pair, and given his size, I only needed one of his kind for the phaeton."

"Impressive," Graham murmured, one of his hands reaching up to slide up the horse's muzzle and along his cheek.

Jake knickered softly.

"Might I take the ribbons?" Graham asked as Tom moved to step up and onto the phaeton's bench.

Tom allowed a shrug. "He doesn't know the way to Woodscastle," he warned.

"*I* might need reminding," Graham countered with a guffaw. He easily mounted the phaeton and waited for his cousin to be seated before he urged the shire into motion. "Have you seen her lately?"

At first, Tom thought to question who he meant with his query, but he reasoned Graham was asking after Hannah. "Victoria and I had her out to Fairmont Park for dinner a fortnight ago. Cousin Edward wasn't yet home from university, so I knew she would welcome a diversion," he explained. "Only then did I discover she had been invited to dinner by every one of my sisters and two of my brothers over the course of the past month."

Graham winced at the second mention of Edward. Although he had only just learned of the only son of Charles and Hannah, the reminder that Hannah had a child with her husband rankled. He couldn't help but think she should have had his son.

"He's an honorable young man, Graham," Tom said in a quiet voice.

"As Hannah's son, I would expect nothing less," Graham replied as he directed Jake south towards the Knightsbridge Road. "Do you suppose you can arrange an introduction?"

Tom blinked. "I can. He's probably in town by now, given Easter is the day after next. With the Season starting, there will be balls every night beginning this Tuesday."

Graham furrowed a brow. "How does a sixteen-year-old receive invitations to balls?"

Sensing Graham's annoyance, Tom said, "He's an heir apparent. He's amiable, clever, handsome, and has a small fortune. Every matron with a daughter barely old enough to marry will want an introduction, and probably the matrons as well."

"I hate him already," Graham murmured.

"I hadn't noticed," Tom countered with a roll of his eyes. "Just remember. He already has his mother's love. No one will replace him in that regard," he warned. "But... Hannah is still a fairly young matron. There's no reason to think she won't welcome suitors now that she's out of mourning."

Graham allowed a heavy sigh. About to ask who those suitors might be, he couldn't when Jake had to dodge a runaway cart and horse and two children who were darting in and out of various carriages and carts. "Is it always like this?" he asked in alarm, marveling at the amount of traffic he had to drive around or avoid in the intersections.

"I rarely drive this direction this time of the day," Tom replied, glad for the change in topic. "I'm usually headed north, and Jake is always as anxious as I am to get to Fairmont Park."

Graham gave him a questioning glance. "Attentive stableboy?"

Tom barked a laugh. "And my wife. As I mentioned earlier, Victoria trains horses," he said. "For racing," he added, waiting for Graham's reaction.

He wasn't disappointed.

"I thought you married a duke's daughter."

"I did. She is. Estranged for a time from Somerset, but now that her father is doing better—"

"What happened to Somerset?" Graham asked in alarm, referring to Jeremy Statton, Duke of Somerset.

"He was..." Tom sighed. "He was being poisoned," he replied in a hushed voice.

Graham nearly pulled Jake to a halt as he regarded his cousin with a look of shock. "By whom?"

"Well, not his wife, if that's what you were thinking," Tom assured him. Elizabeth and Jeremy had a marriage well known for being a love match. "His heir, as it happens. Jeremiah gambled to excess and needed his inheritance to cover the vowels. Thought the fastest route might be Somerset's early demise."

"Good God," Graham breathed, expertly driving Jake around a delivery cart that was stopped in the middle of the street. "Was he arrested? Or is he exempt from prosecution given his status as an heir?" This last was said with a sneer, a clear indication Graham didn't agree with how aristocrats could avoid penalties despite having committed major crimes.

"He was arrested. He's in Newgate now, in fact, awaiting Parliament to reconvene. He expects he'll get off with a slap on the wrist, but rumor has it Somerset wants him found guilty and stripped of his current and future titles and transported."

Graham furrowed a brow as he directed Jake to take the turn onto the Knightsbridge Road. "Can he do that? What happens to the dukedom?"

"Michael, the second-born son, would inherit. Which would be a boon to the dukedom."

"How so?"

"Michael has managed to protect his father's—and the dukedom's—assets despite Jeremiah's attempts to bleed them dry. Protect his own and see to it Victoria's were invested, as well."

Graham took his eyes off the road long enough to regard his cousin with a gleam in his eye. "Let me guess. Her assets are protected by some investment *you* are managing."

Tom angled his head back and forth. "You have the right of it," he admitted, a dimple appearing in his right cheek. "It's... it's how we met. Michael asked that I pay a call. He wanted to be sure her monies couldn't be taken by Jeremiah. I didn't expect the meeting to amount to anything."

"But?"

Tom inhaled. "Thanks to her sizable investment—and her choice of steam buses to invest in—we have a steam bus line running up north in Yorkshire. Eventually it will be replaced by the railway that's being built there, but when that happens, the assets will be transferred to another town in need of reliable transportation, and the investment will simply continue."

Graham's eyes darted to Tom for a moment before he once again had to pay attention to the traffic. "And this... Fairmont Park?"

"It was an unentailed property of the Somerset dukedom," Tom replied.

"And now you own it."

"I don't, actually."

Furrowing a brow, Graham said. "Then—"

"I bought it and gave it to Victoria as a wedding gift."

Graham let out an exclamation that was a combination of a curse and a word of disbelief. "Thanks for nothing, you cur. Now you've gone and raised the stakes for the rest of us poor saps who might be considering matrimony," he scolded.

"Says the man who can have the entire east wing of Woodscastle any time he wants it," Tom countered, referring to their boyhood home.

"I rather doubt that," Graham countered.

"Your parents have been living in the townhouse in King Street for the entire winter. They like it there. They like that it's in town. And they like that they're across the street from Hannah's parents."

Graham winced at the reminder of how his family was connected to that of Tom's—Graham's aunt Christiana was Tom's mother, and Tom's grandmother was Hannah's mother. "Are they well?"

Tom nodded. "James is mostly deaf," he said, referring to his grandfather. "And Lady Simpson doesn't look a day over forty."

"So I'll recognize her, at least," Graham reasoned as traffic finally cleared and Jake was able to increase his trot into a full-out run toward Chiswick.

"You'd best, if you know what's good for you."

Grimacing, Graham said, "She was the reason Hannah agreed to marry Harrington, was she not?"

Tom rolled his eyes. "I know you'd like to blame it on her, but she has told my mother that she always held the opinion that you and Hannah would end up together."

Frowning, Graham said, "Then... then why *did* Hannah marry Harrington?" She had tried to explain it to him that last night they were together, but he had his mind on other matters at the time and had no desire to be thinking about Charles Harrington.

Memories of that night had sustained him for a very long time. Had warmed him on cold winter nights and kept him sane during the days when he felt desperate loneliness in Boston.

Clearing his throat, Tom gave his cousin a quelling glance. "Because he asked for her hand in marriage. Seven times over the course of a single week."

About to argue, Graham let out his breath in a long sigh. "I would have. Eventually."

"Well, if you have any hope of ever having her as a wife, you'd best be the one to ask her next," Tom said. "She's out of mourning, and the betting book at White's is filling up fast with possible matches."

Graham winced as he directed Jake to take the turn onto Burlington Lane. "Is this right?" he asked, marveling at the height of the trees that lined the drive leading up to Woodscastle. With winter finally over, many already displayed the bright green leaves of early spring.

"Looks familiar," Tom replied with a grin. "I'll introduce you to the staff and then expect you for dinner at Fairmont Park Monday night. I know you'll want to spend a couple of days with your parents."

"Do your mother and father still live here?" Graham asked as he studied the tree-lined lane leading to Woodscastle.

Tom allowed a shrug. "When they're not at Cherrywood in Derbyshire. They were there for Christmas, returned for a month, and then left again last week for Yorkshire. Father wanted to review a couple of the railway lines that are under construction, and Mother went along because Emily is finally married, and there's no one left for her to worry over."

Graham shook his head. "I still cannot believe little Em is married."

Tom grinned. "James is both my friend and a second cousin, so I was glad for them."

Graham shook his head. "Did you truly agree to the match?"

Allowing a sigh, Tom said, "I recall feeling angry with them both for about one minute."

"Just the one?"

Tom nodded. "Then I realized I was jealous. It was so easy for them. As if they were destined for one another. Because they were."

"And then you met Lady Victoria."

"Well, I had already met her, but barely," Tom admitted with a guffaw. "So I understood."

The brick structure of Woodscastle slowly appeared from between the leaves of the tree-lined lane, and Graham let out a low whistle. "Looks better than when I left it," he commented.

"Father had the bricks cleaned last year," Tom acknowledged. "Roger's family was living here for a time, but he took a position at Barclay's Bank and bought a townhouse in Cheapside," he added, referring to his oldest brother.

"Any coaches left in the carriage house?"

Tom nodded. "There are. And there are still the two grooms you already know, so you'll have a means to get about town on the morrow if you don't wish to drive yourself. Or tonight, should you wish to make an appearance at Brooks's."

Furrowing a brow, Graham asked, "Will you be there?"

Tom said, "No, but your father still goes on occasion. Imagine his surprise should he find you there."

Graham nodded as he considered what he had ahead of him. To see to it a ship's cargo was delivered to Wellingham Imports in the morning, and then a reunion with his parents at their offices. If he had time in the afternoon, he would pay a call at Harrington House.

There was someone he needed to see, and apparently another he needed to meet.

As for Brooks's, that all depended on how much sleep he might manage in the next few hours.

# CHAPTER 6

## COUSINS REUNITE

*An hour later at 300 Oxford Street*

Edward Harrington stepped down from the Mayfield coach and regarded the front façade of Grandby and Son. His uncle had started the investment firm long before he ever married Christiana Wellingham, and Tom, their second-oldest son, had joined his father in the venture immediately after completing his education at Oxford.

Making his way to the front door, he was about to open it when a hand reached in front of him and snagged the handle before he could. Startled, he turned to find Tom staring at him with a look of amusement as he opened the door.

"I thought that was you," Tom said with a grin. "What good timing you have," he added as he waved his cousin— one of only two—into the building. "I've only just returned from Woodscastle this very moment."

Edward allowed a huge grin. "As a newly married man, it's a wonder you even bother coming to work every day," he teased.

"Your cheekiness will earn you white tickets if you're not

careful," Tom warned with a grin as he joined the younger man in the long corridor that led to his secretary's counter.

"I heard you married for love," Edward countered.

Tom regarded the heir to an earldom with a look of suspicion. "I did. And although I did take some time with my bride the week of our wedding, I do have responsibilities here. Once Father has concluded his business up in York-shire, he has promised he will see to the office whilst Lady Grandby and I follow the racing circuit." He turned his attention to his secretary. "Mr. Adams, a round of tea, if you would."

"Right away, sir," Adams replied. "Good to see you again, Mr. Harrington." His eyes suddenly widened. "Or is it *Lord Harrington* now?"

Edward gave a start and exchanged quick glances with his cousin. "Not that I'm aware," he replied, although he said so with a hint of uncertainty.

"On the occasion of your seventeenth birthday, I expect," Tom said. When he realized he might be sharing a secret, he added, "I'm quite sure Mayfield has plans for you. We recently hosted your mother for dinner, and she mentioned it."

"Ah," Edward acknowledged.

They moved into Tom's office, and Edward hurried over to the shelves containing Tom's treasures. "Why, you'll have your own museum before long," he murmured as he admired the ancient artifacts.

"I never thought being on the board of the British Museum would have me looking at relics in a new light," Tom admitted. "Having the blunt to pay for them makes it easy to collect."

"One of my classmates was lamenting his lack of funds. Seems he used his entire allowance for the past two years on collecting ladies of the evening."

"And you?"

"I still have most of mine. Cousin Roger set up an account for me at Barclay's Bank," he said, referring to Tom's older brother.

"You're a wise young man," Tom said as he poured them both brandies from a decanter. "It's rare I get to do this more than once in a single day," he added as he offered one of the glasses to Edward and then held up his in a salute.

"Oh?"

"You're the second cousin to pay a call on me today, and I only have two cousins."

Edward's eyes widened. "Mr. Wellingham was here?"

Tom gave a start. "Indeed. How is it you know of him?"

The younger man settled into the chair in front of Tom's desk and raised the glass to his nose. He took a sniff before he sipped a bit of the brandy, sighing with satisfaction. "He's the turtle."

Blinking, Tom settled into his own chair and regarded Edward with a furrowed brow. "Turtle?" he repeated, just then remembering Graham's comment before they left the office for Woodscastle.

"We are speaking of Graham Wellingham, are we not?"

Tom nodded.

"My mother told me a story about the two of them. A long time ago. I don't think she expected I would remember, but from her manner of speech, I know she held him in high regard."

Taking a sip of his drink, Tom set aside the tumbler and said, "They were the best of friends in their youth. Truth be told, I always thought they would end up married."

Edward considered his cousin's words before he asked, "Do you know why they didn't?"

Blinking, Tom considered how to respond. "Your father was very persistent in his pursuit of your mother."

"Seven rings in seven days," Edward replied. "My grandmother made mention of it with a good deal of pride."

"The older matrons always make it sound as if jewelry is the way to a woman's heart," Tom murmured.

"And you do not agree?"

A grin appeared on Tom's face, a grin that soon widened into a full smile. "In my case, I found shoes were more appreciated."

"Shoes?" Edward repeated, his brows furrowed.

"Custom shoes. And boots. Lots of them. My wife has a crushed foot from when a horse stepped on it. Before I met her, she only owned a pair of custom riding boots that fit her perfectly."

Wincing, Edward drained his brandy and set the glass on the desk. "I will remember that should I favor a girl with a crushed foot," he murmured. After a moment, he said, "I should like to meet Mr. Wellingham. Do you know how long he will be in London?"

Tom straightened in his chair, suddenly suspicious of the younger man's motives. "The rest of his life, I expect. He's turned over the operations of the Boston office of Wellingham Imports to his partner there."

Edward's eyes widened. "Might you know where I can find him? Tonight?"

Taken aback, Tom asked, "If I tell you, what, pray tell, do you intend to do?"

"Introduce myself, of course," Edward replied. "I have always wanted to meet the turtle. Discover if he's of a mind to renew my mother's acquaintance."

"You would *welcome* that?" Tom asked, still suspicious.

Edward nodded. "In the story my mother told me as a youth, the turtle was beaten by a horse, but the horse disappeared."

"And the turtle remained," Tom guessed.

"Indeed."

"Was the horse… your father, perhaps?"

Edward stared at his cousin for a moment before he finally allowed a nod. "I believe so."

Deciding it was safe to tell Edward what he knew, Tom said, "I might have suggested Graham pay a call at Brooks's this evening. In the event his father is in attendance."

His face brightening with his news, Edward said, "My grandfather is a member there. Perhaps I can suggest we make an appearance. Especially if he hasn't already spent all of his gambling allowance this month."

Tom blinked. "Mayfield has an allowance for gambling?" he asked in disbelief.

"Don't you?" Edward countered.

Settling back in his chair, Tom considered the query before he broke out into a chuckle. "I suppose I do," he admitted.

"Will you be at Lord Weatherstone's ball this Tuesday evening?"

Tom gave a start at the change in subject. "We have an invitation, of course," he hedged.

"And the proper shoes, apparently," Edward teased. "Does your wife require further incentive to attend the best ball of the Season?"

Not having spent a Season with Victoria, Tom had no idea if she looked forward to the balls and soirées, the *musicales* and the garden parties. "I think I shall leave early this afternoon and pay a call at Ludgate Hill," he murmured. "See what bauble I can find to ensure we do attend. Lord Weatherstone's ball is never one to miss."

Edward grinned. "Now that's a good idea," he said. "Thank you for the news about your cousin." He stood up and Tom followed suit. "Now that my mother is out of mourning, I expect I will have to fight off a string of would-be suitors this week."

"Have you taken up bare-knuckle boxing?" Tom asked in a tease.

Edward balled up his fists and struck a pose suggesting he would gladly take on an opponent. "I would prefer not to fight, but I would not back down should one become necessary." With that, he lowered his fists and gave Tom a bow. "Thank you for the brandy. Rather a nice treat in the middle of the day."

Tom watched Edward depart, curious as to what the young man had in mind. Besides his heightened curiosity, he also experienced the oddest sensation. He had hosted both of his cousins on this day, and they looked remarkably alike.

But then, they were related, he reminded himself.

# CHAPTER 7

## BILLIARDS BEGETS A BARON

*ater that night, Harrington House*
"I see you've been practicing," Edward complained when his grandfather sunk not one, but two balls on the first break of billiards.

"I have indeed. After you embarrassed me at Christmastide, I thought I had better spend some time in here after dinner every night," Mayfield replied as he set up his next shot. "So I do. If I do well, I head to Brooks's for a drink and sometimes stay for the eleven o'clock supper."

Edward allowed a grin, glad to hear his grandfather was still a member of the club that catered to a different clientele from that found at White's. "Will you be doing that tonight?" he asked hopefully. Despite having consumed most of the seven-course meal they had finished only the hour before, Edward would welcome the opportunity to eat again before settling into his bed.

Besides, he was hoping to make the acquaintance of a certain gentleman.

Mayfield gave the question some thought before he took his shot. When none of the balls disappeared into the leather pockets, he murmured a curse. "I suppose you'll be hungry in an hour or so."

Lining up his shot, Edward pretended an air of nonchalance. The queue ball struck a red one, sending it into a corner pocket. "I can always make room for another meal, sir," he admitted with a brilliant smile.

"Well, then let's finish up this game and make our way there. I suppose you already know how to play hazard?"

Edward pretended ignorance. "My mates and I have played faro on occasion, but not for money, of course," he claimed, deciding it better he not admit they gambled as a means to pass their white tickets to the loser. The game had kept him from having to work off a single demerit, not that he had acquired many over his time at the boy's school.

"Is that how you get rid of your white tickets?" Mayfield guessed, a bushy brow lifting in amusement. Edward's second shot sent a ball nearly careening over the edge.

His face reddening, Edward said, "I rarely earn a white ticket, sir."

Mayfield lined up his attempt to sink a blue ball. "How are you at whist?" The blue ball disappeared into a pocket and Mayfield quickly sunk another ball.

"I know how to play, of course," Edward admitted. "You taught me."

"Up for a game tonight? My allowance gives me a certain amount to gamble with every month, and I haven't yet taken advantage." The earl's next shot left a ball at the very edge of a pocket, and he cursed softly.

Edward furrowed a brow as he lined up his shot and sunk the teetering ball. "Your allowance, sir?" he teased. Before his grandmother had told him about their arrangement with respect to gaming, Edward would never have believed an earl would be limited by how much blunt he was allowed to gamble.

"Allowance, indeed. Your grandmother warned me some fifteen years ago that if she heard I lost more than a certain amount at the gaming tables, she would include a mention of it in that damned rag of hers." He cursed again when Edward's next attempt sunk another ball. "There are times I wonder why I bought that business for her, but it makes so damn much money for the earldom..." He shrugged. "Keeps me out of trouble, I suppose."

Despite the seriousness of Mayfield's delivery, Edward struggled to keep a straight face. "May I inquire as to how many times your gambling losses have been featured in *The Tattler*, sir?"

The earl glowered a moment before he allowed a hearty laugh. "Only once. Your uncle Alistair took me for five-hundred pounds one night, so we were *both* featured in the next issue. *That's* never happened again."

Edward allowed a low whistle before he chuckled. He sobered when his ball spun off at an odd angle and knocked another so it was perfectly aligned with the queue ball. "I would think your son by marriage would know better than to beat you at whist."

Allowing a guffaw, Mayfield said, "Well, it wasn't whist at which he beat me." At Edward's look of surprise, he added, "Hazard. He's never done it again, but that's probably because he doesn't throw the dice much these days." The earl sunk the perfectly aligned ball and straightened with a huff of satisfaction. He easily sank the last ball. "Brooks's it is."

His eyes darting to one side, Edward asked, "Am I allowed to go into the club, sir? I'm... I'm not yet a member."

"You'll be my guest, of course. When you're up for election, I rather doubt there will be any black balls. You're a baron now, after all."

"Sir?" He remembered what Tom had inferred—that he

could expect to gain his late father's courtesy title on the occasion of his next birthday.

"You are my heir as well as the Baron Harrington," Mayfield stated. "'Bout time you were seen in Society as such."

Excited at the prospect of attending the men's club, as much for the experience as for who he hoped to find there, Edward gave a nod. "Very good, sir. Shall I... shall I tell my mother I'm going?"

Mayfield furrowed a brow. "Well, if you don't, you'll be in a good bit of trouble at breakfast. But don't go asking her permission. Just... just tell her you're going with me."

Giving his grandfather a bow, Edward said, "I'll be ready to leave in just a few minutes."

He hurried off to the first floor parlor, slowing his steps as he made his way over the threshold.

"Did you let him win?" Hannah asked in a hoarse whisper, a grin teasing the corners of her mouth. She held the bowl of a steaming teacup between the palms of her hands, as if she was using it to warm them.

"I kept it close, but I did let him win, which means we're off to Brooks's," he replied in a quiet voice. "We'll probably return after the supper is served at eleven. I wanted to let you know before I took my leave." He paused and then straightened. "Oh, and it seems I have the title of baron now."

Hannah blinked, about to put voice to a protest. But instead, she gave him a brilliant smile. "Well, now that you know you are a baron, I expect you to do as your grandfather wishes," she finally said. "But do try to limit your losses."

Edward gave a start at hearing her words, wondering if she had overheard his grandfather's declaration. "I cannot lose if I do not play," he countered with a smirk. He bent down and kissed her on the cheek before he gave a bow and took his leave of the parlor.

# CHAPTER 8

# AN UNEXPECTED INTRODUCTION

*ater than night, Brooks's, 60 St. James Street, Mayfair*

"I expect there will be some murmurs of surprise when you enter with me," the Earl of Mayfield said as he and Edward made their way toward Brooks's.

Due to the number of carriages parked along St. James Street, their town coach had been forced to park a good deal away, and although the driver offered to drop them in front of the club, Edward had suggested the walk would do them both good after such a large dinner.

"I would expect nothing less," Edward replied. He might have been declared a baron—and that was only a courtesy title belonging to the Mayfield earldom—but he was still rather young to be attending a men's club that featured all manner of gaming. He had heard rumors there was even a cockpit in the basement.

"I'll vouch for you, of course, and stake you twenty pounds," the earl continued. "After you've reached your seventeenth year, I'll see to it there's an election for your membership."

Edward clamped his mouth shut when he determined it might be left hanging open at the earl's declaration. "Is that really a good idea? I haven't yet started my classes at Oxford."

Mayfield scoffed. "Although it's commendable you wish to attend, I may decide it's not worth your time. Better you remain in London and learn how to run the earldom."

Rather alarmed by the comment, Edward furrowed a brow. Many claimed when he did so, he looked just like his uncle—and his mother's twin brother—Henry Simpson. "Is there something you're not telling me?" he asked as he motioned that they should slow their steps. The front door of the club was only a few yards ahead.

Turning to regard his grandson, Mayfield allowed a sigh. "I am nearly sixty-seven years old. Already a few years older than my father was when he died."

"But you have made it clear you shall be alive as long as Grandmama, and Mother claims she will live to be a hundred."

Mayfield blinked. "Did she now? *Hmph.*"

A dimple appeared in the base of Edward's right cheek. "Something about not allowing another man to have his way with Grandmama, if you should die before her?"

His eyes widening, Mayfield looked thunderstruck, and then he laughed. Loudly.

Edward glanced around them, aware that a few passersby had noticed his grandfather's outburst. "I rather doubt Grandmama would do such a thing," he started to say.

"She wouldn't," Mayfield said with confidence. "But you're right to remind me I am not yet at death's door." He turned to discover they were instead at the front door of Brooks's. "Although this place will be the death of me should I lose more than my allowance for the month," he added with a guffaw.

The two entered, and Edward noted how the earl barely

paused to allow an impossibly tall footman to remove his greatcoat. His own was removed from his shoulders by another footman, and then he was suddenly in the club.

A rather elegant club.

He struggled not to appear boggled by the lush furnishings, by the dark wood paneling and high coffered ceilings, by the thick carpeting that absorbed most of the sounds of tinkling glassware and conversation, or by the stares of several older gentlemen who paused in whatever they had been doing to give him a passing glance. Almost as quickly, they returned their attentions to their games of chance, and Edward finally exhaled the breath he'd been holding.

"I promised Morganfield a game of whist," Mayfield said as his gaze swept the large room. Various gaming tables were scattered throughout, most populated by aristocrats or gentlemen of genteel breeding.

For years, the club had been the bastion of those who owned country estates. On this night, nearly every chair was filled. "He took fifty pounds off me last month, and I intend to get it back," he added, referring to David Carlington, Marquess of Morganfield.

"Is it permissible for me to simply watch the play? Or... or must I play and place bets?" Edward asked as his attention went to the faro tables.

"You can watch, but do look as if you're thinking of joining a game," Mayfield replied, his gaze still wandering about the room. His attention was captured when a tall gentleman waved in his direction. "Ah, looks like I've found my prey."

Without a backward glance, Mayfield headed to the table at which the Earl of Trenton and the Marquess of Morganfield were sitting with a young man who might have been Morganfield's heir.

Haddon, Edward realized. His cousin Juliet's husband.

Edward watched as his grandfather made his way to the whist table. About to head in the direction of the faro tables, his attention was captured by the arrival of another rather tall gentleman.

Handsome in a rough sort of manner and broad of shoulder, the gentleman stood near the entrance and surveyed the room as if he had never been there before. His brown hair was a bit longer than was usual for an Englishman, but he was clean-shaven. Although Edward was sure he had never been introduced, he was also sure he knew him from somewhere.

After a moment, he realized why.

He had seen a younger version of the man in a painting. He struggled to remember where it had been hanging.

Over a mantel, in a parlor. *Across the street from Grandmother's house*, he thought as his eyes widened. *At the Wellingham's townhouse!*

He hurried over to the man.

"Pardon me, sir. You look familiar, but I cannot seem to place you," Edward said as he held out his right hand. "Edward Harrington, at your service," he added.

*G*raham Wellingham regarded the young man who stood before him, stunned by his youth, his words, and his appearance.

*Familiar?*

He was quite sure he had never met the boy before, and given his apparent age, Graham was sure he hadn't even been born before Graham was last on British shores.

Graham had only come to Brooks's on this night because he had a thought his father might be in attendance. A glance around the room proved Thomas Wellingham was probably at the townhouse in King Street, no doubt enjoying the company of Graham's mother, Emma.

Graham struggled to remember what the young man had said, his brain a bit foggy from lack of sleep.

*Edward Harrington.*

Blinking several times, Graham once again experienced a moment of vertigo before the room seemed to right itself. "Graham Wellingham," he stated, not sure how else to respond to the whelp's comment.

And then the word 'Harrington' permeated his sleep-deprived brain.

"Good to make your acquaintance, Mr. Harrington," Graham said. "Since I have just today arrived from Boston, how is it I am familiar to you?"

Edward's eyes widened. "You did say, 'Wellingham', did you not, sir?" he asked as an eyebrow arched.

"I did," Graham acknowledged, curious as to why such a young man would be in Brooks's. He also thought he looked familiar. Like a young man he had known in his youth. "As in Wellingham Imports," he added with an arched brow. "My father's business."

When the young man's countenance changed before his eyes, Graham was compelled to add, "My father's cousin is the Earl of Trenton."

Edward's eyes widened even more, and Graham realized why the young man looked so familiar. He had the same eyes as Graham's mother. Eyes shared by all the Fitzsimmons, in fact. But all thoughts of eyes flew from his brain upon hearing Edward's query.

"Are you by chance the... the *turtle?*"

Stunned by the simple question, Graham blinked. He glanced around the club, looking for anyone he might know. When no one who glanced in his direction seemed to recognize him, he settled his gaze back on the young man who stood before him displaying an expression of awe. "Who told you?"

His head shaking as if to clear it, Edward said, "My mother, sir."

Inhaling slowly, Graham fought off another round of vertigo before he said, "Is there somewhere we might... sit?" His gaze once again swept the room, his attention settling on a few who stood at the faro tables and then on some of the card tables, where whist seemed the game of choice on this night. Smoke billowed from an occasional cheroot.

Edward spied a set of upholstered chairs set next to a bookcase. A fireplace was lit, although it was doubtful it provided the room's only warmth. There were enough patrons to keep the large room comfortable.

He motioned for Graham to follow him, and he hurried to the chairs as if he feared another party might claim them.

"May I buy you a drink?" Edward asked when he paused in front of one of the chairs.

Graham furrowed a brow. Given the elegance of the club, he decided ordering an ale would be uncouth. "I could do with a brandy," he replied as he settled into the other wing-backed chair.

From seemingly nowhere, a footman appeared to take their order. "Two brandies," Edward stated, as if he had been at the club before and knew what to do.

The footman said, "Very good, sir," before he bowed and hurried off.

"Forgive my impertinence, but how *old* are you?" Graham asked as he watched Edward take the adjacent chair.

"I'll be seventeen in a fortnight."

Graham regarded the young man with suspicion. "And your mother?"

Edward screwed up his face in concentration. "Five-and-thirty?" he replied. Then his eyes rounded. "No, she's six-and-thirty."

"I meant, *who* is your mother?" Graham asked, although he already knew the answer. The boy's resemblance to Henry Simpson—Hannah's twin brother—could not be mistaken. He supposed the resemblance to the Fitzsimmons was because his grandmother, the Countess of Mayfield, was a Fitzsimmons. "Hannah?" he added, anxious to hear the answer.

Nodding, Edward brightened. "She is. The former Miss Hannah Simpson. And you... you are her turtle?"

Graham shook his head, hoping his reddening face wouldn't be apparent under the gas chandelier that hung above them. "You are her son?"

"I am," Edward acknowledged.

"She told you about... the horse and the turtle?" Graham asked, his sleep-deprived brain barely able to make the connections. He stared at the younger man, and for a moment, he was reminded of how he once looked in a mirror.

Since they were both related to the Fitzsimmons, it stood to reason there would be a resemblance.

Edward nodded. "I think my father was the horse," he said. "Ran fast, took the lead—"

"Got the girl."

"But..." Edward allowed the sentence to trail off as he gave his head a shake. He rarely felt sorrow over his father's death these days, so the moment of melancholy surprised him.

"I am sorry for your loss," Graham offered. His initial annoyance with the young man dissipated at the reminder that Edward's father had died.

"Thank you, sir. That's rather... kind of you considering my mother should have been your wife."

Graham's mouth dropped open in astonishment at the same time a glimmer of hope formed in his heart. "How... how do you know this?" he asked.

Edward glanced around before he leaned forward and said in a lowered voice, "I made her tell me," he admitted. "Last year, after my father died. I always knew he wasn't her first love."

A number of thoughts tumbled through Graham's head just then. Perhaps he had forgone the opportunity to return to town and had simply fallen asleep in his old bedchamber at Woodscastle, and now he was experiencing a vivid dream.

Or perhaps he really had taken Tom's suggestion that he attempt to find his father at Brooks's and one of his friends from school was playing a trick on him. This young man was merely a plant. An urchin dressed up to resemble a young aristocrat and taught to speak perfect English.

But he knew this all had to be real.

What else could explain how it was Edward knew the tale of the horse and the turtle?

What else could explain how the young man could look so much like Henry Simpson? Unless he was Henry Simpson's son—a cousin to Hannah's son and in on the ruse— but, according to Tom, that was almost impossible.

Henry hadn't yet been caught in the parson's mouse trap.

Henry hadn't yet found the perfect woman for him, and it was doubtful the young man was Henry's by-blow.

Given their ages, Graham and Henry really did need to consider marriage soon, for their chances of seeing their heirs age enough to be educated and ready to inherit their estates was growing slim.

Noting the young man's look of expectation, Graham remembered the comment, "I always knew," and decided to take the bait. "Knew? Knew what?" He once again glanced about, as if he thought someone might be playing a cruel trick on him. His fists clenched at the thought that he might have to challenge someone to a bare-knuckle fight on his first night back in England.

Edward Harrington finally allowed a shrug. "I knew Mother held a candle for someone besides my father. She would never admit it, of course."

Graham stiffened, sure a trap was being set. Sure Hannah's son intended him harm. And if not harm, then public embarrassment. Given the number of men in the club, it would be easy enough for the young heir-apparent to the Mayfield earldom to do so. "So, now you wish to pummel me to a pulp in the alley out back?" Graham asked with annoyance.

Edward's eyes once again rounded. "Not at all, sir," he replied with a shake of his head. "I want my mother remarried. Preferably to you." He paused when Graham simply stared at him. "That is... if you're still of a mind to marry her."

# CHAPTER 9

## TWIN TALK OF POSSIBILITIES

*M*eanwhile, at the Simpson townhouse in King Street

Henry Simpson regarded his twin sister with a smirk. "Look at you. You can't even stay awake past midnight."

Hannah jerked upright, her eyes suddenly wide open. "Oh, my apologies. I don't know why I'm so sleepy." She glanced around the parlor. "Where are our parents?"

"Off to bed, of course. It's a wonder Father stayed awake through dinner," Henry replied with a grin.

"Mother didn't seem the least bit tired," Hannah remarked as she straightened on the settee. She had come to her parents' townhouse after Edward and the earl had left for Brooks's, deciding a late night was warranted as a means to practice for the upcoming Season.

Her brother took her wine glass from her hand, the claret within barely drunk. "I don't think she was tired until you started to yawn," he said, rebuke evident in his voice. "She was very glad to see you, though, as was Father. They've been worried about you."

"Me? But... but *why*?"

Henry gave his head a shake. "You're a widow out of mourning. Mother expects you'll have a string of suitors at your door starting this week, and Father fears you'll end up married to a fortune hunter."

Her mouth dropping open in shock, Hannah was about to respond when Henry reached over and placed his finger beneath her chin to lift it. She quickly closed her mouth but ensured her sound of disgust was audible. "I am *not* going to marry a fortune seeker," she argued. "I don't even think I shall marry again, in fact."

Her attempt at stifling a yawn had Henry chuckling. "You're welcome to spend the night in your old bedchamber, sister," he offered. "If you'd rather not make the trip back to Harrington House. I can send the coachman back with word that you'll return in the morning."

Hannah gave her head a shake. "Although the offer is appreciated, I wish to have as much time with my son as I can whilst he's home from school."

Henry took a seat next to her on the settee, careful to avoid sitting on any of her wide skirts. He had frequently cursed the newer fashions, preferring instead the gowns of the era before George IV was coronated. Before William and then Victoria were crowned. The shape of a lady's legs were more easily discerned, especially when the wind blew. At least the current gowns did a better job of displaying a woman's waist and the extent of her bosom, but he was always terribly curious about their lower limbs.

"Well, you'd best sleep late in the morning," Henry suggested. "Starting Tuesday night, you will have to stay awake well past midnight. The entertainments are due to begin, and your son tells me he has invitations for nearly all of them."

"About that," Hannah said as she turned her head in his direction. She regarded him with suspicion. "How is It a boy not even seventeen years of age has invitations to balls and soirées and such? Invitations *I* do not have?"

Henry's eyes darted to one side, and for a moment, Hannah was struck by how much he looked like his nephew, Tom Grandby. "Well, he is a baron now, and you know these events are always in need of unattached males," he reasoned.

Hannah's eyes widened. "What did you do?"

Ignoring her query, Henry continued. "As for you, I suppose it's not general knowledge that you're out of mourning now. Perhaps you can mention it to your mother-in-law so she can include an article in the next issue of *The Tattler*?"

Hannah gave him a quelling glance. The very last thing she wanted was a mention in London's premiere gossip rag. "What did you *do*?" she repeated. "With regard to my son, I mean."

Rolling his eyes, Henry regarded his sister with another smirk. "Well, I may have made a few suggestions here and there," he finally admitted. "Spread the word he would be home for Easter, so to speak."

Hannah scoffed. "But, why? He's too young to be considering marriage."

Allowing a long sigh, Henry finally said, "But you and I are not."

Blinking, as much to fight off sleep as to sort her brother's words, Hannah asked, "You're thinking to finally take a wife?"

Henry nodded. "It's past time I do. I didn't mean to wait this long."

"Then why did you?"

Henry's eyes darted to the side, and Hannah was once again struck by his resemblance to Tom. Only his blonde hair was diffcrent. "You looked just like Tom when you did that," she accused. "The moment he told us he was marrying

Lady Grandby," she added as her eyes widened. "Have you... have you someone in mind for your wife?"

Shaking his head, Henry said, "I do not. Which is why I thought it best I accepted the same invitations as your son received and act as an escort for the two of you."

Hannah furrowed a brow. "I'll go with you, of course," she said. "Make sure you're not proposing to the first woman who gives you a passing glance."

It was Henry's turn to scoff. "I am not so easily impressed by the fairer sex."

"You have always been rather harsh in your assessment of us," Hannah accused.

Henry gave a start, his brows furrowing before his back settled against the settee. "Is it really too much to expect to find someone like... like Mother? Or you?" he asked rhetorically.

Dumbstruck, Hannah stared at Henry for several seconds. "The very last woman I would expect you to want for a wife is me, which has me wondering why you would be in pursuit of such a creature."

"Well, now who is harsh in her assessment?" Henry countered as he leaned his elbows onto his knees. His head dropped into his hands. "I just mean that I do not wish to end up with an insipid English miss."

"I was once an insipid English miss," Hannah argued.

"But you didn't fawn over every unattached male who glanced in your direction."

Hannah's gaze turned from his and looked inward. "True," she whispered. "Because I had already set my cap on my future husband."

Henry regarded her for a moment before his attention once again went to his hands. "I'm sorry he died," he whispered. "I know I believed you only—"

"He is not dead," Hannah interrupted. Then her eyes

darted to one side, much like her brother's did when he was sorting a problem. "At least, I've no reason to believe he is no longer of this earth."

Henry blinked, his brows once again furrowing. "The future husband you spoke of was not Harrington?"

Hannah gave him an expression of annoyance. "You know he was not."

"Then why did you marry Harrington?"

Hannah's continued annoyance was apparent in her voice. "Because he asked. Because he was besotted with me. Because Mother didn't tell me not to, and Father encouraged me to. Practically begged me to. Because..." She sighed. "Because it was the right thing to do at the time."

Henry dipped his head back into his hands. "I guess I... I always thought you felt affection for Harrington."

"I did," Hannah replied, as she fought back the tears that threatened. The thought of climbing into the Mayfield town coach and spending the night in her own bed no longer held any appeal. She would only wake up to discover once again that her husband was no longer alive.

But Edward was home. She had him to look forward to seeing every morning at breakfast for the next week.

Well, she hoped he would be home by now. She had cringed when she learned Mayfield had insisted Edward join him for an evening at his club. Hannah feared her father-in-law had arranged for a courtesan to entertain her son until Henry told her Brooks's didn't offer that sort of service.

*Mayfield will just play whist*, Henry had assured her. *And Edward will be left to find his own game of chance, or someone to engage in conversation.*

*That doesn't make me feel any better,* Hannah had said.

· · ·

"There must be some young lady you have thought about making your wife," Hannah reasoned, deciding it was time they discussed Henry's prospects.

Henry was about to accuse her of changing the subject, but he had seen her eyes brighten with unshed tears and thought better of it. "There is a rather comely young woman who works for the Wellinghams," he said on a sigh.

Hannah stared at him. "A housemaid?"

He nodded before he cleared his throat and grinned. "I am teasing, of course."

For just a moment, Hannah was sure he *wasn't* teasing, but she decided not to press the issue. "I suppose you've read the latest issue of Debrett's?" she asked, referring to the book that detailed the progenies of the aristocratic families of Great Britain.

"Twice," he admitted. "Although there are a couple of possibilities, I rather doubt their mothers will agree to a marriage to a commoner," he argued.

"We are a bit on the fringe, are we not?" Hannah murmured in reply. Although their mother was the daughter of a duke and aunt to a current duke, their father could claim no relation to a peer of the realm. Given their parents' ownership of about half the townhouses in King Street, Henry stood to inherit not only a vast sum of money, but the houses, as well.

Sometimes wealth was a better draw than aristocratic lineage these days.

"Have you been holding off taking a wife until Father dies?" Hannah asked in a whisper. "So you'll have the inheritance?"

Henry shook his head. "No. He gave me most of my inheritance when I reached five-and-twenty," he replied.

Doing her best to hide her surprise, Hannah furrowed a

brow. Her dowry had been her inheritance, bestowed on Charles Harrington when they married. At least Charles had been quick to establish a settlement for her and any children they might have, claiming he hadn't taken any of the dowry for himself. Given his allowance and what he stood to inherit once Mayfield died, it made sense he wouldn't require the dowry. "So... why have you waited?"

Giving his head a shake, Henry allowed an audible sigh. "I haven't *waited*, exactly," he said softly. "I just haven't... I just haven't found anyone I wish to wake up to every morning."

"Not even a housemaid?" Hannah asked in a whisper.

Henry stared at her for a long moment before he tore his gaze away. "Would you be vexed if I courted such a creature?"

Hannah shook her head. "Not if she made you a happy man," she replied in a whisper.

"What do you suppose Mother would say?"

Rolling her eyes, Hannah reached out to place a hand on his arm. "She of all people would understand," she replied in a quiet voice. "After all, she married a butler."

A grimace appeared on Henry's face before he could hide it. "I do not think the circumstances are the same."

"Why ever not?"

Henry straightened in his chair. "A butler's status is far higher than that of a housemaid."

"They're both in service," Hannah argued. "Who is she?"

"I'm not sure."

Hannah stood up from the settee and regarded her brother with a look of disbelief. Her hands went to her hips. "Of course you are."

Henry shook his head. "I've seen her. I've never spoken to her," he added, once he realized Hannah wasn't about to give up her line of questioning.

"What's her name?"

"I've no idea," he claimed. "I've only seen her from my bedchamber window. When she was on the street." When Hannah indicated he needed to continue, he allowed an audible sigh. "When she's just stepped from a town coach in front of the Wellingham's townhouse. Every Monday morning just after dawn. I only first noticed her about three weeks ago."

Hannah stared at him for a moment as her brows furrowed. "Blonde hair? Cut short and curly? About my height?" She held a hand up level with the top of her head.

Henry frowned. "Maybe."

"I've no idea who she is," Hannah stated, her attention on the glass of claret he still held. Her eyes betrayed her delight, though.

"What?!" Henry's mouth dropped open in exasperation, which had Hannah reaching out with a finger toward his chin. He snapped his mouth closed before she could do so.

"I really don't. But now I have an idea of where to start with my inquiries," she teased, an impish grin appearing that had her looking years younger.

His eyes once again darting to one side, Henry said, "I suppose you'll ask Mrs. Wellingham?"

"I might," Hannah hedged.

Henry stared at his sister for several seconds. "Will you tell me what you discover?"

Hannah rolled her eyes. "You will be the first I tell," she promised. "But this does not absolve you from doing what you can to discover her identity for yourself."

Looking as if he'd been scolded by their father, he dipped his head and scowled. "Understood."

Hannah waved for a footman to join them in the parlor. "I've decided to spend the night here," she announced. "Could you let my coachman know and have him send word of my whereabouts to Harrington House? And return for me at ten o'clock—?"

"Eleven o'clock," Henry interrupted. "Breakfast won't be served until Mother is up and about, and that's usually after nine on Saturdays."

Hannah's expression screwed into one of annoyance. "Eleven o'clock?"

The footman nodded. "Very good, my lady." He turned on his heel and rushed from the parlor.

"What are you planning?" Henry asked, suddenly apprehensive.

Hannah gathered her reticule and took the glass of claret from Henry. "Other than going to sleep? Nothing," she replied, just before she drained the glass. She leaned against Henry's side and kissed him on the cheek. "Go to bed, Henry." Without waiting for a reply, she took her leave of the parlor and made her way to her old bedchamber.

She was out of Henry's hearing range when she added, "Tomorrow is another matter, however."

*H*enry watched his sister's retreating back, sure she was plotting something. He thought about chasing her down. Thought about insisting she forget everything he had said about the comely Wellingham housemaid.

But he also knew he wanted an introduction to the young woman.

What if she was who he had been imagining in the middle of the night? A young, blonde-haired woman tucked up against his side, one of her legs betwixt his, and a bent arm resting on his chest?

He let out a soft curse when he felt his body respond with desire, his pantaloons becoming far too tight. Although he had considered asking Emma Wellingham if she might introduce him to her maid, perhaps he would have his sister arrange an introduction.

At least it would allow him the courtesy of helping the young woman step down from her coach on Monday mornings and step into it on Saturday afternoons.

Perhaps after that, he could ask that she join him for a luncheon.

He shook his head, annoyed when a yawn interrupted his thoughts. Heading for his own bedchamber, he allowed his mind to imagine far too much of the housemaid wearing far too little.

# CHAPTER 10

# A PLAN FOR A REINTRODUCTION

*M*eanwhile, back at Brooks's, Mayfair

"Did I say something wrong, sir?" Edward asked as he regarded the gentleman who sat across from him. When he noted Graham's reaction—saw how the older man seemed to struggle to remain upright in his chair—he added, "Sir, are you well?"

The sensation of vertigo once again had Graham wavering as he stared at Mayfield's heir. Failing that, he allowed a curse of disbelief as his eyes nearly rolled up into his head. Then he remembered Edward's query. "Not wrong, exactly. Just... unexpected."

*If you're still of a mind to marry her.*

"How so?"

Blinking, Graham was about to allow his gaze to sweep the room when he noticed the footman had delivered his brandy. He took a long drink and then closed his eyes in appreciation. Although French brandy was easy to obtain in Boston—imports from France were frequent and lucrative for Wellingham Imports' Boston office—Graham hadn't drunk anything other than ale during the three-week Atlantic crossing. "Let us just say that I would never expect the whelp of my nemesis to encourage a marriage between his mother and me," he said, his brows furrowing in confusion. "Which has me wondering... what are you about?"

Feeling a bit foolish, Edward allowed a shrug. "My Mother is just now out of mourning. I am aware of rumors that there are several members of the aristocracy that wish to court her, or otherwise engage her... time," he explained in a quiet voice. "But I do not want her subjected to their... attentions."

Graham blinked. And blinked again. "I should think Hannah capable of making her own decisions with regard to whom she spends her time with," he replied, not even realizing he had used her given name.

"Me as well, but shouldn't we be a bit... *intentional* in all of this?" Edward countered. "See to it you are the *only* one she allows to court her?"

Graham couldn't argue with the young man's logic. "How do you propose I manage it?"

A brilliant smile appeared on Edward's face. "Come for dinner at Harrington House. Tomorrow night," he said with such glee, Graham was left wondering if the entire meeting was a ruse to make him out as some simpleton. As a pretender to Hannah Simpson Harrington's affections.

"I expect I shall be having dinner with my parents on the morrow. I've only just returned to London today."

"Sunday night, then."

"The Harrington House servants don't have the day off?" Graham countered, amazed he could come up with the excuse to beg off so quickly. "Besides, Sunday is Easter."

Edward blinked. "Good point. Monday night, then."

Deciding the young man wasn't about to give up, Graham resisted the urge to sigh out loud. "What time?" he asked, suspicion evident in his voice. He thought of the dinner invitation he had received from Thomas, and he really didn't wish to send his regrets. The opportunity to spend time in Hannah's company couldn't be missed, however. Even if the Earl and Countess of Mayfield and Hannah's son were present.

"Dinner is usually at eight, so... seven o'clock? We'll have coffee and walnuts in the parlor before the dinner bell," Edward said with excitement.

Graham furrowed a brow. "Are you sure it would be acceptable to Mayfield?" he asked.

Edward nodded. "Of course. I shall tell him of it tonight. He's just over there, playing whist with Morganfield and Haddon and..." His eyes narrowed as he attempted to determine the identity of the fourth player at the whist table.

"Trenton?" Graham offered, his lips curling into a grin when he recognized the blond-haired, blue-eyed earl that sat across from Mayfield. "He hasn't changed a bit."

Glancing in the direction of the table in question, Edward said, "His oldest son looks just like him."

"Gabe the Younger?"

"Indeed. He was caught in the parson's mouse trap just a couple of months ago," Edward said with a smirk.

Graham gave a start. "Gabe is married?"

"Indeed. To a potter he met at the British Museum," Edward replied. "She's... probably a bit older than he is, but they are a handsome couple, and they married for love," he added in a quiet voice.

"The only reason to wed," Graham countered quietly.

Edward's eyes widened. "I do hope I shall end up in such a situation."

Graham regarded the young heir and allowed a sigh. "Then you shall have to inform your mother and your grandfather of your intent so that a marriage is not arranged on your behalf. As I recall, it seemed it was the way of the world when I was last in England."

Edward dipped his head. "Not so much, these days," he said. "Although I expect there will be young ladies I am supposed to find suitable, I do not intend to marry until I am well past twenty."

"So… three or four years, then?" Graham asked, a smirk appearing. He could barely remember having turned twenty.

"Mayhap seven or eight," Edward countered. "Unlike you, I have not yet had a visit from Cupid."

Graham furrowed a brow. "What makes you think I had a visit from Cupid?"

Settling back into his chair, Edward said, "You're coming to dinner Monday night. To claim my mother. You wouldn't be doing that if you hadn't already taken a direct hit to the heart."

Stunned at the young man's insight, Graham was left speechless for a few minutes. He used the time to savor the brandy and consider how to respond. "What if she has set her cap on another?"

The young man across from him shook his head. "Was there not a bargain betwixt the two of you?" he asked. "One that assured *you* would be her husband if my father could not be?"

Graham stared at the Mayfield heir apparent, doing his best to hold back a curse. "She told you about the bargain?"

Edward captured his lower lip with an eye tooth as his eyes darted to one side. "Under duress, perhaps," he admitted.

Frowning, Graham asked, "How much duress? What did you… what did you *do* to her?"

Allowing a wicked grin, Edward said, "The kind only a devoted son can impose."

"Bastard," Graham accused, not so lightly.

"Doubtful," Edward replied. "For that would make me *your* son." The words were out of his mouth before he could stop them, so he did his best to keep his chin up and his gaze steady as he stared at Graham.

Stunned at the young man's words, Graham gave a shake of his head. "Is that what you believe?"

It was possible, he supposed. Hannah had lain with him that last night before he departed England. Begged him to bed her, for she had learned something about the man she was to marry, and she was unsure if she could abide a marriage without the hope of romantic love.

So he had taken her virtue, but only because he had hoped her mind might be changed. Hoped she might break off the engagement. Hoped she might instead agree to wait for him to make his fortune and marry him.

Someone had convinced her to go through with it, though. Perhaps she even knew that night she would marry Charles, no matter what transpired between them.

The note he found pinned to his pillow the following morning had him leaving for Boston, bitter but unable to hate the only woman he had ever loved.

Edward blinked several times before his head hit the back of his chair. "I only wish to know the truth of the matter."

Graham gave a shake of his head. "Did you have a reason to doubt your mother's virtue?"

His head dipping, Edward finally shook his head. "The Duke of Ariley is my great uncle, but apparently my grandfather was a butler. Sorting my mother has not been an easy task," he said in a quiet voice.

Hissing, Graham found it easy to come to Hannah's defense. "Miss Hannah was one of the most virtuous women in all of England. Her father's former occupation had nothing whatsoever to do with how she was raised, other than she had an appreciation for those in service and a thorough understanding of life as an aristocrat. As her son, you would be wise to embrace both lineages and live the best life you can knowing what you know," he scolded.

Edward regarded Graham with a furrowed brow for some time before he said, "I wish someone would have said those words to me when I was much younger."

Graham shrugged. "Better late than never."

Nodding, Edward drained his brandy and said, "Agreed."

His own brandy glass empty, Graham said, "Lord Harrington, are you not?"

Giving a start, Edward said, "I learned just this evening that I have the courtesy title of baron, but... I have not yet used it."

"Use it," Graham replied. "No matter your youth. Even if Lady Mayfield lives to be a hundred and Mayfield is forced to follow suit, you'll one day be an earl. It's best you get used to the idea."

Laughing at the mention of his grandfather having to live as long as his grandmother, Edward said, "I suppose you're going to tell me not to bother returning to school?"

Graham regarded the younger man for a time before he said, "Do you know your Latin?"

"I do," Edward answered in Latin.

"Some Greek?"

Edward recited a quick response in Greek. "I am fluent in French, as well, but I've no idea why I had to learn it."

"Probably to appease your mother."

His face reddening, Edward glanced in the direction of the Earl of Mayfield before he said, "You had to learn it, too?"

Graham allowed a nod. "My parents aren't even aristocrats," he murmured, and then he struggled to suppress a yawn. "Apologies."

"Are you well?"

Graham squeezed his eyes shut and straightened in the chair. "Besides lacking a good night's sleep for the past three weeks, I am."

"Have you a place to stay, sir?" Edward asked, his brow furrowed.

Sure he detected a hint of genuine concern, Graham cleared his throat. "The entirety of the Woodscastle estate, it would seem. None of my cousins—nor my parents—seem to have use of it at the moment."

Edward nodded. "That is a relief, sir. But should you have required lodgings for the night, I would have been happy to offer a guest bedchamber at Harrington House."

Arching a brow in surprise, Graham was about to admonish the young man when he realized Edward was serious. He wasn't teasing. He wasn't setting up Graham for some kind of public humiliation. "That is rather kind of you," Graham murmured. "But given Hannah is your mother, I suppose I shouldn't be surprised."

"She is a charitable woman," Edward agreed. "Unlike other women of her station, she does genuinely care about the less fortunate." He displayed an expression that suggested he was proud of his mother, but then he gave a quick shake of his head. "Not that you, sir, are less fortunate."

"Thank you for the clarification," Graham muttered. "Unless something drastic has occurred in the past few weeks, I cannot count myself among the less fortunate. Indeed, I do believe I shall soon be taking on my father's responsibilities at Wellingham Imports. Perhaps not right away, but within the year. One day I shall inherit his share and eventually my mother's, at which point I shall be the majority owner."

"Mr. Wellingham wishes to retire?" Edward asked in surprise.

Furrowing a brow, Graham allowed a shrug. "My mother

has already arranged her replacement in the hopes they can spend more time in Derbyshire."

"At Cherrywood?" Edward asked, referring to the country estate owned by the Burroughs family. Although the direct descendants of the Duke of Ariley rarely visited the large manor home surrounded by a parkland and gardens, Gregory Grandby and his brood—along with Thomas and Emma Wellingham—had adopted it as their home for the holidays.

Graham blinked. "Yes. How is it you know about Cherrywood?"

His shoulders lifting in a shrug, the young man said, "As the grandson of Lady Simpson, I have spent many a summer and a few Christmastides at Cherrywood."

Allowing a chuckle, Graham finally nodded. Edward had more of a right to call Cherrywood a second home than he did. "I suppose you have," he murmured. When another yawn threatened, he said, "Pardon me, but I really should take my leave."

Edward dared a glance in his grandfather's direction, noting how the whist players were concentrating on their cards. They probably hadn't even noticed his conversation with Graham Wellingham. "So you will come for dinner? Monday evening?" he asked. "I should like very much to be the one to introduce you to my mother."

Graham winced. "That would have required you be born about the same year as me."

"Reintroduce," Edward clarified. "I know she will be so happy to see you again. I should like to be present when her turtle appears in the parlor."

Once again wincing at the nickname, Graham rolled his eyes. Realizing the young man wasn't going to be deterred, he said, "Dinner, then. Seven o'clock?"

"Perfect," Edward replied. "Harrington House, in Park Lane."

"I know where it is," Graham replied. He turned his attention to his brandy glass and said, "Thank you for the drink. I do believe it's past time I take advantage of my bedchamber at Woodscastle. I'll see you Monday at seven o'clock at Harrington House." He stood and gave himself a moment to be sure he was steady on his feet before he bowed.

"It's been an honor, sir."

Graham regarded the young man for a long moment. "As for me, as well." Feeling as if he might pass out at any moment, Graham made his way to the exit and then to the town coach parked down the street.

He knew Edward watched his departure, and despite his land legs not yet firmly in place, Graham was determined not to embarrass himself as he made his way to the Woodscastle coach.

"Where to, sir?" Mr. Allen asked from the driver's bench.

Graham couldn't help but chuckle. "Home. You'll no doubt have to wake me when we arrive."

The driver gave him a nod of understanding. "Will do, sir."

The coach didn't even make it to Jermyn Street before Graham was sound asleep.

## CHAPTER 11

## A GRANDSON EXPLAINS MUCH

*A few minutes later, still at Brooks's*
Edward finally found his way to the faro tables and watched the play until he was sure he understood the rules. When the dealer gave him an expectant glance, he nodded and placed a twenty pound note on the table.

The play was quick and rewarding, his suspicions as to the odds favoring a player confirmed when he won more than he lost.

When his winnings had increased to one-hundred-and-twenty pounds, he gave the dealer a tip and pocketed the rest as he watched the foursome playing whist stand almost in unison. From his grandfather's expression, Edward was fairly sure the earl had lost most, if not all, of his allowance during the play.

When Mayfield finally joined him at the buffet for the supper—Edward had already helped himself and was in line for a second helping—he grumbled about the Marquess of Morganfield's ability to cheat without being caught. "He's practically family now that Haddon is married to Juliet," he said with disgust.

"How much did you lose to Morganfield?"

Mayfield stiffened, his eyes darting to one side. "You cannot tell your grandmother," he warned.

"You expect she will ask me?" Edward asked in surprise.

The earl nodded. "I have no doubt."

Edward fished in his pockets and handed over half his winnings.

Frowning Mayfield asked, "What's this?" as he rifled through the fifty pounds of bank notes.

"This is the money you shall show grandmother when she asks if you enjoyed yourself on this night," Edward replied.

"Where did you get this?" Mayfield asked as he stared at the stack of notes. "I only gave you a twenty pound note."

Edward motioned toward the faro tables. "Might I recommend you share the money with grandmother? Suggest she buy herself some frippery? I will do the same with the rest of my winnings."

"But, *why?*" Mayfield asked, his bushy brows furrowing in confusion as they took seats at a dining table.

"It will go a long way toward smoothing things over when we arrive home an hour later than we said we would," Edward said before tucking into his meal.

His eyes widening in fear, Mayfield pulled his chronometer from his waistcoat pocket and allowed a curse. "You've a good head on your shoulders, Harrington. If I was looking at you, I would think you were six-and-thirty."

Edward dipped his head. "I hope you'll still think that when I tell you who I have invited to come for dinner the day after tomorrow."

Mayfield furrowed a brow. "But we don't seat a formal dinner on Sunday evenings," he argued, picking at his food.

Tapping his chronometer to indicate it was well past

midnight, Edward said, "The day after tomorrow is Monday."

"Ah, so it is," Mayfield murmured. He ate his supper, continuing to complain about having been cheated as Edward simply listened and watched those around them. When his grandfather had finished his meal, they stood up to leave and Mayfield asked, "Who have you invited to dinner?"

Edward motioned to where the footman was holding the door for them, and Mayfield allowed the other footman to help with his greatcoat while Edward saw to his own.

"That man you were speaking with earlier this evening?" Mayfield guessed as they took their leave of the club and headed to where their coach was parked. "He's the one you invited to dinner?"

"Indeed," Edward replied, surprised his grandfather had even noticed him while he played whist. His attention seemed entirely focused on the game.

"Who is he?"

For a moment, Edward was tempted to say, "My father," but Graham's lecture about Hannah had him doubting what he had come to suspect over the past few years.

Then he considered answering with, "My future step-father," but thought better of it.

Instead, he said, "The future owner of Wellingham Imports and a cousin to the Earl of Trenton. He's just today returned from Boston."

"Looking for an investor, no doubt," Mayfield grumbled.

Allowing a guffaw, Edward said, "He has no need of our blunt, sir."

Mayfield grunted his disbelief. "If not blunt, then what does he want?"

Edward regarded his grandfather by the dim light of the lantern that hung on the side of the town coach and said, "Only his due. And I intend to see that he gets it."

Mayfield paused a moment, regarding his grandson with a furrowed brow. Then he stepped up into the town coach and settled into the velvet squabs. He watched as Edward took the seat opposite, surprised when the young man didn't offer any more information about what he'd been doing— and with whom—whilst at Brooks's.

"What's going on in that head of yours?" Mayfield asked, suspicion evident in his voice.

Edward furrowed a brow. "Sorting. I've been sorting, sir."

"Numbers?"

"Men," Edward replied. "Suitors, actually." Even in the dark, Edward could tell his grandfather had come to the wrong conclusion. "For *mother*," he clarified.

"But... she hasn't *had* any suitors," Mayfield argued.

"She will. Starting Tuesday, with the first ball of the Season," Edward argued. "She's out of mourning now, so I expect there will be a steady stream of widowers and older bachelors intent on gaining her hand in marriage."

Mayfield stared at his grandson in wonder. "How is it you know this?"

Edward sighed. "Really, Grandfather. All the years I have spent at Eton have shown me the various scenarios that can occur when someone dies," he replied. "And I intend to have a say in who my mother marries."

His eyes widening in both surprise and respect for his heir, Mayfield said, "Well, I have to admit, I am impressed, young man. So impressed, in fact, I think I shall make good on my earlier suggestion and *order* you to remain at Harrington House."

Edward gave a start. "You were... you were *serious* about me not returning to school?"

Mayfield sighed. Loudly. "Truth be told, I could use you and your sensibility now," he murmured. "I am growing old, and I find I am not as interested in running the earldom as I should be. My man of business is on the verge of quitting me, given how long it takes for me to answer his queries."

"Not as interested?" Edward repeated, hearing a slight slur in his grandfather's words. He hadn't thought the man drunk when they left the club, but now he thought he might be quite foxed. "Does that mean... you have not? Been running the earldom, I mean." He remembered the state of the exterior of Harrington House upon his arrival and now wondered if all the Mayfield properties were in similar states of disrepair.

Rolling his eyes, Mayfield whispered, "I do what I must, but no more than that. If it wasn't for J. Arthur Peabody, the earldom would belong to the Crown. The Mayfield earldom deserves better. But all I want to do is fuck my wife, sleep, eat, drink, and to beat Morganfield at cards."

Edward blinked, sure his face was bright red at hearing what his grandfather wanted to be doing with his grandmother.

He had heard the rumors, of course. Rumors that Mayfield was quite enamored with his countess had floated about Mayfair for Edward's entire life.

Edward had only paid witness to their carnal activities once, when he was in the Harrington House library looking for a book and ended up trapped there. He hid behind some bookshelves for nearly an hour as his grandparents tupped in one of the leather sofas and then over a library table. "And when you're sober?" he asked, just to test the earl.

Mayfield frowned. "Fuck my wife, eat, drink, and beat Morganfield at cards," he repeated. He leaned forward and lowered his voice. "Got her in the office of that rag of hers a few times. Over the desk, and once, we..." He stopped speaking when he saw how Edward had his hands pressed against his ears. "What?"

Edward shook his head and tentatively removed his

hands from his ears. "Really, sir, I shouldn't wish to hear what you do to my grandmother in the privacy of your... bedchamber... or... or her office," he stammered.

Allowing a loud laugh filled with amusement, Mayfield shook in the squabs and finally sobered. "I suppose you are a bit young yet," he said on a sigh. "Haven't tupped a barmaid, have you?"

"I have not yet bedded a woman," Edward admitted with a grimace. "Although most of my classmates have managed it to some degree."

"Why haven't you?" There was no censure in the query, even if it was expected a boy of sixteen would have had at least one encounter with a prostitute.

Edward winced. "If you must know, sir, I have an aversion to contracting a venereal disease," he said in a quiet voice. "After seeing the evidence of such on three of my classmates, I do not wish for such a fate for myself."

A low rumble erupted from the earl. "Ah, that is rather wise of you," he murmured. After a long moment, he asked, "Will you stay in Mayfair for the Season?"

Not ready to give his grandfather an answer, Edward said, "Perhaps we should sleep on it this night and discuss it over breakfast in the morning."

Mayfield leaned into a corner of the coach and sighed rather loudly. "Agreed. I suppose we should do the same as it applies to your mother's next husband."

Alarmed, Edward straightened. "Oh, that's already been sorted. As I mentioned earlier, I met him this evening. He's a good man."

"What?" Mayfield asked as he attempted to sit up, obviously deep enough in his cups to have already forgotten their conversation just outside of the club. "Who?"

Edward shrugged a shoulder. "The one she was supposed to have married in the first place," he replied.

Mayfield wavered on his seat, the swaying town coach adding to his unsteadiness. "Oh?" was all he could think to say, his alcohol-impaired brain having a hard time keeping him awake. It did manage to serve up one bit of reasoning before he succumbed to sleep. "You do realize you would not exist if she had."

Watching as his grandfather's head fell into the corner of the coach and hearing the man's soft snores, Edward allowed a long sigh.

Well, he wasn't about to agree completely on that point. He could not change what had happened before he was born.

But he could certainly have a say in what happened next.

CHAPTER 12

## A REUNION OF SORTS

*A* *bit over an hour later, Woodscastle, six miles southeast of London*

Refreshed from his brief nap in the town coach, Graham made his way to the library. A candle lamp was still lit on his father's mahogany desk, so he took a seat in the leather chair in front of it. He pulled out a sheet of parchment bearing the Wellingham Imports mark and wrote a note to his cousin.

*Dear Cousin Tom,*

*It seems I am expected for dinner in two places at the same time. Please do not take offense when you read that I have accepted the offer of dinner put forth by one Edward Harrington, heir to the Mayfield earldom. Seems I have a champion in the young man, and I intend to take advantage of his good opinion and take dinner at Harrington House...*

He paused to pull out his chronometer and winced when he saw the time.

Where had the day gone?

*Monday evening. I shall pay a call at your office to smooth things over. In the meantime, please give my regards to your bride. You have my permission to tell her my sordid story if it helps my cause.*

*Yours truly,*

*Your indigent cousin, Graham*

Graham shook some sand over his hastily penned missive and poured the excess into a small porcelain bowl already half-filled with the stuff. He folded his note into an envelope and sealed it, relieved the stamp in the wax revealed only a "W". At some point, he would pay a call at a stationer's and have a proper seal made with his initials.

He regarded the missive as he allowed his mind to wander, and he remembered the baron's assessment of his mother. For a moment, he had been left wondering if the two had been speaking of the same woman.

The Hannah he knew would never have been a hermit. She never would have been satisfied spending her days holed up in a house, no matter how grand. The Hannah he remembered was vivacious. She smiled easily. She flirted and flitted and made him mad with wanting her.

She teased him when she knew she shouldn't, and then apologized profusely when he pretended offense. He recalled how he sometimes took his due—a stolen kiss well away from prying eyes—and adored how she blushed but didn't scold him.

Which always left him wondering if she teased him just so he would kiss her.

The minx.

Glancing at his chronometer again, he realized it wouldn't be long before he'd have to make his way to Wapping. He had a shipment of tobacco, beaver skins and pelts to take to Wellingham Imports once the sun was above the horizon.

Suddenly aware he wasn't alone, he glanced up to discover the butler, Humphrey, regarding him from the threshold. "Evening, Humphrey."

"Good morning, I believe it is, sir," the butler replied with a nod. "Will you be requiring a valet?"

Graham shook his head. "Not tonight. If I am not awake by seven o'clock, can you knock on my door? There's much to do on the morrow."

"Very good, sir."

"Oh, and would there be any clothes appropriate for dinner at an earl's house in my wardrobe? Or my father's, perhaps?"

The query had Humphrey giving a start. "Not that would fit you, sir, given your extraordinary height. Or that would be in keeping with current fashion," he added with a wince.

"Ah," Graham responded. "Then I suppose I shall need to see to acquiring some appropriate clothes on the morrow." Although he had left his trunk on board the ship, he knew his Bostonian wardrobe would not include whatever it was British noblemen were wearing at dinner these days.

"Might I suggest a shop in New Bond Street? It sounds as if you do not have the time for a tailor to make you a bespoke suit."

"I don't suppose there's a shop close to the warehouse?" Graham asked with a pained expression.

Humphrey shook his head. "You will find the area around Wellingham Imports has changed considerably since your last visit."

It was Graham's turn to wince. "How so?"

The butler merely shrugged. "It's not *bad*, sir," he said. "Just different. It seems your father set a precedent for the type of business that exists in that area of London now, and with having to take on additional warehouse space, Wellingham Imports no longer fits in one building."

Graham thought of the mishmash of businesses that existed near the Boston docks, some of questionable legitimacy. He hoped Wellingham Imports wasn't surrounded by such disreputable concerns. "Perhaps you should wake me at your earliest convenience," he said on a sigh.

"Very good, sir."

Humphrey took his leave of the library as Graham settled back in the comfortable chair. He had a thought to make his way up to his bedchamber, but he was sound asleep before he could put the plan into motion.

## CHAPTER 13

## A PLOT IS PONDERED

*The following morning* Hannah awoke with a start, her heart hammering in her chest as the sensation of confusion settled over her. The pink tulle and satin canopy above her was familiar but entirely unexpected.

Green velvet. It was supposed to be green velvet.

Remembering where she was helped to assuage the sense of panic she'd felt as she struggled to open her eyes.

Her parents' townhouse. In King Street. The memory of the night before came flooding back, and she took a deep breath. When she sat up, she let out a screech.

"Oh, beggin' your pardon, my lady. I did na' mean ta give a fright." The words were said by Preston, the lady's maid who had been seeing to her mother for the past two decades.

Hannah stared at the lady's maid for a moment before she lifted her hands to cover her face. "I'm so sorry, Preston. I forgot where I was."

"I know how that is," the lady's maid replied as she waddled her way to the drapes and pulled them open. "I would have let ya' sleep late, but I had orders from Mr. Simpson that you be ready for breakfast."

Her eyes darting to the Baroque clock on the fireplace mantel, Hannah inhaled sharply. "That cannot be right," she whispered.

"Oh, it's right, my lady," Preston replied as she moved to the fireplace and worked to ignite the kindling for the lumps of coal.

"Is breakfast already served?" Hannah asked as she stepped from her childhood bed. She secretly thanked her father for having seen to it the floors in the bedchamber were completely covered with Axminster carpet. Given the chill in the air, she knew the floor beneath would be cold.

"Not for another half-hour, accordin' to your brother. What will you be wantin' to wear this morning?"

Hannah moved to the dressing room, unsure of what gowns she might have left behind. A quick perusal had her sighing. "This one, since it's the only one still half-fashion-able," she said on a sigh. She handed the maid a day gown of peach muslin embroidered with green leaves.

"This one is rather gorgeous on ya'," Preston remarked as she moved to pull a pair of stockings from a bureau. "How would you like me to style your hair?"

"Something quick. Just a bun," Hannah replied. "I don't want to be the last one in the breakfast parlor." She allowed Preston to help her into her chemise and corset. "What day is this?"

"Saturday, my lady."

*Saturday.*

"My brother hasn't left for the bank?"

The lady's maid shook her head. "He doesn't go to the bank on Saturdays, my lady."

Not about to question Henry's good fortune in not having to work on Saturdays—perhaps clerks of his advanced skills weren't required every day—Hannah then realized why it was he could pay witness to a maid taking her leave of the Wellingham townhouse on Saturday afternoons.

"Pray tell, Preston, do you know the name of the young woman who has been working across the street? At the Wellingham's townhouse?"

Preston opened the day gown and held it out for Hannah to step into. "Their three servants are all older, my lady."

Frowning, Hannah turned so Preston could do up the fastenings at the back of her gown. "Then who is the woman who arrives every Monday morning and takes her leave Saturday afternoons?"

Preston blinked. "Oh, you must be referring to the artist."

It was Hannah's turn to blink. "Artist?"

"Oh, aye. Mr. Wellingham hired her to paint his wife's portrait. Since Mrs. Wellingham can only sit for an hour or so before she has to leave for her position at their company, Miss Overby lives there during the week to work on the paintin' and returns to her home for Sundays."

"Miss Overby?" Hannah repeated, her eyes widening in delight.

"Yes, my lady." Preston's eyes narrowed. "Do you know the artist?"

"Blonde hair? Cut short and curly?"

"Aye."

Hannah grinned. "I think I do," she whispered as she took a seat at the dressing table.

"Has she painted your portrait?"

"Unfortunately, no." The reminder that she and Charlie hadn't had a family portrait done since Edward was breeched had her feeling disappointment.

"Lady Simpson likes to pay a call on her in the middle of the day. I think they have tea together. Her ladyship is always in a fine mood when she returns. Says it's a joy to spend time with a young lady who knows what she wants for her life. Whatever that means."

Staring at the lady's maid's reflection in the dressing table mirror, Hannah asked, "And what might that be?"

Preston shrugged. "She's not said, as far as I know, my lady."

Hannah winced, realizing if she wanted to know more, she would have to ask her mother. She would need to do so without Henry present, though, for she was quite sure the woman they were discussing was the one that Henry had decided was a housemaid.

Well, he was certainly in for a surprise.

Grinning, Hannah watched as Preston brushed her hair and then twisted it into a quick knot on the top of her head. Perhaps she would have to pay a call on the young woman before she returned to Harrington House.

*A half-hour later*
"Good morning, Mother, Father," Hannah said as she sailed into the breakfast parlor and then bent to kiss her parents on their cheeks. "So good of you to have hosted me last night."

"You are welcome any night," James said as he reached for her hand and kissed her knuckles. "You look radiant, especially in that gown. It's my favorite on you."

Hannah gave her father a quelling glance. "You are the master of fabrications," she replied as she took her usual seat. In all the years they had shared breakfast, they always sat in the same chairs.

Her brother, Henry, gave a nod in her direction. "Sister."

"How are you on this beautiful morning?" she countered.

Henry regarded her with suspicion. "Surprised to see you in such fine form given your countenance last night."

Her brows furrowing, Hannah said, "Last night my countenance was tired, and now it is not." She nodded to the footman who offered her a cup of tea and then said, "Thank you," to the servant who delivered a plate filled with a variety of breakfast foods. "I do appreciate an appropriate breakfast," she added as she tucked into her meal.

Although the breakfasts at Harrington House were always filling, they were done in the manner of a buffet, and only a certain selection of foods were offered on any given day.

She couldn't fault the countess for the oversight. Temperance Harrington was an excellent hostess, but her attentions of late were on *The Tattler*. She tended to spend hours in her office where the weekly newsheet was written and printed, which for a time had Hannah wondering if the countess was entertaining a lover there when Patience Waterford, Countess of Aimsley, wasn't in the office.

After paying witness to how the earl behaved with his wife, Hannah soon realized Temperance's lover was not the pressman or another aristocrat but rather her own husband.

The two were hopelessly in lust with one another.

Any doubts she might have had were always assuaged when Mayfield returned from having paid a call at *The Tattler's* offices, his manner jovial and his words bordering on the scandalous. *My countess could have been a courtesan*, he had once said. *Or a celebrated mistress. So I am glad she is my wife.*

Hannah had simply smiled and nodded, hoping her reddened face wasn't apparent.

How was it Charlie hadn't grown up to be like his father? He would never say anything so crass. He would never say anything that might call attention to himself. Never do anything that might draw unwanted attention. Perhaps his mother's avocation had him hiding his true self.

The thought had her momentarily scowling.

"Really, Hannah. You must mind how you appear when you're thinking less than charitable thoughts about your brother," Sophia said, just before she took a sip of her tea.

Hannah gave a start. "But, I wasn't think about Henry," she argued, a forkful of eggs halfway to her mouth.

Henry drew a hand across his forehead and followed it with a "Whew! You looked positively livid just then," he murmured.

Blinking, Hannah struggled to paste a pleasant expression on her face. "I apologize. I was... ruminating."

"Is everything all right at Harrington House?" her father asked, his bushy brows furrowed with concern.

"Oh, it's fine, really. I was just... lamenting over not having had another family portrait done prior to Charlie's death."

Sophia's eyes lit with excitement. "We should have that done again," she said, her breakfast forgotten. "And I know just the artist who could do it! I'll make the arrangements today."

"Really, Mother. Isn't the one of us enough?" Henry asked. He set his coffee cup in its saucer and grimaced as if his sip of the brew was objectionable.

"Now, Henry," his father said. "It's been more than three decades since our last family sitting. Perhaps it is time we do it again. I'm certainly not getting any younger."

"Where would you even hang it?" Henry countered, obviously not pleased with the idea.

"Above the fireplace in the front salon, darling," his mother said brightly. "Although I do like having a large mirror there, a current family portrait would be so much more appropriate."

Sophia Simpson had been hosting more of her friends in the ground floor salon given it didn't require her elderly guests to climb the stairs to the parlor on the first floor.

Hannah's eyes suddenly widened. "It's a capital idea," she said as she straightened in her chair. "Perhaps Miss Overby could do it when she's finished painting Mrs. Wellingham." She wasn't surprised when her mother beamed in delight, but she noted her brother's reaction and wondered at why he displayed a pout.

"Who is Miss Overby?" James asked.

"Oh, she's the daughter of Lady Overby," Sophia replied. "And... oh, I can never remember her husband's name."

"William," Hannah offered, relieved to learn that the portrait painter was indeed related to Lily Overby, the wife of an importer for Wellingham Imports. More importantly, she was the illegitimate sister of Gabriel, Earl of Trenton.

"William, yes, that's him," Sophia said as she clapped her hands together. "He's been promoted by Thomas again. Why, if Graham never returns from Boston, I expect Mr. Overby will end up running the business alongside Mr. Vandermeer's oldest son."

The mention of Graham Wellingham had Hannah inhaling sharply. She lifted her napkin to cover her mouth, pretending she had burned her tongue.

Her brother noticed. He was about to put voice to a platitude, but Hannah's sharp glance in his direction had his jaws clamping shut.

"How very fortunate for Mr. Overby," Hannah murmured, turning her attention to her breakfast.

The conversation moved to the weather, and after a few more minutes, Hannah took her leave of the breakfast parlor with the excuse that she really needed to return to Harrington House.

Although her mother's and brother's reactions to her

announcement were entirely expected, the one her father aimed in her direction was not.

One of consternation.

So when she was about to step into the Mayfield town coach for the trip back to Harrington House, she wasn't surprised when James joined her at the curb. "I am fine, Father, really," she said as the driver opened the coach door.

"Do not despair, for your mother does not know what I do."

Hannah furrowed a blonde brow. "And what is it you know?"

James allowed an impish grin. "Plan to attend Lord Weatherstone's ball on Tuesday night, and you shall find out."

Her eyes widening in wonder, Hannah was prevented from asking for more information when her father gave her a deep bow and returned to the house, his quick steps belying his advanced age.

## CHAPTER 14

## A FAMILY REUNION

*eanwhile, in Wapping*
Having arranged for dray carts to take the *Alanzaar's* cargo to Wellingham Imports the day before meant Graham didn't have to be at the docks right at dawn. Now he watched as the last of the crates were loaded onto the carts, his chronometer just then registering ten o'clock.

"Is this all of it?" Graham asked as he regarded the array of vehicles lined up next to the *Alanzaar*. The ship's early arrival the day before had been a blessing for Graham—he didn't do well on the water and, as a result, was still unsteady on dry land—but it had meant there wasn't a team of laborers to offload the cargo until later in the day.

"Isn't that enough?" Mr. Croft asked as he gave Graham a look of chagrin. "Most of what was on board was yours." Croft, the ship's chief mate, had overseen the unloading of the crates, ensuring those marked for Wellingham Imports were ready for transport that morning.

Giving the chief mate a nod, Graham accepted the last sheet of papers associated with the cargo. "It never looks as large when it's loaded like this," he said.

"And it will look even smaller when it's been uncrated," Croft reminded him.

Graham allowed a bark of laughter as he shook Croft's hand. "Good to meet you, sir." Then he stepped into the Wellingham coach, and the parade of coach and carts made its way toward London.

*M*eanwhile, at Wellingham Imports, London

Thomas Wellingham stood outside his first floor office, leaning on the railing to regard what appeared to be chaos on the warehouse floor below. Burly men pushed crates this way and that as even burlier men loaded them onto delivery vehicles. Horses neighed in protest as they were forced to wait until carts were full before they could be put into motion. Then they disappeared out the rectangular openings in the warehouse wall at the opposite end of the building.

"You look as if you're lording over your domain," Emma Wellingham teased as she crested the wooden stairs that led from the entry of Wellingham Imports' main building.

Dressed in a sky blue day gown and pelisse and a felt hat of a slightly darker blue, she could have been any matron out for a walk near Puddle Dock. Instead, she was the head accountant for the company she owned with her husband, arriving a bit later than usual to begin her workday.

Chuckling, Thomas turned to give her a peck on her cheek. "I'm actually on the lookout for a particular delivery," he countered. "How did it go with Miss Overby this morning?"

Emma grinned. "Very well, I think. I have been dismissed, which is why I'm here a bit earlier than I thought I would be."

"Dismissed?" he repeated, his brows furrowing.

Her grin widening into a smile, Emma said, "She won't need me to pose any longer. Thinks she might even finish the painting later today, which is timely. Apparently Lady Simpson wants her to paint the Simpson family portrait next."

"Well, that's good news," Thomas replied, anxious to see the finished product. He had commissioned the young artist to paint his wife's portrait several months earlier, but given Laura Overby's sudden popularity, she had put him off until a few weeks ago. "Do you like what you've seen so far?"

Emma shrugged. "To tell you the truth, I haven't looked at it." At his expression of surprise, she added, "I thought you were."

He shook his head. "I haven't dared to take a peek. She always leaves a cloth over it," he claimed.

"Well, I guess I want to be surprised," Emma murmured.

"Are you worried she hasn't rendered you truthfully?"

"I'm worried she has," Emma replied with a giggle. "I cannot imagine why you thought it necessary for this painting to be done at my age."

Thomas gave a start. "I want it for my office."

"I do hope you're not expecting it to be like the one in Mr. Vandermeer's office," she warned. The large painting on the wall opposite Todd Vandermeer's desk was of his wife Deborah, but it was hardly a portrait. That painting was of her mostly-nude back and her profile, a satin drape barely covering her bare bottom.

To his credit, a red flush appeared on Thomas' face. "I'd have to keep the office locked all the time," he replied with a guffaw. "Lest there be a parade of your clerks coming in to take a look at their boss's bare bum."

Emma didn't have a chance to scold him when a commotion near one of the large openings in the opposite wall had them both turning at the same time.

"Isn't that Mr. Allen?" Emma asked, when she recognized the driver of the coach, a groom from Woodscastle. Several dray carts pulled in behind the coach and fanned out to fill up the available floor space.

Thomas straightened as a grin lifted his cheeks. "It is, indeed." He glanced at Emma, but before he could say anything else, she was already hurrying back down the stairs, her bell skirts lifted well above her ankles.

He followed her, hoping they weren't about to be disappointed.

Although he preferred having his only son in charge of the burgeoning Boston office, Thomas knew Graham would one day have to take over the London operation. Given how much the company had grown since Graham was last on British shores, it was far better he come home now and reacquaint himself with the business than to have to take over upon Thomas' eventual death.

A squeal of delight had several warehouse workers pausing in their labors, turning to see Emma embracing her son even before he had made it completely out of the coach in which he had arrived.

A loud laugh announced Graham's final step onto the warehouse floor. He was soon joined by his father, who rushed up to first shake his hand and then pull him into an hug.

"By the gods, how tall are you?" Thomas asked as he regarded his son with a huge grin.

"Six-feet-two is all. Mayhap an inch or more taller," Graham replied, hiding the wince he felt upon seeing his father. Nearly two decades had passed since he had last seen his parents, and although his mother still appeared much as he remembered her, his father had visibly aged. Gray hair had replaced the medium brown, and his cheeks were thinner, more hollow. He still stood straight, though, and he wasn't thick around the middle.

"I come bearing gifts, or at least everything I could manage to get on the *Alanzaar*," Graham said happily, his gaze taking in the enormity of the warehouse. When he saw the evidence of newer bricks extending beyond the original south wall, he realized why it seemed so much larger than when he had last seen it. The east wall had been moved out, nearly doubling the size of the main warehouse.

"Looks like you had the entire ship's hold," Thomas remarked as he took in the sight of all the dray carts.

"Almost all of it. Some bloke had arranged for several crates of artifacts to be brought here to England."

"Artifacts?" Emma repeated.

"Yes. For the British Museum," he complained. "Can't imagine there's any room left there for the stuff."

Emma suppressed the urge to grin, realizing her son knew nothing of the expansion currently happening at the country's largest museum—and his cousin Tom's involvement in it. "I don't suppose you noticed the name of the bloke who arranged for those shipments?" she teased as she waved a hand in the direction of the very crates to which he referred.

Graham furrowed a brow before he rolled his eyes. "Tom didn't say a word about it when I paid a call on him yesterday," he complained.

"Looks like you've brought us enough here to keep us busy until the day after tomorrow," Thomas said as he motioned for Graham to follow him.

Graham offered his arm to his mother, and Emma took it with a smile. "You look as if you're getting enough to eat," she said.

"I am. Spent the night at Woodscastle, and Humphrey

had breakfast ready for me in the dining room early this morning."

Emma's mouth opened in surprise. "You arrived last night?"

He immediately regretted his words. "I apologize. I thought you would be at Woodscastle," he said. "Tom gave me a ride there. Filled me in on his situation."

"I'm so sorry you didn't know to come to the townhouse," Emma murmured. "But I suppose it was good you spent some time in your cousin's company."

"Tom is certainly a different man than he was when I last heard from him in October," Graham remarked.

"Lady Grandby is the perfect wife for him," Emma said as they climbed the stairs to the offices.

"Which is his assessment as well," Graham agreed. "He's invited me to dinner on Monday evening, but..." He winced at remembering the invitation he had accepted for dinner at Harrington House.

"But?"

"I met someone. Last night. He insists I have dinner with his family Monday night."

"You'll have dinner with us tonight, surely," Emma said, hoping she didn't sound as if she were begging.

"Oh, I am counting on it, as is the cook at Woodscastle," Graham replied with a grin. "Tomorrow night, as well, since it's Easter." They paused in front of Thomas' office door and waited while he opened it.

Emma entered and hurried to a set of double-doors in the back wall. She opened them both, which had light flooding the front office, before moving to where a stove not only provided heat but the means to make hot water for tea. She retrieved a tea set from a cupboard along with a canister of biscuits.

"I remember when this used to be your office," Graham

said as his gaze swept the room. The south windows, much larger than they had been when he was a young boy, overlooked the Thames. A landscape painting, done by his aunt, Samantha Fitzsimmons Range, still hung where he remembered it, although now the wall was a fashionable painted ivory paneling rather than the dark wood it had been before.

He noted how thick carpet now covered the entire floor, and Emma's small escritoire had been replaced with a larger oak version, this one containing numerous drawers and cubbyholes stuffed with papers. Neat stacks of ledgers, quills and an ink pot filled the flat surface.

"It still is, darling," Emma murmured as she placed a kettle on the stove.

"You don't work with the clerks?"

She shook her head. "I did for a time, but their wives objected to a woman sharing their office," she said as she rolled her eyes. "So, I moved back in here."

"After some renovation, I see."

Grinning, she motioned for him to take a seat in the sofa that took up the short north wall. A low table was positioned in front of it, and an upholstered chair sat adjacent to the sofa.

"Indeed. I arranged for gas lines to be installed in all the offices and the warehouse ceiling, added the lighting, and had carpet put down up here. The carpet has made such a difference, especially in the clerks' office. It's quieter up here —the sounds from downstairs aren't so noticeable—and the offices seem much warmer in the winter months."

Graham watched as his father joined them, his attention on the paperwork that Graham had given him when they first stepped into the office. "Doubled the warehouse, too?" he half-asked.

Thomas allowed a grunt. "That was a challenge, but necessary. May be again soon if business continues as it has."

"If your father had his way, this building would be attached to the the one that's located north of here. But the city wouldn't allow the road to be blocked," Emma explained.

"Imagine that," Graham murmured, attempting to hide his humor.

"I was willing to have a pass-through built to allow traffic to the Thames," Thomas argued.

"But let me guess. Wellingham Imports would have been the only concern allowed to use it," Graham said with a grin.

Thomas regarded his son with a combination of chagrin and appreciation. "It made sense at the time," he replied.

"So what did you do?"

"Well, we already owned the building east of here, so we put it to use. Added stables on one side and then made it into the export house."

"It's smaller, so cargo has to be moved out more quickly," Emma explained as she poured hot water into the teapot. "Especially after the sheep have been sheared."

"Wool exports," Graham murmured, understanding her comment.

"At the same time Merino wool arrives from Portugal," Thomas put in. "Banks Textiles up in Darlington will take whatever we can bring in."

"And the transport business? To get the goods to wherever they're to go? Are you still using horse-drawn coaches, or...?"

Emma allowed a sigh as she settled into her chair and poured tea for the three of them. "As much as we would prefer to use steam-powered coaches—and we have a few— the tariffs are making it hard to justify employing them."

"Steam powered buses have been welcomed in London since they provide reliable transportation and stick to a schedule," Thomas remarked, "but not so much out on the country roads."

"Yet, Tom has invested in a number of them," Graham argued, remembering some of his conversation with his cousin from the afternoon before.

"For the time being," Thomas agreed. "He may have to move those investments to railways entirely, though. They don't seem to suffer the challenges steam-powered vehicles are having to overcome in order to stay in business."

"And our business?" Graham asked before he took a drink of his tea. "If it's anything like what's happening in Boston, Sinclair will be needing to hire on an assistant of some sort," he added, referring to his partner in the Boston office.

Thomas and Emma exchanged quick glances. "As always, there's too much business," his mother said before she offered him the plate of biscuits. "I already sent word to Mr. Sinclair that he may hire a secretary."

"It's a good thing you've decided to return to England," his father said before helping himself to a biscuit. "Which has me wondering. Why now?"

Graham's eyes darted to his mother, and she immediately stiffened in her chair. "Because I wrote to him on the matter of Lord Harrington' death," she admitted.

His brows furrowing, Thomas pulled his gaze from Emma to regard his son. "You still hold a candle for Hannah?" he asked in a quiet voice. "I would have thought you might find a girl in Boston. The daughter of a merchant? Or a politician? A rich widow?"

Graham shook his head. "Although they seem to think I would make a suitable husband, I am determined to renew my acquaintance with Lady Harrington," he explained.

"You're holding her to the bargain?" Thomas asked, a soft *huff* sounding at the end.

"I am," Graham acknowledged with a nod, a bit annoyed his mother had apparently shared the secret with his father. "And given her mourning period is over and the Season is about to begin, I can think of no better time to collect."

Emma dipped her head. "I do wish the two of you the best," she murmured. "And that you'll find Hannah as amiable as you remember her."

"But?" Graham prompted, sure she was about to add another sentiment to her comment.

"Will she find *you* as amiable? You are not the same young man who left here nearly seventeen years ago," she said in a quiet voice.

Graham's first reaction was to argue. To scold his mother for what he saw as impertinence. But he let out a sound of disbelief as the corners of his lips lifted. "I believe she will find me more so," he replied. "I am still the man she remembers. I still hold her in high regard. Besides, I have a champion on my side. One that can make all the difference."

"Oh?" Thomas asked. "You mean her mother, of course?"

Graham bristled at the reference to Lady Simpson. For the entire time he'd been in Boston, he believed the Duke of Ariley's aunt was the reason Hannah agreed to marry Charles Harrington. He could almost hate the woman for what he had assumed was a power play on her part to see her daughter wed to the heir to an earldom.

His father's words now called that assumption into question. "You are referring to Lady Simpson?" he asked carefully.

Thomas nodded. "Of course. From the day you were born, she has said you and her daughter would be wed."

Graham's brows furrowed. "Even after Lord Harrington proposed to Hannah?"

Thomas looked to Emma, whose lowered lashes suggested she knew the truth of the matter. "Emma?"

Emma allowed a short sigh. "Your father is right. Lady

Simpson still wished for her daughter to be your wife, even when she knew of Lord Harrington's interest."

For a moment, Graham felt ill at the thought that he had cursed Hannah's mother nearly every day for the week leading up to his departure from England. Learning she wasn't responsible for Hannah's acceptance of Charlie Harrington's proposal had him asking, "If not Lady Simpson, then who encouraged Hannah to marry Harrington?"

"Her father," Thomas replied, an expression of pain crossing his face.

"Mr. Simpson?" Graham repeated in disbelief. "But... why?"

Emma moved up to sit on the edge of her chair, eager to stifle any thoughts of anger her son might be considering. "So his daughter would one day be a countess," she whispered. "Quite a coup for a man who had at one time been a butler, don't you think? You hadn't put forth a proposal, and apparently you had told Hannah you wouldn't be looking to marry until you could ensure your own fortune," she said. She dipped her head. "Which made it sound as if you didn't think Wellingham Imports would be yours to inherit one day."

Graham blinked. "I've always known I would inherit at least part of the company," he argued. "But I didn't wish to rely on an allowance to keep Hannah in good stead." He paused, an expression of hurt settling over his features. "And she knew I would propose when I was good and ready."

"Are you now?" Thomas asked, his voice gentle. He remembered well how hurt Graham had been when he learned of Hannah's betrothal. How Graham had suggested it was time to start the Boston office, and how he wanted to be the one to do it. Remembered how Graham immersed himself in learning the details of Wellingham Imports' operation—even though he knew them well—

before he set out for Liverpool and then boarded a ship bound for Boston.

Graham gave a start. "More ready than you can know."

"You're prepared to court her?" Emma asked, as she refilled his teacup.

"I am."

"There will be others, now that she's out of mourning," Thomas warned.

"Doesn't matter. Hannah will accept my suit," Graham claimed.

Emma's eyes widened. "You seem terribly sure of yourself."

"I am. It seems the current Lord Harrington wants me to marry his mother," Graham said with a grin. "And who am I to argue with my future stepson?"

Emma and Thomas exchanged looks of surprise but said nothing. After all, what could they say to such a pronouncement?

# CHAPTER 15

# A PENDING PORTRAIT
# PORTENDS A PROBLEM

*ater that day, at Harrington House*
Penning a congratulatory letter to her niece, Emily Grandby, for her recent wedding to James Burroughs, Hannah paused to reread her words.

She had been sure the newlyweds were on the Continent enjoying a wedding trip. Instead, she had learned from her nephew, Tom Grandby, that they wouldn't leave London for a honeymoon until later in the year. Apparently, James' duties as his father's replacement at the Bank of England made it impossible for him to take time away just yet.

Feeling ever so guilty over her tardiness with her good wishes, she had arranged for a Chippendale console to be delivered to their townhouse as a wedding gift. Word had come from the studio that the maple and cherry wood furniture was to be delivered this Tuesday.

With any luck, her missive would arrive before the gift.

About to fold and seal the letter, Hannah was startled when the Harrington House butler interrupted her. "Potter, what is it?"

"Mr. Henry Simpson has paid a call and wonders if you are in residence, my lady."

Hannah stiffened, immediately thinking something might have happened to one of their parents.

"He said it has nothing to do with your parents," Potter added, as if he could read her mind.

Relaxing, Hannah glanced around her salon. "Have him join me here, and could you have a tea tray delivered?" She dared a glance at the Rococo clock on the fireplace mantel.

Given the time of day, she decided her mother was probably at the Wellingham townhouse having tea with Miss Laura Overby. Henry had probably planned his exit from the Simpson townhouse to coincide with his mother's departure.

"Of course, my lady." Potter backed out of the salon as Hannah quickly folded her letter to Emily and then moved to take a seat in her favorite upholstered chair.

A minute later, Henry appeared on the threshold. "Sister," he said with a bow.

From his expression, Hannah couldn't tell if he was the bearer of good news or the harbinger of bad. "Brother," she countered. She patted the chair adjacent to hers. "I've ordered tea, but I can certainly have the butler bring brandy if you'd prefer."

Henry gave her a quelling glance. "A bit early in the day for brandy," he commented. "Tea is fine. I've merely come about the issue of this... this family *portrait* Mother wants painted."

"You're not in agreement we should sit for it?"

Grimacing, Henry took the chair she had indicated and settled into it with a heavy sigh. "I am not," he admitted.

"Why ever not? An hour a day is all you'll be required, at most," Hannah insisted, remembering what Preston had said about the length of time Emma Wellingham sat for the painter in the mornings.

"A woman?" he replied curtly. "Painting portraits? It's not seemly."

Hannah blinked. "I cannot believe you just said that," she replied in surprise. "I thought you seemed especially fond of the wedding portrait our nephew had done," she added, referring to a painting of Victoria and Thomas Grandby that hung over the great hall fireplace in Fairmont Park. "Miss Overby painted it."

This she knew from having had dinner with Tom and Victoria the fortnight before, a dinner party which included Henry and several other relatives of the newly-weds. The name of the artist hadn't meant so much at the time Lady Grandby mentioned it, but now it was vital information.

Henry gave a start. "She did?" he asked, just as a maid delivered the tea tray.

Hannah motioned for the maid to set it on the low table in front of her. "Indeed. Victoria said she was very professional. Always on time for their sittings and quite concerned for their comfort." She leaned forward and prepared the cups for tea.

"Older woman, I imagine," Henry murmured. "Has to be given the level of skill apparent in that wedding portrait."

Offering him a cup of tea, Hannah did her best not to grin at his expense. "Hardly," she said as she turned to pour a cup for herself.

"The lace in that gown of Lady Grandby's was rendered in such detail, it could not have been done by someone too young."

"And yet it was," Hannah murmured.

"You've met her?"

Hannah shook her head. "I have not, but Mother has had tea with her. She is quite impressed with Miss Overby."

Henry shook his head. "If she is so accomplished, how is

it I've not heard of her before?" he asked as his brows furrowed.

"Well, we're not related to her," Hannah replied. "And I rather doubt your position at the bank would have the two of you crossing paths."

"I suppose she's peculiar," Henry groused.

Hannah blinked. "Henry! I doubt that."

"Why?" Henry's simple query came at the same moment he straightened in his chair and regarded her with challenge in his eyes.

For a moment, Hannah thought he would have made an excellent soldier. Or a barrister. The enemy would cower in fear at seeing the cross expression he aimed in their direction.

In fact, she had been the victim of that look of annoyance far too often of late. Far more than she had been while they were growing up together in their parents' townhouse.

For a moment, she wondered if he directed the same expression at their parents. At his superior at the Bank of England. At the clerks who referred to him as their superior. At his friends whilst they were at their club.

When had Henry Simpson grown cross—and stayed cross—with the world?

"That look might work on one of your lowly bank clerks, Mr. Simpson, but not on me," she chided, her initial delight at what she knew about Miss Overby replaced with annoyance. Her brother's mood was rubbing off on her, and she didn't like it.

Not one bit.

Henry rolled his eyes. "Then... then why do you defend her?"

Tempted to tell him what she knew about Laura Overby —that the young lady was this very moment ensconced in the Wellingham townhouse completing a portrait of Emma Wellingham—Hannah spitefully decided to withhold the information in favor of giving him the facts as they might appear in a copy of *DeBrett's*.

"Miss Overby is Lily Overby's daughter."

Henry allowed a shrug. "Who is Lily Overby? I know Mother mentioned something about her over breakfast, but I cannot say I paid much mind."

Sighing her disbelief at hearing his query, Hannah explained, "Lily Overby is the Earl of Trenton's illegitimate sister. She married William Overby, who was at one time Thomas Wellingham's caddy at Wellingham Imports." When he didn't say anything to interrupt, she added, "He's a broker there now. Miss Overby is one of their five children. The oldest, I'm quite sure."

A look of confusion passed over Henry's face. "If the Earl of Trenton recognized Lily as his sister, why would her daughter need to work as a painter for her living?"

Hannah shrugged, tempted to share with him what she knew from Preston. Keeping the secret was so much more fun, though. "Perhaps it's not a vocation as much as it's an avocation. Or perhaps she simply enjoys painting. I suppose you would have to ask Miss Overby to know for certain," she suggested, her brows waggling.

She knew Henry would never pay a call at the Overby townhouse, so she thought to tease him with more of what she knew. "I do believe Lady Overby was a lady's maid at one point." Her eyes widened. "To Emma's half-sister, Lady Samantha. Before she married the Marquess of Plymouth," Hannah added as excitement increased in her voice. "Before Trenton found her and acknowledged her as his sister," she added happily.

Henry regarded his sister with a look of chagrin. "You are entirely too excited by the oddest of circumstances," he accused.

"I am, and I am not about to apologize for it." She

sighed, realizing he still wasn't convinced as to the importance of the painting. "Please sit for the painting, Henry. If not for me, do it for our Mother. Our last one is over thirty years old."

Wincing—Henry hated when Hannah played the Mother card—he rolled his eyes. "I shall like to think on it for a time," he replied.

"Well, don't ruminate too terribly long. I rather imagine Mother has already scheduled our sitting."

*M*eanwhile Sophia Simpson hadn't only arranged the times for her family to sit for Miss Overby, she had also determined exactly where in the Simpson townhouse she wanted them to sit. She had even encouraged the young artist to join her for a quick trip across the street so that she could show Miss Overby the first floor parlor.

"In front of the fireplace," she said when Laura Overby asked where in the room she had in mind for a backdrop.

"But, your parlor will smell of oils. Mineral spirits," Laura argued. "Although the odor doesn't linger long."

"Oh, it will be fine," Sophia replied. "I rarely host visitors in here these days." She motioned to a couple of chairs, and they moved to stand before them.

Laura furrowed a blonde brow. "Well, if you're sure. The marble mantel does provide an elegant background, and the morning sun from the two windows will cast you in a favorable light." She waited for Sophia to settle into a brightly patterned upholstered chair, noting how it could have been a throne given how the duke's sister positioned herself.

"At my age, any light is favorable," Sophia replied with a look of delight. She motioned for Laura to take a seat.

Giving the older woman an impish grin, Laura sighed

and glanced around the rest of the parlor. "You've decorated it perfectly, my lady," she murmured as she took the proffered chair. She had to resist the urge to audibly sigh at how comfortable it was. "I so wish for the day I might have such a parlor."

"Why, don't you have one already, my dear?"

Laura gave a start. "I still live with my parents in Curzon Street," she argued. "I've not yet married."

Sophia's eyes lit with mischief. "I know I have asked you before, but have you had any suitors? Since I last asked?"

Her eyes widening with humor—it had been but a fortnight since Lady Simpson had asked her the first time—Laura said, "I have not. Although I am old enough, I... I haven't exactly had a come-out."

"Because?" Sophia prompted, her back straightening as if she intended to pounce.

Laura dipped her head. "My mother has offered—several times—but I fear a young man might assume her ties to the Earl of Trenton mean I possess a larger dowry than I do. I shouldn't wish to unintentionally trick a young man."

Understanding replaced Sophia's initial look of delight. "It is awkward, is it not, to be so closely related to a peer and yet be a commoner?"

Her brows furrowing, Laura regarded the older woman a moment before she said, "I don't know that it's awkward so much as it's far more common than I had any reason to believe."

Sophia blinked. "Common?"

Laura nodded. "Why, Mrs. Wellingham's uncle is a viscount," she said, referring to Lord Chamberlain. "Mr. Wellingham is a cousin to my..." She paused to consider the relationships. "Uncle Gabriel, the earl. You have told me you are the daughter and the aunt of a duke, and your daughter is a baroness. Your son, no doubt, has connections as well."

Rather enjoying Laura's argument, Sophia grinned as she leaned in her direction and said, "His cousin is a duke, but Henry is quite satisfied with his status as a commoner. He is gainfully employed at the Bank of England, owns his own townhouse which he claims is undergoing renovations, and he shall inherit this house upon his father's death."

Laura winced at the mention of death.

"Death is inevitable," Sophia murmured with a shrug. "But I have warned my husband that he cannot die until after I have, since I have every intention of becoming a Merry Widow if he does." She grinned in delight at seeing Laura's face blush a bright red.

"My lady!" Laura scolded. She couldn't maintain her look of shock, though, when she saw Sophia's expression. Then a maid appeared with a tea tray, and their conversation ceased for a moment as the young woman poured tea and then took her leave of the parlor.

Sophia sobered as she reached for the cups, added lumps of sugar to both, and offered one to Laura. "My James has never warned me that he would take a lover upon my death, but I would never wish to deny him his need to be... *needed*. To be loved by another. He was in service as a younger man, you see, and it's been his mission in life to continue in that vein."

"In service?" Laura repeated. "He was a...?" She stopped, afraid to guess whatever level of servant James Simpson had been at one time.

"A butler. A very good butler," Sophia said.

Laura was almost relieved at hearing this news. She hadn't yet met the man, but she had seen him on the street, when he was taking his leave of his townhouse whilst she watched from the Wellingham's residence.

Mr. Simpson always appeared the epitome of refinement, his clothes perfectly tailored and his posture befitting a man of means. And yet she never had the impression he put on airs.

Sophia's gaze darted to the painting of the family that had been done when the twins were but four years of age. "He looked much like that back then."

"He's quite handsome," Laura remarked. "As are your children. And you don't seem to have aged at all."

Sophia scoffed. "That painting was done three decades ago."

"Thirty years?" The sound of disbelief was apparent in Laura's voice. She immediately attempted to calculate the children's ages in her head based on the age she thought they might have been in the painting.

"Two-and-thirty years, actually, given the twins' current ages," Sophia replied, her gaze settling on the image of Henry "I always thought Henry would be wed by now, but..." She sighed and gave her head a shake. "I almost wonder if he's decided to remain unmarried because he feels as if he cannot on account of my James and me."

Laura furrowed a brow. "Perhaps he simply hasn't met the right woman," she suggested.

Sophia's eyes darted in her guest's direction, and she allowed a grin. "Perhaps."

The two enjoyed their cups of tea as Sophia secretly plotted an introduction for her son and the painter. Although Henry might consider courting the young lady on his own, Sophia was fairly sure he would need a push in the artist's direction.

And Miss Laura Overby would have to be prepared for a collision.

# CHAPTER 16

# AN INVITATION ARRIVES

*S*aturday afternoon, Harrington House breakfast parlor
"My lady, a Fairmont Park footman delivered this for you," Potter said as he held out a silver salver.

Seated at the breakfast table, Hannah regarded the bright white missive with a look of surprise. She had already begun eating her luncheon, using the time alone to review the invitations Edward had brought with him from school.

Once again, she boggled at the sheer number he had accepted for the coming week. There were several balls, two soirées, a garden party, and a *musicale*.

"He said he's to wait for a response," the butler added as he dipped his head.

Hannah blinked and gingerly took the missive from the tray. "I do hope all is well with my nephew and his bride," she murmured as she slipped a thumb beneath the wax seal and unfolded the fine stationery.

*To my dearest aunt, Hannah,*

Hannah couldn't help the burble of laughter she felt at reading *those* words.

She was Tom Grandby's *only* aunt.

*Although it has only been a fortnight since you last graced us with your presence, the love of my life and I would like you to join us once again for dinner this Monday evening. With the entertainments beginning Tuesday night (we have received our invitation to Lord Weatherstone's ball, and we will be in attendance), we thought to start the week with a small dinner party for our closest friends.*

*I do apologize for the short notice. Marriage has made me realise I must be open to the idea of last-minute plans and appointments. Else, how would I know the joy that can be had at someone else's behest? This, I am sure, is something with which you have already been familiar.*

Hannah inhaled sharply, stunned at reading her nephew's words. Apparently, Tom was enjoying his marriage.

If that's what he meant by his words.

But what else could he mean?

Remembering Potter was waiting for a response to pass along to the footman from Fairmont Park, Hannah resumed reading.

*I intend for you to find joy in your attendance, for I have a surprise of monumental proportions. Or, in the event you have already been surprised by this particular surprise, you will at least appreciate the opportunity to spend time with those who hold you in the highest regard.*

*Please do join us.*

*Sincerely,*

*Tom and Victoria*

*(Your favorite nephew and niece)*

Hannah tittered, a hand covering her mouth. She had no idea what Tom might have in the way of a "surprise of monumental proportions," but she was certainly willing to discover it for herself.

She turned to Potter and said, "Do tell the footman that I shall attend Lady Grandby's dinner party," she said, deliberately not mentioning her nephew.

Surely Tom would find humor in her verbal RSVP, and then have a reason to tease her Monday night when she arrived at Fairmont Park. "I shall plan to arrive at..." She glanced back at the invitation and realized there wasn't a time mentioned. "Six o'clock," she said, remembering the last dinner at Fairmont Park had been served at seven of the clock.

"Very good, my lady," Potter said before he bowed and disappeared.

Hannah was still grinning when it dawned on her that the invitation didn't include Edward.

Rifling through Edward's invitations, she discovered he didn't have any for Monday evening.

Well, she would certainly surprise Tom when she showed up with Edward on her arm. But if Edward had already made plans with one of his friends in town, she would simply attend the dinner at Fairmont Park by herself and mention her son was in town for the first week of the Season.

Feeling ever so proud of herself, Hannah beamed when she was joined by the earl and his countess and then finally Edward.

Complaining his grandfather had kept him up far too late with their trip to Brooks's, Edward tucked into his luncheon, his hunger apparently insatiable.

Lady Mayfield was beaming in delight, and when Hannah asked what had her so happy, Temperance pulled out a wad of pound notes from a pocket. "Mayfield won at cards last night, and he's given all of it to me," she said happily. "Which means I'll be shopping for fripperies this afternoon. Would you care to join me?"

Hannah exchanged a glance with her son, who had paused in his eating to wink at his grandfather. "Indeed. My son has reminded me I am in need of new clothes for the Season. It seems we have invitations for the entertainments."

"I am so glad to hear it. I feared you might be forgotten," Temperance said, waving away the luncheon entree in favor of some cubed fruit.

A twinge of melancholy had Hannah inhaling. All the invitations that were opened before her had all been addressed to her son. Invitations her brother had arranged on his nephew's behalf.

So why hadn't he done the same for her?

Hannah was about to continue her conversation with Lady Mayfield, but Temperance only had eyes for her husband, and he for her. Hannah wasn't surprised when they rose in unison and announced they had business in the library.

When Edward finally lifted his head from his plate, his stomach apparently filled to capacity, he mentioned his need to find the latest version of *DeBrett's*. He bowed and was about to take his leave of the breakfast parlor when Hannah suddenly straightened.

"Oh, do not go to the library," she ordered.

Edward turned on the threshold. "Why ever not?"

Hannah's eyes darted to the side. "Your grandparents are in there. And I'm quite sure they are not reading," she replied, her face blooming with color.

Edward considered her words a moment before he let out a guffaw. "Grandfather is so horny!" he announced.

"Edward!" Hannah scolded, having a hard time resisting the urge to laugh at hearing his proclamation. The Earl of

Mayfield had obviously said *something* during their time at Brooks's the night before.

When she couldn't hide her humor any longer, though, she added, "He may not be the one at fault on this day."

Edward blinked and then allowed a brilliant grin when he remembered the money he had shared with his grandfather the night before. "Mother!" he nearly shouted.

Hannah grinned in delight. "You can look at *DeBrett's* later," she said. "In the meantime, it's high time you spent some time with your peers. Off with you," she ordered with a wave of her hand.

His brows furrowing as he sobered, Edward said, "Promise you'll pay a call on your modiste for a new ball gown?"

Reluctantly agreeing to his mandate, Hannah nodded. "I will pay a call at Madame Suzanne's this afternoon. Your grandmother has asked me to go shopping with her."

Edward didn't need to know that Suzanne's in Oxford Street featured ready-to-wear gowns. The very last thing Hannah wanted to do on this day was to stand in a modiste's shop and be poked and prodded by seamstresses armed with pins and needles.

Far better to just buy something ready-made.

Something for Monday night's dinner at Fairmont Park and something appropriate for Lord Weatherstone's ball on Tuesday.

With any luck, she would be in and out of the shop in less than an hour.

## CHAPTER 17

## A PORTRAIT REVEALED

*everal hours later, at the Wellingham townhouse in King Street*

When a sharp rap sounded on the red-painted door of 3 King Street, the housemaid, Mrs. Dahlia Larsen, opened it.

A liveried footman handed her a bright white missive. "Is Mr. Wellingham in residence?" he asked.

Dahlia narrowed her eyes, taking in the sight of the rather tall footman wearing the livery of Fairmont Park. "Well, ain't you a sight for sore eyes?" she responded, a grin teasing the corners of her mouth. She was old enough to be the servant's mother, but he didn't need to know that.

"I'm quite sure I wouldn't know," the footman replied. His eyes darted to the side, though, apparently unsure of what Dahlia meant by her words.

"What news do you bear?" she asked.

"This, my lady," he replied, as he held out a folded note. "I've been told I needn't wait for a reply."

Frowning, Dahlia accepted the missive as if she thought it might explode. "I'll be sure it's passed along to Mr. Wellingham," she replied. She watched with interest as the footman bowed and headed toward a small coach bearing a gold crest on the door. The footman appeared as if he had to bend nearly in half in order to step into the coach, which meant Dahlia was afforded a generous view of the man's posterior.

Despite having been married to one of Wellingham's grooms for thirty-five years—or maybe because of it—she tittered in delight.

Lingering far too long in the open doorway, as much for a breath of fresh air as to watch the coach pull away from the curb, Dahlia's attention went to the large Simpson town-house across the street.

As her gaze went up the four stories, she gave a start when she realized someone was staring at her from a third story window. Pretending she didn't notice, she continued her perusal of the house and then the one next to it. When her gaze darted back to the third story window, the drapes dropped in front of the face so quickly, she almost wondered if she had seen a ghost.

"Well," she huffed. She turned around and was about to close the door when Emma Wellingham appeared from the parlor.

"What is it, Dahlia?" she asked, her attention on the street beyond the door.

"I'd say it was a Peepin' Tom, but he was looking out instead of in," Dahlia said. "Not sure why he was starin' at me so, but he's not now." She held out the missive. "A footman just delivered this for Mr. Wellingham."

Emma frowned as she took the envelope. She had only just arrived from Wellingham Imports the hour before, deciding she could take the afternoon off in favor of seeing to arrangements at home now that Graham had returned. "Did you recognize whoever it was who was staring?"

Dahlia shook her head. "Didn't get a clear look, Mrs.

Wellingham. Oh, and Cook asked if you wanted tonight's dinner served here or at Woodscastle."

About to answer, Emma realized she hadn't given a thought to that night's dinner location. Although Laura had said her presence wasn't required for her to finish the portrait, Emma chose to spend the early afternoon in the parlor in the event the young woman needed her to resume her pose. "Since Graham is staying there, we should probably do it at Woodscastle. We'll spend the night and then can leave for church in the morning," she said as she considered how complicated life could be with two households and not enough servants to fully staff both.

"Very good, ma'am. I'll let the cook here know and have Mr. Allen take me to Woodscastle."

Emma nodded her understanding, glad the older woman would see to the logistics. When she turned to go back into the parlor, Laura stood on the threshold and gave a curtsy. "I'm finished with your portrait, my lady."

Excitement and a hint of worry had Emma pausing before she followed the artist into the parlor.

"I haven't quite finished the other one we discussed, but..." She allowed the sentence to trail off. "I'll have it finished later today. I wanted you to see this one first."

She led Emma to an easel on which rested the larger of two canvases, and she pulled away a Dutch cloth.

Emma inhaled softly, her eyes widening as she took in the sight of herself—an image the opposite of what she saw in a mirror but otherwise rendered perfectly. "Oh," she breathed. "You made me look so young," she said with a grin. She leaned forward, studying the sheer fabric overdress that allowed her teal blue satin dinner gown to show through. The details of the rosettes decorating the edge of the bottom ruffle had Emma gasping. "It all looks so real," she murmured.

"I know it's a style not to everyone's liking," Laura replied. "But I don't know how to do it differently."

"But this is perfect," Emma said as she continued to admire the other details in the painting. The vase of flowers atop the plinth next to which she stood. The strands of her hair, arranged in an ornate style with one long blonde lock resting on a shoulder. The sheen and folds of her teal satin gloves. The necklace of sapphires and diamonds Thomas had given her on the occasion of their twenty-fifth wedding anniversary. The matching bracelet and earrings, the jewels rendered so there were stars of light reflecting from them. "I could stare at this all day."

"You'll have to step aside so I can join you doing it," Thomas murmured, his profile appearing in Emma's peripheral vision.

Emma gave a start. "Thomas! You startled me," she accused, a grin appearing when she saw how he was admiring the painting. She glanced back at Laura and gave her a wink.

"Now I almost wish I had agreed to stand with you." Thomas said as he stepped back.

"I wish you had," Emma agreed. She turned to Laura. "Could you do one of Mr. Wellingham?"

She nodded. "I could, but it would have to wait until I am finished with my next commission," Laura replied.

"Oh? And who is the lucky subject this time?" Thomas asked.

"Subjects, sir. Lady Simpson and her family," Laura replied. "I'm to start on their portrait this Monday."

Emma's eyes widened in delight. "Then you shall continue to stay with us during the week," she said.

"But, I couldn't impose. I've already—"

"It's not an imposition in the least," Emma argued. "That is... if it's not an imposition for you," she added, her brows suddenly furrowing with worry.

Laura shook her head. "Actually, it's not. Truth be told, I've enjoyed my time here. It's made me realize I do want a home of my own."

"You practically have one given we're not here very much," Thomas murmured, his attention back on the painting. "Tell me, does it usually take this long for you to complete a painting?"

Laura and Emma exchanged quick glances. "Miss Overby has actually finished two portraits," Emma replied.

"Almost two. I still have a few hours before the other one is finished."

"Another one?" Thomas repeated, straightening to regard the artist with curiosity.

"She's been working on another commission at the same time she's been doing this one," Emma put in, hoping to keep her secret for a few more days.

"Ah, very good," Thomas replied. "Well, you'll have the house to yourself this afternoon. I'm taking my wife out to Woodscastle for dinner with our son."

"Then I shall see to it the front door is locked upon my departure this afternoon," Laura said.

Thomas furrowed a brow. "You haven't met our son, yet, have you?"

Laura's eyes widened. "I have not. Until a few minutes ago, I don't believe I even knew you had one."

Emma and Thomas exchanged quick glances, mischief in their expressions. "We'll introduce you next week," Emma promised. She turned back to Thomas. "We need to be off to Woodscastle. Graham is probably wondering where we are."

"Understood," Thomas replied. He turned to Laura. "Thank you for rendering my wife so beautifully."

Laura grinned. "You're welcome, sir."

· · ·

*few minutes later*

Thomas assisted his wife into the Wellingham town coach and followed her in. Even before he had taken his seat next to her on the bench, he asked, "Just what have you in mind for our son and Miss Overby?"

Emma settled into the squabs, an expression of surprise on her face. "Nothing," she insisted.

"I saw that look in your eye," he accused. "You're up to something."

Allowing a sigh, Emma said, "If Graham and Hannah do not end up together as we have always thought they would, then I am of the opinion Miss Overby would make a suitable wife for him," she admitted.

"Emma," he said, a warning tingeing his voice. "She's a bit young for him, don't you think?"

His wife allowed a sigh. "Young, but the perfect age to bear children," she countered.

"But you're not planning to do anything untoward?"

She shook her head. "Of course not."

Not entirely convinced, Thomas wrapped an arm around her shoulders and pulled her closer until she settled her head onto his shoulder. "I suppose you can't help it," he murmured, turning his head so he could kiss the top of hers.

Emma allowed a secret smile.

She wanted a grandchild, and given her son's age, she almost didn't care who he married.

Almost.

# CHAPTER 18

# IN THE WRONG PLACE AT
# THE RIGHT TIME

*An hour later, at 3 King Street*

Graham Wellingham gazed out the wavy glass of the hansom cab as it made its way east on Oxford Street toward King Street. A few pasteboard boxes were riding on the seat next to him, his purchases from a day spent reacquainting himself with London's shops for men.

Determined to dress appropriately for the dinner at Harrington House two nights hence, he availed himself of the advice of no less than three tailors and the current owner of the hat shop, Fitzsimmons and Smith, for what he should be wearing in London these days.

Seeing Ambrose Smith with gray hair and mutton chops for sideburns had been both a pleasant surprise and a reminder of how much time had passed since Graham had last visited his late grandfather's hat shop.

George Fitzsimmons, his mother's father, had died long before Graham was born, but George's legacy lived on in the hats that Ambrose continued to produce for his eponymous shop. Graham was fairly sure his mother still collected a small stipend in exchange for the use of the Fitzsimmons name in all the labels of the top hats that were sold there.

Although there were a few he remembered from before his time living in Boston, he marveled at the variety of hats that now existed—for both men and women. The latest version currently rested on his head, a beaver of conservative design and height. Given his own height, he hardly needed one of the stove pipe styles that would have added another four inches.

The sudden sway of the cab had Graham struggling to see a street sign on the side of a building. Even before spotting the King Street label, he recognized the townhouses that had at one time all been owned by the Simpsons. Only a few of the houses were still theirs these days, the rest having been purchased by their residents when James Simpson elected a quieter, more retired life after the birth of the twins.

The cab slowed to a halt, the whinny of an annoyed horse sounding from in front. Surveying the façade of the town-house adorned with a "3" on its red brick face, Graham was heartened to see it was clean of soot. A few early spring blooms colored the greenery in two pots that flanked the entrance. Behind the door, he expected to find his parents and the promise of an evening eating a sumptuous dinner and hours to catch up on the latest *on-dit*.

He gathered his boxes into one arm and paid the driver. Unsure if a butler was employed, he opted to simply step into the vestibule and see to his own hat and greatcoat.

Finding the house quiet, he made his way to the parlor, sure he would find his mother enjoying a glass of claret. "It's just me, Mother," he called out as he stepped into the parlor.

And stopped short.

A young woman who was definitely not his mother was regarding him with large blue eyes and an expression of shock.

· · ·

*I*n the middle of a particularly fine brush stroke, Laura gave a start and stepped back from the easel at the sound of the front door opening. Given that Dahlia and the Wellinghams had all taken their leave, she was quite sure she was the only one in the townhouse. At the sudden appearance of a rather tall gentleman, she straightened and briefly wondered if she might be close enough to the fireplace to grab the poker. Her paintbrush would hardly work as a weapon.

"You're not my mother," the man said as he stopped in his tracks.

"I'm not anyone's mother," Laura said with a shake of her head. She watched as the intruder glanced around the parlor, apparently unsure of his surroundings.

He furrowed a brow. "This is Number Three, is it not?"

Laura nodded. "It is."

Appearing flummoxed, he asked, "And the Wellinghams still live here?"

"They do," she affirmed.

His eyes darted about. "Are they... in residence?" he asked as he took a few steps in her direction.

She shook her head. "They are not," she replied as she took two steps back, her paintbrush held up as if she might use it as a dart. Perhaps the threat of the bright red paint at its tip might act as a warning to the intruder.

"Might you be expecting them? Soon?" he asked as he stepped around her easel and glanced at the canvas that was mounted on it.

Laura watched as he did a double-take and then took a step back in her direction. She would have taken another step back, but her backside was already pressed against the front of an *escritoire.*

"Well, I've found my mother," the man said as he blinked. He glanced back at her. "An excellent likeness, although I admit I cannot attest to the exactness of her..." He inhaled and let the breath out in a *whoosh*. "Backside," he whispered.

"Thank you," Laura replied, not quite sure what else she could say. "Am I to understand Mrs. Wellingham is your mother?" she asked.

Graham's attention had gone back to the painting. "She is," he murmured as he bent and examined the painting more closely.

"It's not quite finished."

"Are you quite sure?"

"Of course I'm sure," she countered. "I am the artist, after all." When he turned around again, she inhaled softly. "Graham?"

"I am," he acknowledged as he bowed. His brows furrowed as he seemed to struggle with determining her identity. "You have me at a disadvantage, my lady," he finally admitted. "You seem familiar, but..."

Blinking at the courtesy, Laura said, "Laura Overby," as she dipped a curtsy.

Graham blinked. And blinked again. "*Laura?*"

Her eyes widening—she could hardly believe he would remember her, let alone her name—she said, "I am."

"I saw your father this morning. At the warehouse," he said with excitement. "He's certainly come a long way since his days as a caddy for my father," he remarked.

Laura relaxed, happy to hear his words. "He has been promoted many times since then."

"And you... you are a painter?"

"I am. I do portraits. I actually just finished one of your mother."

When he indicated the one on the easel, she shook her

head. "Your father doesn't know about this one," Laura said as she quickly dropped a cloth down from the easel so the painting was hidden. "Your mother commissioned it as a surprise for him. He commissioned the other," she added as she gestured toward a much larger painting.

Mostly covered with a Dutch cloth, Graham was about to see that it was a more traditional pose, one that made Emma Wellingham appear as if she was an aristocrat.

She wasn't. Not quite, anyway.

"It's beautiful," Graham breathed as he gently pulled away the white cloth and leaned forward to study the painting.

"Thank you."

"Have you any idea of where she and my father might be?" he asked as he straightened, his attention still on the painting.

Laura's eyes widened. "On their way to Woodscastle. They're expecting to find *you* there. To join them for dinner," she replied with some consternation.

Graham rolled his eyes. "Ah. A bit of a mix-up on my part. I assumed we would be eating here. I'll just..." He glanced around. "Hail a hansom cab and be on my way." He paused, his brows once again furrowing. "Are you in need of a ride anywhere? We can share a hackney," he suggested.

Laura shook her head. "The Overby coach should be here at any moment to take me home," she replied. "We could give you a lift to Woodscastle, if you'd like."

Graham scoffed. "Woodscastle is six... seven miles away."

"A long drive would be most welcome about now," she argued. "I've been standing most of the day. Most of the week, actually." Even on a rough road, the thought of riding in a coach through a part of town she rarely saw would be a welcome treat.

Reluctant to agree, Graham glanced around the parlor. "Have you a lady's maid or a chaperone to accompany you?"

"I do not. Scandalous, isn't it?"

Graham stiffened. "Truth be told, I've been in the United States for the past eighteen years. I've no idea how things are done here these days."

"Good. Then you can pretend everything has changed."

A knock sounded at the front door.

"Your coachman?" Graham asked as he made his way to the parlor door.

"Probably. I just have to retrieve my valise from my bedchamber," Laura said as she passed him and headed up the staircase.

Graham watched her go before he moved to open the door.

As expected, the coach driver stood on the stoop. He frowned at seeing Graham. "I'm here to collect Miss Overby," he said with a bow.

"She'll be right down," Graham said as he donned his hat and collected his boxes. "I do hope it won't be an inconvenience for you to drop me at Woodscastle," he added as he held the door for Laura. She appeared from inside the house carrying her luggage in one hand and a key in the other. Once Graham stepped out of the house, she turned and locked the door before dropping the key into her reticule.

The driver's eyes widened until Laura said, "Tucker, we're taking Mr. Wellingham to Woodscastle. In Chiswick."

"Yes, Miss Overby." He bowed again and moved to open the coach door, stepping aside to allow his passengers by.

He closed the door behind them and stepped up to the box.

.  .  .

*eanwhile, across the street*

His labored breaths becoming more so, Henry Simpson watched as the young woman stepped from the Wellingham residence, her valise clutched in one hand as she locked the door with the other.

From her expression, it appeared she was quite pleased. Happy, even. Perhaps this week's labors had been light, or her duties were those she enjoyed doing.

Well, he supposed from her happy expression that she had enjoyed her work. That she was satisfied with what she had accomplished.

He could imagine how it might be to spend time in the company of someone who took pride in their work. Who enjoyed it. Who looked as happy Saturday afternoon as she had appeared in the early hours of Monday morning.

He sighed and vowed he would introduce himself when she arrived Monday morning.

His rumination was interrupted when he noted that she wasn't just in the company of the coachman.

A rather tall gentleman followed her. Followed her and paused as she stepped into the coach.

Bent and followed her right into the coach.

Henry stepped back from his window, sure he had cursed out loud.

Clutching his chest, Henry felt panic and disbelief. Pain and confusion.

It seemed that the woman he had been imagining might one day be his already belonged to another.

The happy thoughts he had allowed only the moment before quickly dissipated, and for the first time in his life, Henry Simpson felt despair.

# CHAPTER 19

# MISTAKEN ASSUMPTIONS

*A few minutes later*

The glossy black town coach bearing the crest of the Mayfield earldom turned south onto King Street, its occupant peering out the window. Even though several townhouses had doors painted a different color than they had been when her parents owned them, those along this stretch of King were familiar.

Having grown up in one of them, Hannah Simpson Harrington remembered the names of every resident in the neighborhood, especially those who had children her age.

One townhouse had her particular attention on this day, and not only because it was across the street from the one in which she had been raised.

The Wellinghams owned it. Although they had also called their country estate in Chiswick home for most of their lives, the townhouse offered a place to stay when they didn't wish to make the trip south. That meant there were occasions when her best friend was close.

Graham Wellingham hadn't been so for nearly two decades, though. Although she had known their relationship would change when she had her come-out, she had no reason to expect Graham Wellingham would flee London upon her acceptance of Charles Harrington's proposal.

She expected a scolding. A rebuke. A speech about living up to bargains, for she had made one with Graham.

She didn't expect he would simply leave London without saying good-bye.

She had gifted him her virtue the night before his departure, a deliberate act meant to seal her bargain with him and afford her a night with the only man she had ever truly loved.

To this day, she had never regretted that night. She had never told anyone about it, nor had Charlie suspected anything on their wedding night.

Now that she thought about it, she supposed from his tentative behavior and unsure moves that he had never bedded a woman before her.

At least Graham had written upon his arrival in Boston. Apologized for his sudden disappearance. Begged forgiveness for not being in London for her wedding.

His postscript had been quite the entertaining read. Something about how despite what she might look like when she was widowed and eighty years old—wrinkled skin, white hair, rheumy eyes, stooped posture, and claws for fingers—he would hold her to her bargain, and she could expect he would marry her.

Well, she was widowed, and she had been for almost exactly a year. Her hair wasn't yet completely gray, and she still carried herself with the posture of a young lady having recently completed finishing school. Her eyes were clear and her fingers were still much as they had been when Graham was still in London.

She had written him with word of Charlie's death, but when she didn't receive a reply after six months, she began to wonder if he was still in Boston. Perhaps he had finally married, or perhaps he suffered from poor health, his hair gray and his skin wrinkled, his eyes rheumy and his fingers having turned to claws.

Rolling her eyes at her imaginings, Hannah regarded the pasteboard boxes that were stacked on the velvet-clad bench across from her. They contained two of the most beautiful ball gowns she had ever had the opportunity to own.

She had entered Suzanne's in Oxford Street expecting to find only one ball gown and perhaps a new dinner gown or some fripperies. Given the impending Season, she had no reason to hope there would be much left from which to choose.

But the owner of Suzanne's had approached Hannah with word that she had set aside several gowns for her in the event she required something for an early Season ball.

Hannah had thought to kiss the older woman, she was so happy. Two had fit to perfection and were wrapped in tissue and contained in the pasteboard boxes. A third was this very moment undergoing the removal of one of its bottom ruffles, the dress obviously designed for a woman much taller than Hannah.

It was while she was modeling the third gown for the seamstress that her attention had been caught by a passing hansom cab. The equipage wasn't the reason for her interest, but rather the face that had been framed in the window facing the shop.

Hannah remembered blinking. She remembered stepping toward the shop's front window, the seamstress attempting to follow her on her hands and knees as she continued to pin up the ruffle. She remembered staring at the man whose gaze suggested he was dazzled by the sights found in Oxford Street.

When the hansom cab was no longer visible from her

vantage, she had finally returned her attention to the matter at hand and apologized profusely to the seamstress.

"He must have meant a great deal to you," the young woman had said as she continued poking pins into the ruffle.

Hannah had gasped at hearing the words. "I cannot believe it was who I thought it might be," she had responded. "It cannot be."

But the more she thought about the man in the cab window, the more she wondered.

There was only one way to find out if Graham Wellingham had received her letter. She was sure the answer lay beyond the door at 3 King Street, and that's the address she gave to her driver when she took her leave of Suzanne's and practically ran to her coach.

When the driver pulled up to the curb in front of 3 King Street, she waited until he opened the door for her before she stepped out and hurried to use the brass knocker. Her brows furrowed when the door didn't open—surely a servant would answer, even if the Wellinghams weren't in residence.

She knocked again and even tested the door handle to discover it was locked when she was aware she was no longer alone.

"They have taken their leave," her brother said as he offered her his arm.

Not the least bit startled by Henry's sudden presence, Hannah allowed a sigh of frustration. "Did they have valises? Or... or trunks?" Hannah asked, her gaze finally turning onto Henry. "You look ill," she added with worry.

"And you look resplendent, as usual," he answered as he motioned for the coach driver to pull over to the other side of the street.

"Thank you," she replied, thinking he was hiding something. "You only just saw me this morning. What has happened?"

Henry looked both ways before he led them across the street. "I admit to having occasionally watched out my window this afternoon," he replied. "While I was writing my correspondence. The Wellinghams took their leave—along with Mrs. Larsen—not even an hour ago. There was only one valise among them."

"Which means they are to spend Easter at Woodscastle, no doubt," Hannah reasoned.

"An hour later, the curly-haired young woman took her leave, accompanied by a well-dressed man I could not identify. He looked familiar, but..." Henry shook his head. "Needless to say, I have reason to believe the woman I have been watching from afar is already claimed."

Hannah blinked. "You assume that just because the young woman had an escort, she is unavailable to you for courting?" she countered in disbelief.

"What else am I to think?"

"That her escort was a brother, or her father, or a—"

"Her husband," Henry interrupted.

Furrowing her blonde brows, Hannah said, "If he was tall, he was probably a footman," she countered.

"To escort a housemaid to her home?" he asked rhetorically. "Unlikely."

Hannah was about to admit she had confirmed the identity of the woman Henry had thought was a housemaid until earlier that day. She had discovered that Miss Overby was not only unmarried, but she hadn't yet accepted an offer of marriage because she hadn't yet been courted by anyone. She hadn't even had a proper come-out.

Before Hannah could admit what she knew, their father opened the door of the Simpson townhouse and pulled her into an embrace.

"Father. It's only been a few hours since I was last here," she protested. She stepped back and regarded him with curiosity. Always impeccably dressed—he could easily pass for an aristocrat despite his former position as a butler—James Simpson was finally showing his age. Liver spots were scattered about the backs of his hands, and his thinning hair was almost entirely white. His posture, however, was surprisingly good, and he still towered over Hannah.

"How is my favorite daughter?" he asked as he waved them both into the house.

"Your *only* daughter is exhausted from shopping for ball gowns and fripperies," she replied with a grin before she bussed him on the cheek. "I *am* your only daughter, am I not?"

James appeared flummoxed for a moment before his wife, just then entering the vestibule, said, "Of course you are, darling. Your father would never dare bed another woman but me." She turned her attention on her son. "You don't look so well, Henry."

Henry rolled his eyes. "So I've been told."

Sophia furrowed a brow before she turned her attention back to Hannah. "To what do we owe this honor? I didn't expect to see you again until Monday morning. I sent word to Harrington House that the artist can begin our portrait at eight o'clock. I know that's terribly early, but Henry must be off to the bank by nine—"

"Must I be *in* this painting?" Henry asked, an expression of pain once again crossing his face.

Reacting as if she'd been slapped, Sophia regarded him with worry. "Something *is* wrong," she murmured.

Hannah widened her eyes and jerked her head sideways, hoping her mother would notice and cease her questioning. "I'll be here bright and early, as will Henry. He'll be on the lookout for a particular young woman, after all," Hannah teased.

"Not any longer, I won't," Henry groused.

Understanding had Sophia allowing a long sigh. Her suspicions were confirmed when she noticed how Hannah stared at her, her eyes wide and her head jerking as if she were suffering some sort of tic. "Well, good. Because I have someone I wish for you to meet—"

"Mother," he scolded.

Sophia exchanged quick glances with her husband before she said, "Come. I think it's time you had a cup of tea with some brandy in it." She turned her gaze onto Hannah. "Will you join us, too?"

Noting the time on a nearby clock, Hannah shook her head. "I must go, Mother. I'll barely have time to change for dinner as it is," she said as she kissed her mother on the cheek and did the same to her father. She was about to kiss her brother on his cheek, but she hesitated, sure he was on the verge of tears. "Courage, Brother. I promise you. She is *not* married."

Before Henry had a chance to question her words, Hannah took her leave of her childhood home and stepped into the Mayfield coach, half-tempted to have the driver take her to Woodscastle. Even if Graham wasn't there, at least his mother would tell her if he was expected in London any time soon.

In the end, she had the driver take her to Harrington House. After all, if Graham Wellingham was back in London and if he intended to hold her to her bargain, wouldn't he pay a call there?

## CHAPTER 20

## A COACH RIDE REVEALS
## MUCH

*M*eanwhile, somewhere near Kensington

As the Overby town coach rumbled over the cobbles on its way to Knightsbridge Road, its occupants were entirely unaware their departure had been witnessed by one Henry Simpson. Their conversation soon turned to include the bank clerk, however.

"I'm very glad to know your family has grown even more and your parents are well," Graham said, his gaze occasionally darting to the scenes beyond the coach windows as they made their way.

"Did you even recognize my father when you saw him at Wellingham Imports?" Laura asked, relaxing into the squabs. Given her distant cousin's size, she worried there might not be room in the coach for her legs and his, but they soon arranged themselves so they weren't sitting directly across from one another. "He said you had not been in England for a very long time."

"About eighteen years," Graham acknowledged. "But I would know your father even from a distance," he claimed. "Other than a few gray hairs, he has not changed much at all." He paused a moment. "Which has me wondering about my parents' neighbors. Have you met the Simpsons?"

Laura's eyes widened with delight. "Oh, yes." She sobered a bit. "Well, Lady Simpson, at least. She's been joining me for tea in the afternoons whilst I paint your mother's portraits."

"Is she well?"

"Oh, very," Laura assured him. "Other than pining for more grandchildren."

Graham stilled himself and tried not to stare at the young woman. "By way of... Henry, no doubt?" he guessed.

Nodding, Laura said, "She is worried because he has not yet taken a wife."

Not entirely surprised by the comment—he had occasionally exchanged letters with Henry—Graham said, "There are those of us who must make our fortune before we consider matrimony."

Laura shook her head. "Lady Simpson claims he has always been able to afford to marry, but apparently he's not even courting anyone. Did you know him well?"

Graham had to resist the urge to let out a guffaw at the reference to Henry's financial situation. He was quite sure Henry would have been able to afford a wife before he even completed university. "I did indeed, and not just because our parents' townhouses are so close," he replied. "He was always very amiable when we were in school," he added, noticing that Laura seemed especially interested in his assessment of Henry.

"I have seen him," Laura said, not adding that she had done so by watching from the guest bedchamber window in the Wellingham's townhouse as well as from the front parlor window. "But we've not been introduced."

Straightening in the squabs, Graham said, "I can introduce you."

Laura dipped her head. "I expect Lady Simpson will do so Monday morning. I'm due to begin a family portrait of the Simpsons at eight o'clock."

His head jerking at hearing her pronouncement, Graham stared at her. "The entire family?"

She nodded. "The four of them, yes. I feared the time would be too early, but Mr. Simpson must not be late to the bank, so the early time is necessary."

"Eight o'clock in the *morning*?" Graham repeated, his eyes widening in disbelief.

"Indeed. But Lady Simpson insisted, since there is light in the parlor at that time of the day. I, of course, wondered about Lady Harrington, but her ladyship assured me the baroness would be dressed and ready."

Graham held his breath at the mention of Hannah and then allowed a knowing grin. "She was always a bit of an early bird," he murmured.

"I've not yet met her," Laura said. "But my mother insists she is amiable."

"As does her son."

Laura furrowed a brow as she regarded him. "You have met the Earl of Mayfield's heir? But not been reacquainted with his mother?"

Allowing a shrug, Graham said, "That about sums it up."

"You seem disappointed."

Graham inhaled. "I am. I..." He let out the breath and decided he could tell his cousin his intentions. "You see, I've returned to England to make her my wife."

Laura blinked. "Does *she* know that?"

Despite the seriousness of the situation, Graham couldn't help but chuckle. "She will."

"I rather imagine she'll be attending all the entertainments now that she is out of mourning," Laura said, remembering what Lady Simpson had told her.

"I intend to be at every one of them," Graham stated. "And given her son's... *intentions* for me, I rather expect my invitations will begin arriving Monday."

"Intentions?" she questioned. "That sounds rather ominous, but your manner in which you said it would suggest it is not."

Graham grinned. "It seems Edward Harrington is my champion when it comes to his mother."

"Oh!" she replied in delight. "He wants you to marry his mother," she murmured on a breath.

"A situation I intend to exploit at my first opportunity to do so."

Laura seemed to think on his claim for a moment before she said, "Will you go to Harrington House?"

He nodded. "I've been invited to dinner on Monday night," he replied, barely able to contain his excitement.

"She'll be at the Simpson townhouse that very morning for the sitting," she reminded him.

"If I am back in town, I may arrange to pay a call. How long do you suppose she'll be engaged in... in sitting?"

Laura grinned at the query. "Only an hour every morning for a few days at least. Possibly a week or more. Mr. Simpson must depart for the bank no later than nine-oh-five every morning but Saturday, according to Lady Simpson."

"He must hold a position of some importance?" Graham half-asked.

"He's a clerk and will be promoted to head clerk upon the current head clerk's retirement. In a fortnight, I believe is the schedule."

His eyes widening at hearing the news, Graham said, "Surely he will take a wife given his promotion. In social circles, he'll no doubt be considered a real banker, which means..." He gave a huff.

"What?"

"When I was last in London, the *ton* included bankers and wealthy tradesmen in addition to the aristocracy," he explained, "which means Henry's status will be elevated. I do hope he'll have time for the likes of me."

Laura's gaze moved to the window, her expression pleasant but her lips pressed together as if she feared what she might say.

Graham regarded her a moment before his eyes narrowed. "Are *you* betrothed?"

"I am not," she replied, almost too quickly.

"But you wish to be."

Hiding her mouth with a gloved hand whilst she cleared her throat, Laura finally said, "It all depends, I suppose."

"On?" For a moment, she stared at him, and Graham realized his query was far too personal. "Forgive me. I... I forget myself," he said on a sigh. "Forget where I am. In America, people are far too forward with their queries. Far too curious, but then, we were also far too free with our answers."

A wrinkle appeared between her brows. "I suppose it makes for less gossip if everyone knows everyone's business."

"Oh, there's still gossip," Graham said with a grin.

"Well, I hesitate to speak of betrothals given my avocation. I don't wish to give it up, you see. The painting, I mean, and accepting commissions. But Father says there is no man who would allow me to continue my painting for profit after we are wed."

Graham frowned. "I rather doubt that is true," he replied. "There must be an open-minded man somewhere here in England. Someone who would appreciate a woman who can help with the expenses, although I would be concerned should you end up with a man who doesn't earn his own keep."

"If he's not in London, I rather doubt I will meet him," she replied with a roll of her eyes.

"True," Graham agreed. "Still, I shouldn't recommend you give up on marriage just yet. You're still young. You're biddable. Your uncle is an earl. When Trenton commissions a family portrait, you will find your prospects increasing tenfold and suitors lining up to escort you to the park."

A blush suffused Laura's face. "I appreciate your words. I do," she replied.

"But you already have someone in mind?"

The pink blush deepened to a near scarlet, and Laura's eyes once again darted to the window. "As I've said, I've not yet been introduced to him, so I cannot say—"

"You would be perfect for Henry," Graham said in a hoarse whisper. "At least, the Henry I knew before I left." He gave his head a shake. "We have exchanged correspondence over the years, of course. I cannot say that he has changed much, other than he is more serious about the world than he was as a young man."

Laura leaned forward. "You mustn't say anything to anyone," she hissed.

Graham blinked. "Even if I might persuade him to consider you, should he be so blind as to not have already noticed you?"

Stilling herself on the bench, Laura held her breath a moment as she remembered the face that had watched her from a third story window. "I believe he *has* noticed me," she countered with a frown.

"How long have you been working on the paintings of my mother?"

Laura furrowed a brow at hearing the change in subject. "Three weeks."

"So, you've been arriving in King Street...?"

"Monday mornings. Usually by seven o'clock."

"And leaving?"

"Much as I did today," she said on a shrug. "Late afternoon on Saturdays."

A brilliant smile lit Graham's face before he let out a guffaw. "Oh, he's noticed you, mark my words."

"Really, Mr. Wellingham—"

"I am Graham to you just as I am to the rest of your family," he said. After a pause, he added, "I will not speak of you when I am reacquainted with Henry, but I would be happy to introduce you should the opportunity arise before Monday morning."

Laura stared at her distant cousin and finally allowed a nod. "Very well. But I rather doubt there will be such an opportunity. Your mother was quite clear that she and your father are to have you in their presence for the entire day tomorrow."

Graham winced, realizing there wouldn't be an opportunity to see Hannah if his parents expected him to remain at Woodscastle for the entire day of Easter. "Well, then, I guess this means Lady Simpson will have to do the honors," he replied with a hint of disappointment.

For at that moment, Graham wanted to be present when Henry and Laura were formally introduced.

Especially since Hannah would be there as well.

# CHAPTER 21

## AN IDENTITY REVEALED

*M*onday morning, seven o'clock, Simpson townhouse

Henry was ready to ignore the sound of the coach coming to a halt on the street in front of the Simpson town-house. Given the time, he had already decided it was the same coach that had departed only the Saturday before, its passengers the curly-haired woman from the Wellingham household along with her protector.

*Her husband*, he thought, given the tall man's consideration for the young woman. Then he remembered his sister's comment.

*I promise. She is not married.*

Hannah hadn't had a chance to explain what she knew.

Curiosity prevailed, and Henry moved to the window to peer out.

The coach was indeed familiar, as was the driver, who stepped down and then escorted the young lady to the door. He handed her a valise, and she disappeared behind the red door.

Allowing a sound of dismissal, Henry was startled when

he turned to find his valet, Hopkins, regarding him from the threshold of the bedchamber.

"Morning, sir. I hope I am not too early."

"Just in time," Henry replied as he indicated a folded strip of silk. Although he usually wore a linen cravat to the bank, he had decided he best don a silk cravat to pose for the painting.

"Did you have a good Easter, sir?"

Henry inhaled, not about to admit he had been in a blue mood for the entire day. His heart felt as if someone had torn it out of his chest and stomped on it. He had spent the entire night before chiding himself.

How could he have such a reaction when he hadn't even met the woman who had haunted his dreams?

In the middle of the night, he had taken his member in hand, determined it would be the last time he would do so. All the while, he imagined her beneath him, writhing with pleasure as his lips took purchase on one of her nipples and suckled them until her quiet mewls and soft gasps summoned his ecstasy.

His release had been so welcome and yet so heartbreaking, for when he had awakened expecting her to still be beneath him, he found only mussed bed linens and a pillow.

How would he forget her? What could he do to put her from his mind?

His first thoughts on this morning had to do with finding a mistress. Well past the age he should have married, Henry's devotion to his parents had kept him from leaving and setting up a household in a townhouse he already owned. Had kept him from courting. Had even kept him from dalliances that would have at least seen to his baser needs.

He had half a mind to ask his valet if he had a mistress. The man might be married for all he knew.

Remembering Hopkins' query, he finally answered, "It was much like any other Easter. And yours?"

"Very good, sir. My mother was in fine form at church."

"As was mine, and my sister," Henry murmured, remembering how elegant the women had dressed for the Easter service at St. George's. How their hats, festooned with silk flowers, had brightened an otherwise gray day. "Today will be different from most Mondays, however. An artist is coming to paint our family portrait. An effort I expect will take several days. Weeks, perhaps." The words came out sounding as cross as he felt. "I don't suppose Lady Harrington has arrived yet?"

"Lady Harrington is in the breakfast parlor with Lady Simpson," Hopkins replied as he moved to the bathing chamber.

Henry gave a start before he remembered that Hannah had elected to spend the night at the Simpson townhouse rather than at Harrington House.

Her lady's maid and a rather tall Mayfield footman had arrived the afternoon before bearing a trunk and a valise. The maid took up residence in the same servant's quarters she had occupied before Hannah married while the footman returned to Harrington House.

"Well, I suppose I should not keep them waiting," Henry said as he wondered how he had missed his sister's arrival the night before. Except for the cravat and a top coat, he had already dressed for the day, but he was in desperate need of a shave.

Hopkins mixed shaving cream and, sensing Henry's impatience, saw to applying it without delay. His strokes with the straight razor were quick and practiced.

"Tell me, Hopkins. Have you had the occasion to meet the young woman who has been working for the Wellinghams this past few weeks?" Henry asked as he absently watched his valet's skill with the razor in the looking glass.

"Are you referring to Mrs. Larsen?" Hopkins asked, expertly directing the razor along Henry's jawline.

"No. The younger woman."

Hopkins stepped back and regarded Henry with furrowed brows. "Mrs. Larsen is the only servant they employ at their townhouse, sir."

"Perhaps she's a lady's maid?" Henry suggested. "The young woman who leaves every Saturday afternoon and returns early on Monday mornings."

Hopkins gave him a blank look. "I've not met anyone but Mrs. Larsen and her husband, the groom," he said, removing a hot towel from a rack over the bathtub. He placed it around Henry's face, using the ends to wipe away the leftover shaving cream.

For a moment, Henry reveled in the heat from the bath linen. Perhaps the steam would erase the memory of the woman from his brain. But now that he was imagining what she might look like with a sheen of perspiration covering her body after a particularly spirited round of lovemaking, he found his mind replaying what he had dreamt about only the night before.

How ever would he erase that memory?

When Hopkins removed the towel, Henry blinked. His father stood to the side, regarding his son's reflection in the mirror with a furtive expression. "Father?"

"Don't mind me, son. I just wanted to be sure you didn't have a mind to sneak down the back stairs and escape to the bank."

Henry gave his father a quelling glance. "I will admit the idea has crossed my mind," he replied. "And yours?" he guessed.

His father gave a start. "Not for a moment. I've been

relishing the idea of this painting ever since your mother told me of her plans last week," he claimed.

"Liar," Henry accused.

"Have a care, Henry. I welcome any excuse to hold onto your mother for hours on end."

"Hold onto her? Just how *are* we posing for this painting?" Henry asked in alarm.

James allowed a scowl. "I expect I'll have an arm about her waist, or a hand on her shoulder. Nothing scandalous. Just what have *you* been imagining this morning?"

Glad the hot towel would account for his reddened face, Henry allowed his gaze to lower. "Apologies, Father."

Seeing how his son appeared suitably chagrined, James added, "This will probably be the last opportunity for the four of us to do this."

"Father—"

"Your sister will no doubt be remarried within a month, and I expect you'll finally decide you don't have to remain a bachelor on our account. In fact, I'm of a mind to order you to find a wife with the threat of withholding your inheritance if you do not."

Henry stared at his father, stunned by his words. "You already gave me my inheritance when I turned five-and-twenty—"

"Part of it, yes," James agreed. He flicked a hand in the direction of the valet, and Hopkins left the bathing chamber. "I've been holding onto the rest to give you upon the occasion of your wedding day."

Blinking, Henry straightened in the reclining chair and regarded his father with a furrowed brow. "The rest?"

"Your sister's as well," James added on a sigh. "It's time you both settled with the spouses you were intended to marry. Time you both got on with your lives. You're not getting any younger."

Henry gave his head a shake. "And just who do you have in mind for me to marry?" He would have asked about who his father had in mind for Hannah, too, but at the moment, and for selfish reasons, he was more curious about his prospects.

"Well, we'll know in the next couple of days now, won't we?" James replied, his gaze going to something beyond the window. "If you've a mistress—"

"I do not—"

"Then see to it you put your mind to courting," he ordered. "Hopkins!" he called out.

The valet appeared on the threshold, the silk cravat held in one hand. "Yes, sir?"

"Time for a cravat and a fashionable top coat. The artist has arrived."

"Yes, sir."

Without another word, James took his leave of his son's bedchamber, leaving Henry exchanging curious glances with his valet.

Henry quickly stood up and looked out the window, but no coaches were parked in front of the townhouse, nor did he see anyone in the street below.

The faint thud of the brass door knocker sounded through the window, though, and he turned to his valet. "You heard my father," he grumbled.

A moment later, and Hopkins had the cravat wrapped around Henry's neck and tied into a perfect mail coach knot. The black topcoat followed. Once the buttons were done up, the valet stepped back and regarded his master with a nod. "You are ready, sir."

Feeling as if he was heading for the gallows, Henry nodded in return and made his way down the stairs to the first floor parlor.

. . .

*A*t first, he thought he had misunderstood his mother's explanation. He was sure she had said they would be posing in front of the fireplace in the parlor. She wasn't in the parlor, and neither was his sister nor their father.

The room wasn't empty, though.

He paused on the threshold.

About to move onto the next set of stairs and make his way to the breakfast parlor, he paused when he saw that a young woman, her back to him, was busy erecting a tall easel directly across from the fireplace.

Two upholstered chairs had been positioned in front of the fireplace, each slightly angled toward the other and facing the easel.

Henry watched as the woman mounted a huge stretched canvas on the easel and stepped back, her head angling to one side.

A head covered in blonde curly hair.

Henry blinked. He wasn't aware he made any sound, but he knew he must have when the young woman suddenly whirled around.

She dipped a curtsy, one hand pulling her dark green bell skirt to the side. "Good morning, sir."

Staring at the young woman for a moment too long, Henry finally remembered how to bow. "Good morning," he replied. His gaze swept the parlor, as if he were looking for someone. "I thought I might be late." When she didn't respond but continued to watch him, her eyes occasionally darting to the side, he added, "But it seems I am early."

She nodded, her gaze going to the mantel clock. "I'm not expecting my subjects for at least another ten minutes. I take it you are one of them?"

Henry swallowed. He would have bristled at her use of

the word 'subject' to describe him, but he was still too mesmerized by her. By the myriad thoughts colliding in his head at that moment. By the brief memories of what she had looked liked naked beneath him. By how embarrassed he felt at what he had done with her.

To her.

Wanted to be doing with her right this very minute!

For the creature who stood before him was not quite the comely young woman he had conjured from his brief glimpses of her, but rather a more beautiful woman with perfect posture and a poise usually found in much older members of her sex.

"Is something wrong, sir?" Her eyes suddenly widened as she glanced down at the front of her gown and then around where she stood, as if she thought something had stained the fabric.

Henry shook his head as he scolded himself. The poor woman. They hadn't been properly introduced. No wonder her responses had been so hesitant. Her query—*I take it you are one of them?*—had been made as a prompt, and he had missed his cue entirely.

"Not at all, my lady. Please, forgive the intrusion." He bowed again. "I am Henry Simpson."

She nodded, a grin lifting her lips. "It's very good to meet you, sir," she said as she stepped forward and offered her hand.

Even if she had intended to shake his, Henry was quick to capture the hand and bring it to his lips. "May I know your name? Even though there is no one here to do the honors, surely we can forgo the formality just this once."

She stared at him before her gaze dropped to where her hand still held onto his. "Miss Overby, sir. Laura Overby. My father is a broker at Wellingham Imports."

All at once, Henry remembered everything his sister had

told him about this young woman. Remembered how she had described her. Remembered the gleam in Hannah's eyes, as if she knew something he didn't.

"And your mother is the Earl of Trenton's sister," he murmured, realization dawning even as he said the words.

"Indeed, she is," Miss Overby replied.

*Damn it, Hannah!*

His sister had suspected his *tendre* was for the woman he had thought was a housemaid.

Not just suspected.

Hannah *knew*.

Not once had she mentioned that the woman he had thought was a housemaid was in fact the painter their mother had hired to do their family portrait.

She knew, and she hadn't told him! He had suffered in silence for days.

Weeks.

Well, just a couple of weeks. Nonetheless, his pain and longing and yearning had made him desperate. Made him surly. Made him cross with the world.

Well, Hannah would certainly be learning of his ire on this day. He had every intention of marching down to the breakfast parlor and scolding her for withholding such vital information. Of course, doing so would require he give up his hold on the beauteous Miss Overby's hand, and at the moment, he had no intention of letting go of it.

A petite hand with long fingers. Fingers that ended with perfectly oval nails. Despite her avocation, there wasn't a hint of paint beneath those nails. Not a stain on the smooth skin. Not a bit of evidence she was an artist.

He lowered his lips to her knuckles and pressed a kiss there, sure he felt her hand tremble and a jolt shoot up her arm. Perhaps that was merely the jolt he felt in his own hand at the reminder of the jewel he held.

He heard her slight inhalation of breath, but she made no move to pull away her hand. "And the Earl of Trenton has been a very generous uncle."

"He and his countess are known for their charity," Henry replied.

Even before the last word was out of his mouth, Henry grimaced. The brief look of pain that crossed Miss Overby's face could not be mistaken for anything but a wince. "Their generosity to various charities," he quickly amended.

"Indeed," she replied, jerking her hand from his hold. "Please excuse me. I still require a few minutes to set up for today's sitting." She dipped a curtsy, not waiting for his reply as she turned to arrange a number of pencils on a table.

Henry resisted the urge to reach out and capture her arm, sure he had made a cake of himself. "Of course, my lady. I will take my leave and return with the rest of my family when you are ready for us," he said as he gave a leg and then backed up to the threshold. An expression of pain crossed his face when he turned to head down the stairs.

Cake, indeed.

*Damn, damn, damn, double damnation.*

# CHAPTER 22

# PONTIFICATING ABOUT A PAINTER

*A moment later*
Henry's footsteps were leaden as he descended the stairs.

How could he have said what he had when he did?

*He and his countess are known for their charity.*

As if the Overby family required financial assistance.

They didn't. Certainly not if William Overby was a broker at Wellingham Imports. Every businessman and banker in London knew the import and export concern was the best at what they did. Knew the majority of the business was employee-owned and that pay was better than at other import companies.

As the head clerk at the Bank of England, Henry knew William Overby's account was flush with funds. Had been for years. In addition to his regular account, there was the account that had been set up to see to Lady Overby and their five children upon her husband's death, an account that had been funded by Lady Overby's generous dowry.

*Could a dowry be considered charity?*

Henry cursed himself. Cursed again just as he stepped into the breakfast parlor.

He stopped short when three sets of eyes turned to regard him with various expressions of surprise.

"Henry," his mother scolded. "Whatever has you so cross this morning?"

"Apologies, Mother," Henry replied as he helped himself to a plate. He filled it with bits of everything from the sideboard—toast, poached eggs, bacon, ham—and sat in the one remaining chair.

His sister was sitting in the one he usually occupied, and his gaze fell on her as she quietly sipped tea from a porcelain cup. "I am unhappy with *you* on this day, Sister."

Her brows arching, much like Miss Overby's had done only a few moments ago, Hannah regarded him a moment before she brought a napkin to her lips. "Dear Brother, you have been unhappy with *everyone* these past few weeks."

Recoiling as if she had slapped him across the face, Henry dared a glance at his mother before he dipped his head and tucked into his breakfast.

"Henry," his mother said on a sigh. "Now you have me curious. What is it you think Hannah has done now?"

"Mother!" Hannah said in protest, even though she had almost asked the very same question.

"She deliberately withheld vital information from me," he accused. "Information I should have known prior to my unfortunate introduction to the woman you have hired to paint our portrait," he explained. When he saw how Sophia Simpson's eyes lit up in delight, his own narrowed. "And you're guilty as well?" he half-asked.

"Why, I'm quite sure I don't know what you're talking about," Sophia replied as she set down her fork. "I am quite sure I mentioned Miss Overby by name. What else could you be required to know about her?"

He turned his gaze onto Hannah. "Does she know? About what I thought?" He lowered his voice to a near whisper. "About the woman I thought was a housemaid?"

The picture of innocence, Hannah allowed a one-shouldered shrug. "I did not share your suppositions with Mother, no," she replied. "I thought you would do so. Not that she would have been able to clear up any mistaken impressions, even if you had."

"Hannah," he groused. "How long have you known the housemaid wasn't a housemaid at all?"

Angling her head in her brother's direction, Hannah said in a quiet voice, "I did not know for certain until a couple of days ago. Had you brought up the matter of your affection for Miss Overby with Mother—"

"Affection?" he interrupted.

"—she would have been able to arrange an introduction—"

"There is no *affection*," Henry firmly stated, attempting to keep his voice down.

Hannah blinked as she regarded him, her disbelief evident. Then her eyes narrowed. "Are you saying it was just lust?"

"*Hannah*." The quiet but firm rebuke was offered by James, who placed a bony hand on her shoulder. "Apologize to your brother and your mother, please."

Her shoulders sagging, Hannah said, "I apologize. It was wrong of me to say such a thing."

Sophia leaned forward. "It's not like you to tease your brother so this early in the morning," she said. "Now please explain to me what has happened to make you so peevish."

Hannah's expression softened. "Nothing, Mother."

"Nothing?" her father prompted.

Tears collected in the corners of Hannah's eyes before she suddenly straightened and said, "Nothing. Which is the problem. I would have expected him to call on me by now."

Clearly confused, her father exchanged a quick glance with his wife. She shrugged before turning her attention back to Hannah. "Him? Him, who?"

"He could have at least sent a note, but I've received nothing," Hannah went on, a few tears dribbling down her cheeks.

Glad he was no longer the center of attention, Henry exchanged glances with his father and mother before turning his gaze back to Hannah. "A note from?" he prompted.

Hannah inhaled before she blurted, "Graham." When neither of her parents reacted, she added, "He's been in London for at least three days, I'm quite sure." At her father's look of guilt, she added, "I think I saw him in a hansom cab in Oxford Street when I was shopping on Saturday, but then, when I didn't receive anything from him—a note or even a word of gossip—I thought perhaps I was wrong."

"You were probably wrong," Henry whispered, not the least hint of humor sounding in his words.

"I was going to mention it at the end of dinner last night," Hannah went on, ignoring her brother. "But before I could, Mayfield said something about 'Mr. Wellingham' to Edward. Something about having met him at his club. Imagine my shock when Edward said he would speak with him more on the subject whilst they played billiards!"

"You didn't ask about it?" Sophia queried, her brows furrowed.

"I could not, since it was time for the countess and me to retire to the parlor. Mayfield and Edward were in the billiards salon after that, so I couldn't ask either of them about it, and I took my leave last night before they finished their game." Despite her attempt at appearing brave, a few more tears leaked from her eyes.

"So now you're convinced Graham Wellingham is back in London?" her father asked, his gray brows rising. He didn't seem the least bit surprised by the news.

"I am," Hannah sighed. "We had a bargain," she whispered.

It was then Henry remembered seeing the man who he thought seemed familiar—the gentleman who had helped Miss Overby into her carriage on Saturday afternoon. He straightened in his chair as his eyes widened. "I think I may have seen Graham," he announced. "With Miss Overby."

Hannah's brows rose as she swallowed a sob. "Are you sure? When?"

A moment ago, Henry wouldn't have thought so, but now that he considered how long it had been since he had seen Graham Wellingham, he could imagine how the young man he remembered from his teens would age. How the planes of his face would harden to make him look more like his father. How his eyes were those of his mother and the other members of the Fitzsimmons side of the family. How he might have grown another two inches taller and taken on the physique of a bare knuckle fighter. From moving heavy crates about, no doubt.

No wonder Graham had looked so familiar!

"He was escorting Miss Overby when she took her leave of Number Three last Saturday," he said. "Helped her into her town coach and followed her in," he added, his attention on his mind's eye.

Despite her attempt to reign in her sudden jealousy, Hannah let out a mewl of distress. "Do you suppose...?" she slumped in her chair, her hands wringing together in her lap. "It cannot be," she whispered as she turned to regard her brother. "We had a bargain."

Henry's expression of annoyance from earlier that morning had been replaced. He now looked as forlorn as he felt. "I fear it can," he murmured. "Despite whatever bargain you may have had, dear sister, it seems he and the artist…"

The sound of a throat clearing had the four of them turning to discover Miss Overby just beyond the threshold. She displayed a happy expression quite at odds with those who stared back at her.

"Good morning, Miss Overby," Sophia said brightly.

"Good morning, my lady. I am ready for you in the parlor," she announced.

Sophia swept her gaze around the breakfast table before she returned her attention to the artist. "Thank you, Miss Overby. We'll join you in a moment."

Laura Overby dipped a curtsy and disappeared from view.

Three sets of eyes fell on Sophia as she regarded her grown children and inhaled deeply. "Really, you two. You would think the world had come to an end. Dry your eyes, Hannah. We shouldn't want you looking as if you've been weeping all morning. And you, Henry," she turned her assessing gaze onto her second son, "Chin up. Sometimes things are not at all as they seem. And if you so much as scowl during our sitting today, I shall order Miss Overby to paint you with a ridiculous smile."

Henry gave a start. "But Mother—"

"I don't wish to hear it," Sophia stated as she held up a staying hand. Despite her age, she was up from her chair in a smooth move. "Come along. The light will be best for only another hour, and I don't wish to leave our artist waiting."

"Yes, Mother," Hannah and Henry said in unison as they stood, their moods somber.

The four made their way to the first floor parlor in silence.

## CHAPTER 23

## AN ARTIST'S PERSPECTIVE

*A few minutes earlier*
Satisfied with the workspace she had created in the first floor parlor, Laura glanced about in search of a footman. Mr. Simpson had said to simply let someone know when she was ready for the family to join her, and her ladyship would ensure everyone would arrive in time for their first sitting.

Laura supposed a footman would inform the butler, although no such servant had let her into the Simpson townhouse that morning.

Mr. Simpson had been the one to do so.

Dressed in what appeared to be his very finest evening clothes, he had greeted her as if she were to the manor born, bowing and inviting her in with a hearty, "Good morning, Miss Overby."

She had never felt so welcome.

"I'll see to it your canvas is taken up to the parlor," he had added before offering to take her mantle and seeing to the valise containing paints and brushes. The faintest odor of turpentine followed its movement.

"That's very kind of you, sir."

Then he had stared at her as if she might have grown horns. "Oh, where are my manners?" he asked rhetorically. "I am James Simpson, at your service," he added as he favored her with another bow. "I have the honor of being married to Lady Simpson."

Laura couldn't help the grin that had lifted the edges of her lips. "Of course, sir. She has spoken of you most favorably," she replied, her eyes twinkling at how he beamed in delight. "Why, I do believe she likes you." This last was said with a wink, which had the older gentleman amused.

"Best feeling in the world, it is. To wake up every day with your arms around the one you love." James continued to grin as he led her up the stairs to the parlor. "She is my first and only love."

Laura was struck at hearing his declaration. At hearing such intimate details of the Simpson's life. But the words had been said with such conviction, such devotion, with not the barest hint of avarice or falseness, Laura experienced the pang of jealousy she usually felt at seeing a young couple walking arm in arm in Hyde Park.

At just over twenty years of age and given her avocation, she had begun to believe the opportunity for a marriage based on love would pass her by. That if she had any hope of finding a husband, he would have to be older. Widowed, perhaps. Not as old as Mr. Simpson, of course, but someone who had put off marriage so long that he would not necessarily welcome the change to his lifestyle.

The addition of a wife to a life spent in bachelorhood might mean she would share him with a long-time mistress. That he might have illegitimate children. That he was so accustomed to spending evenings at his club, he would not change his habits just because he had a wife at home.

Children.

Lady Simpson had mentioned how old she had been upon the birth of her twins. Laura winced at the thought of waiting so long to have a baby or two. At least her ladyship had an older son—the heir to her late husband's fortune, who now had a wife and ten children of his own.

"They're as in love with one another as my James and I are," Lady Simpson had said during one of the days they had enjoyed tea in the afternoon.

How was it two people could still be so in love after such long marriages? Had they been in love from the start? Or had they grown to love one another over the decades of a life spent together?

Had raising their twins brought the Simpsons closer together? Had they ever experienced a time when they were not in love?

Given Mr. Simpson's age and what Laura knew of Lady Simpson's first marriage to a man long dead, Laura decided they had to have been together a very long time.

The twins were six-and-thirty!

"*L*ady Simpson said you oversaw the reconstruction of this townhouse," Laura said to her escort as they reached the first floor landing, her gaze darting about to take in the tasteful display of furnishings. Although she had grown up in a beautifully decorated townhouse much like this one, it was half the width of the Simpson home.

"I did," James replied. "I practiced by seeing to the renovation of the other houses on our street first," he explained. "So I was ready for this one when it came time to create larger quarters. This used to be two townhouses, you see, but neither had a breakfast parlor, and her ladyship had always wanted one," he explained, his face once again lighting up at the mention of his wife. "I wanted to be sure there was a nursery, of course, and an enlarged parlor, and, well, it's probably in need of another renovation, but I shall let my son see to it as this house will be part of his inheritance."

Laura had wondered at his words. She had expected the older gentleman to exhibit airs, to behave in a stoic manner. But he was as free with his information as if she were family.

Once they were in the parlor and James was assured she had what she needed, he had taken his leave. "I expect a servant will find the entire family in the breakfast parlor when you're ready for us."

Despite the brief interruption when Mr. Simpson's son had appeared in the parlor, Laura had been left alone to complete her preparations.

She might have finished even sooner if she hadn't been so dumbstruck by what had happened with Henry Simpson. For the long moment he had held onto her hand, she was quite sure he stared at her. Not with recognition, exactly, but with an awareness that had her entire body responding with excitement.

Anticipation.

Longing.

Here was a man—an older man—who seemed to actually see her.

Desire her.

Want her.

For a moment, she thought the lips that had finally kissed her knuckles were instead destined to make contact with her own.

She would have welcomed their touch.

She would have gladly returned his kiss with the same level of fervor he displayed. From the slight scent of shaving cream that lingered long after he left and the smooth planes of his face, she knew he had just shaved. Or been shaved.

Probably by a valet who was an expert at seeing to his perfectly tailored clothes and custom shoes.

Had he pulled her into his arms, she would have gladly allowed him the intimacy. Her entire body had tingled at the thought of being held in his arms. Against the front of a body that displayed the very latest in men's fashion to good effect, which meant that body was trim and fit, but not too lean. His hands hadn't been as bony as his father's, and neither had his cheeks begun to hollow.

His fair hair was still thick and possessed of a smooth wave that left one forelock barely hanging onto his forehead. It would prove a challenge to capture in paint, but she already had a clear idea of how she would accomplish it.

The easiest feature to paint would be his eyes, for their irises were of a blue that was darker than the sky but not quite sapphire, and at that moment he had been regarding her with awe, she thought they held a hint of mischief.

She could imagine those same eyes in their son, a fair-haired tot who would delight in mischief but make her pine for another even as she struggled to paint his likeness in this very room. Why, her easel could be permanently placed exactly where it was, so she could continue her portraitures on the days Henry was at the bank.

She would ensure dinner was served not long after he returned home, so that they could spend an hour or so together in quiet conversation before heading for bed.

His father's words had come back to her in a flash.

*Best feeling in the world, it is. To wake up every day with your arms around the one you love.*

When they had finally decided to forgo the need to wait for someone to provide a formal introduction, all the delightful scenarios she had imagined for a life with Henry Simpson *poofed* out of existence at his mention of the earl's charity.

Did everyone believe her family's largesse was due solely to the Earl of Trenton? Did they not know that her father was a valued employee of Wellingham Imports? That he had earned a fortune during his forty years with the firm? That he had instilled in her and her brothers and sisters—well, her youngest brother was still a babe—the importance of hard work and dedication to a goal?

Apparently not.

Laura fought back a tear and cleared her throat as she looked for a footman, finally deciding she would simply deliver the message that she was ready for the family in person.

Finding the breakfast parlor was easy.

Overhearing the last of a conversation that obviously included her had her pausing well before she reached the opened door.

She hadn't intended to eavesdrop. She hadn't intended to lean closer but remain clear of their line of sight. But she couldn't help herself.

Henry Simpson had seen Graham Wellingham climb into her family's town coach directly after she had. That had been Saturday, when she had offered him the ride to Woodscastle.

There was certainly nothing untoward about doing so— the man was her second cousin!

But Henry's sister must have assumed something entirely different. For the look she had directed to Laura upon her announcement that she was ready for them had been one of hurt coupled with something far more sinister.

Jealousy.

CHAPTER 24

# POSING IS HARD,
# PRETENDING IS HARDER


*In the parlor at the Simpson townhouse* Laura regarded her subjects with a practiced eye, heartened to see that two of them had obviously done this before and knew exactly how to stand and sit.

Lady and Mr. Simpson easily moved into place, her ladyship seated in one chair while her husband moved to stand behind and to the side of her. He placed a protective hand on one of her satin-clad shoulders at the same moment she lifted one of her own to cover it. Then she angled her head and displayed a pleasant expression that made her appear far younger than her eighty years.

Meanwhile, Lady Harrington—Laura hadn't yet been introduced but was sure her ladyship would do the honors in a moment—took the other chair while she batted a gloved hand at her brother, attempting to coax him into place while quietly scolding him.

Laura cleared her throat and gave a curtsy. Although she wanted to avoid glancing at Henry, she couldn't help but make the occasional eye contact as she said, "Good morning.

I am Miss Overby, and I have the honor of painting your family portrait."

"Good morning, Miss Overby," Sophia replied. "Do be sure the other two are positioned correctly. They were far too young the last time we did this."

"Yes, my lady," Laura said as she stepped forward and regarded the younger subjects. Addressing Hannah, she said, "My lady, you'll want to spread your gown a bit wider—"

"Of course. Where should I place my hands?" Hannah asked, her voice sounding frosty. Or perhaps Laura merely imagined it.

"Your gloves are very beautiful, so perhaps it's best to place your hands like this..." Rather than touching Hannah's hands, she held her own out in demonstration. She nodded when Hannah followed suit. "Are there any rings you wish to wear? You don't need them today, of course, but in a few days."

Hannah inhaled softly. "I'll think about it," she replied, her manner less cold.

Laura turned her attention to Henry. "Your posture is perfect, sir," she remarked, her attempt to avoid his gaze failing when he leaned forward and whispered, "I wish to apologize for my earlier comment. I meant no offense as I am well aware of your father's success at Wellingham Imports," he murmured.

Blinking, Laura stared at him, just then remembering her father's accounts were with the Bank of England. If Henry didn't know exactly how much were in those accounts, he would discover their value when he was next at the bank, she was sure.

At the same time, she noted how his sister, who had obviously overheard his words, furrowed her blonde brows. "Thank you, sir. Although I have always known of his position, it wasn't until this Saturday past, when I had the occasion of sharing my coach with my cousin, that I learned just how valuable he is to Wellingham Imports." She reached out a hand and placed it at his elbow, intending for him to bend it slightly as he rested his right hand on his sister's shoulder.

Three events occurred simultaneously.

"Cousin?" Hannah asked, her head lifting to regard the painter.

A jolt shot through Henry's arm at her touch, and he inhaled sharply.

Laura let go of his arm and stepped back, sure the frisson that had passed through her body was evident to everyone in the parlor.

Embarrassed, she directed her gaze onto Hannah. "Cousin, yes. I was but a babe when he was last in London," she said.

"Not your *husband?*" Henry asked, his other hand absently moving to the elbow she had touched, as if he was testing it for feeling.

Furrowing a brow, Laura shook her head. "I am not married, sir, nor am I betrothed." She said this last before she could think twice. For some reason, possibly because of the frissons she had experienced whilst in his company, she felt compelled to admit she wasn't affianced.

"And your cousin?" Hannah asked, her expression conveying a sort of desperation Laura hadn't seen before on such a beautiful woman.

"He is not, either. He's only just returned to British shores a day or so ago." She paused, wondering if she should admit what Graham had told her while they were on their way to Woodscastle. Although he hadn't mentioned Hannah by name, his description of the woman he intended to make his wife exactly matched the woman who sat before her.

No wonder she had directed such a look of disdain in Laura's direction earlier that morning!

She settled her gaze on Henry and once again stepped forward. "I shouldn't wish to keep you all waiting as I compose you," she said loudly enough for everyone to hear. "But if you could just place your hand on Lady Harrington's shoulder like this..." She took his hand in hers and moved it onto Hannah's silk-clad shoulder. "... I believe we have the perfect composition."

The frisson once again shot though her body, and for that moment when her eyes locked with his, Laura was quite certain he had experienced a similar sensation.

Standing so close, she could see the evidence of his arousal in how his trousers tightened.

Afraid the silhouette of her erect nipples had become visible despite her stays, Laura turned and moved to stand behind the blank canvas.

With the light from the parlor windows illuminating the canvas, she picked up a thin charcoal from a nearby table. She began sketching in her four subjects, finally allowing a satisfied grin when she saw how all of them displayed expressions of happiness or contentment. "Remember your positions and your thoughts of this very moment, for this is how you shall pose every morning for the next week or so," she announced happily.

Although she missed Hannah's quick glance in her mother's direction, she didn't miss Henry's wink. Acknowledging it with a quirked brow, Laura concentrated on her work and was soon lost in creating a work of art.

*An hour later*
Aware her subjects had begun to sag after an hour of holding their poses, Laura stepped from behind the canvas and said, "Thank you for your patience. That is all for today. I will see you tomorrow morning."

Not paying any attention to those who allowed sighs of relief or groans of pain at having to stand still for so long, Laura resumed her work, deciding she would take the opportunity to paint James' face as she had the clearest image in her mind's eye of his expression. When she could no longer paint him from memory, she would work on his clothing and perhaps some background elements.

It might have been a few minutes or fews hours later when she was suddenly aware she wasn't alone. "Mr. Simpson," she said as she dipped a curtsy.

Henry gave a bow from where he stood very near where he had been posing earlier that morning. "Miss Overby," he said as he reached for the hand that wasn't holding a paint brush. He bestowed a kiss on the back of her knuckles, his lips lingering far too long.

"You can look if you'd like," Laura said, thinking he wanted to assess her progress. Her gaze flicked to the back of her hand, noting how his long fingers still held it as if it were a fragile glass artifact. For a fleeting moment, she had a thought he was making love to it the way his lips first touched and then finally pursed to suckle the smooth skin.

"I wondered if you might wish to... to take some air. Step away and join me for a ride to the park? Maybe go for a walk to the Serpentine? I've ordered the coach be brought 'round."

Laura lifted the brush from the area of the canvas where she had been painting his father's aged features. "Now?"

Henry blinked and was about to respond when she gave her head a shake. "Of course, now. You no doubt have things to do. Places to be," she murmured as she dropped the paintbrush into a jar of turpentine. She moved her hands to undo the ties at the back of her neck that held her apron in place.

He didn't, really—he had just returned from his day at the bank—but Henry wasn't about to disagree with her. Not when she had apparently made up her mind to join him.

"Allow me," Henry said as he stepped behind her and made quick work of releasing the apron ties.

Laura removed the apron, folding it and laying it over the table on which her palette rested. She glanced down at her gown, wincing at its simplicity.

"What is it?" he asked.

Her gaze going to his fine suit of clothes, Laura was about to change her mind. Apparently, Henry noticed, for he leaned in close and said, "I'll help you with your mantle. It's in the vestibule, is it not?"

The reminder they would be wearing something over their current clothes had Laura relaxing. "Yes, of course. I should probably let Lady Simpson know I'm—"

"She knows," Henry interrupted, hoping he didn't sound like some sort of rake intent on ruining a young maiden. "If you'd like the presence of a maid—as a chaperone—I can prevail upon her lady's maid to join us."

Laura's eyes widened. The ride in the coach would be awkward enough with just the two of them. Adding a maid —someone she didn't even know—would make it even more so. "That won't be necessary, Mr. Simpson," she said with a shake of her head. Then, because she thought to tease him in an effort to see if he could show amusement, she added, "Unless you are a rake intent on ruining me?"

Henry's eyes rounded. "That's not my intent at all," he replied in alarm. When he noticed the twinkle in her eyes, he finally quirked his lips. "I would scold you, but I'm not sure you would receive it the way it was intended."

It was Laura's turn to round her eyes. "Mr. Simpson!" she said in a hoarse whisper. But her broad grin belied her words.

The encounter leaving him hopeful, Henry motioned to the door. "Shall we?"

Laura didn't reply but turned and shook out a Dutch cloth. She settled it over the top edge of the canvas, allowing it to fall over her work just as Henry peeked around the edge.

He turned to stare at her, his eyes wide. "You have captured my father perfectly," he whispered.

A shiver shot down her spine. "He is an excellent subject, Mr. Simpson."

"Henry," he said in a quiet voice. When her brows furrowed, he added, "Call me Henry. Although I admit to a certain aversion to my given name, I do prefer it over *Mr. Simpson.*"

Laura swallowed as she moved toward the door, Henry quickly stepping to her side. "Henrí, perhaps?" she offered, giving his name the French pronunciation.

Henry's eyes widened before a wan grin appeared. "I like that much better."

They made their way out of the parlor and to the stairs, Henry offering his arm. She placed her hand on it and they descended. There were no servants about as he held her mantle for her and then donned his greatcoat as she lifted the hood over her halo of blonde curls. He opened the door, and directly beyond it, the coach stood with its driver holding that door open.

Laura had the impression their departure from the townhouse was kept private as she stepped up and into the sky blue velvet-lined coach.

Did anyone else in the household know they were off to the park?

Thoughts of Henry kidnapping her should have set off alarm bells in her head. Thoughts that their trip to the park might be considered scandalous should have had her begging off and returning to the security of the parlor to continue her work on the painting.

Instead, she struggled to keep a smile from lighting her face as she settled herself into the velvet-covered bench facing the direction of travel and watched as Henry sat opposite her, his woolen greatcoat draping over the edge to reveal its satin lining.

"This is quite elegant," she said once the door was shut.

"It was a gift to my mother from her nephew, the duke," he said. "On the occasion of my parents' fiftieth wedding anniversary."

For a moment, Laura was left wondering if Henry had misspoke "Fiftieth?" she repeated, noting he didn't mention a particular duke by name, although she quickly reasoned it out in her head from what Lady Simpson had told her of her relations.

Henry angled his head to one side. "Indeed. My parents are quite... old."

"Your mother does not look it."

"The Burroughs women all keep their youthful appearance," he agreed. The coach jerked into motion, which had Henry reaching for the strap lest he be pitched forward.

Laura wondered what she might do if he did. If he landed on his knees with his head in her lap, what would she say? What would she do? A flush of color suffused her face at the thought of taking his face between her gloved hands and kissing him.

"Are you warm enough?"

The words brought Laura from one reverie and nearly sent her into another. She could imagine hearing those words at night, after she'd climbed into bed with him, tucked beneath the bed clothes and against the side of his body.

For the moment when their eyes met, she thought her musings were daft. He was merely expressing concern for her comfort. "I am. It's a beautiful spring day," she replied.

"I could not abide the thought of you spending all of it in the parlor," he said as the coach turned onto Oxford Street and headed west. "Standing for so long must be difficult."

"It's kind of you to consider my comfort," she said. "When I tire of standing, there is usually a stool on which I can sit or a chair of a height that allows me to work on the lower portions of a painting."

He nodded his understanding. "How is it you became a painter?" he asked. "Did you have instruction? Or go to a special school?"

Laura shook her head. "I have always drawn. Since I was a small child. When my father brought home a set of paints —I think they were from a shipment he arranged from the Continent—I simply expanded my artistic endeavors to include color," she explained. "I was a bit messy at first, which vexed my mother no end and left me with paint splotches on my hands and face and in my hair."

Henry's eyes lit with humor—and perhaps something else. "Is that why your hair is not long?"

The magic of the moment was lost as Laura absently raised a hand to the hood of her mantle. "My curly hair is... unmanageable," she murmured, her eyes darting to the side and her pleasant expression replaced with one that suggested disgust. "It was forever escaping its pins, and so on the eve of what was to be my come-out, my Mother took the scissors to it and—"

"Created a masterpiece," Henry said.

Laura's eyes widened, a blush coloring her face as she swallowed the rest of what she was about to say. "Hardly," she managed finally. "I hid in the house for a week afterwards."

Henry furrowed a brow. "So, no come-out?"

She allowed a sigh. "No, but it was a blessing, really. I used that week to paint portraits of my siblings. The following week, I gained my first commission when one of my mother's friends saw them. Before I was finished with that one, another followed, and..." She allowed a shrug. "I've been painting nearly every day since."

"But you still enjoy doing it?"

"Oh, yes. Very much," she said with enthusiasm. "I cannot imagine spending my days doing anything else." When she saw how his expression suddenly changed, as if he were disappointed at hearing her words, she added, "Other than running my own household, of course."

When Henry's face once again appeared as it had before, a tingle of excitement shot through Laura. If she'd had any doubt about his intentions, they had just been put aside. "And you, sir? What is it you do for your living?"

Henry straightened, and, for a moment, he seemed torn. "I have been informed only a fortnight ago that I shall be taking my superior's place as head clerk at the Bank of England when he retires this year."

Laura's eyes widened. She remembered Lady Simpson mentioning her son's position during one of their afternoons while taking tea, remembered how happy the woman had been when she spoke of the impending promotion. "Congratulations," she said as she displayed a brilliant smile. "Your mother must be so proud."

A wan grin appeared and then just as quickly disappeared from Henry's face. "Thank you. Truth be told, I haven't yet shared the news with my parents."

It was Laura's turn to wipe the smile from her face. If he hadn't told his parents, then how did his mother know? She had to suppress a grin at the sudden thought that his mother had spies at the bank. Even if she didn't, Laura knew men were the best gossips. Lady Simpson had probably learned of it whilst having tea in someone's parlor. "Are you not pleased?" she asked. "You must be held in high regard by those in charge at the bank."

Henry seemed torn as to how to respond. "It is an honor, of course," he replied.

At that moment, the coach slowed to a halt. A quick

glance out the windows showed they had passed beneath the arch at Stanhope Gate and were already well into the park.

"Would you still like to join me for a stroll?" Henry asked as the driver jumped down from the box. "I asked the driver to take us about halfway to the Serpentine."

"Yes, of course," Laura replied, her gaze on what she could see through the coach window. Despite the cool weather, there were children with their nurses scattered about the grounds. Later that afternoon, the fashionable hour would have members of the aristocracy entering the Hyde Park Gate to parade about Rotten Row in their various carriages and coaches. Some would do so on foot while others might ride horses.

When the door opened, Henry stepped down and turned to assist Laura. "It's actually warmer than I expected," he said as he offered his arm.

Laura placed her arm on his, taking a moment to gain her bearings. The path on which the coach was parked was near the intersection of one that would lead to the King's Road. Remaining on the current path would take them to the southern shore of the Serpentine. "The day is a fine one," she agreed.

Once they had taken a few steps, Laura realized the hood of her mantle prevented her from seeing Henry's profile, and so she turned her head in his direction. Apparently he had been attempting to see hers, for he quickly turned his attention to the path in front of them, as if he'd been caught staring.

"May I ask why it is the honor that has been bestowed upon you has you... vexed?" she asked, guessing at his reaction to learning of his promotion at the bank.

He inhaled slowly before he lifted his other hand to rest on her arm. "You are correct in your assumption," he murmured. "I have been working for nearly two decades to earn the position, and now that I almost have it, I am left wondering..." He allowed the sentence to trail off, as if he didn't have the words to describe his situation.

"What will be next?" she guessed. "What you will have to look forward to?"

Henry nearly stumbled despite the well-trampled crushed granite path beneath his feet. "Yes. That's it exactly," he said with astonishment. "How is it...?" He swallowed the rest of the question when a rubber ball passed in front of them, followed by a young boy who was supposed to have caught it. Another boy, closer to the water's edge, yelled his apologies.

"Don't you suppose we all wonder what is to be next in our lives?" she asked, a small smile appearing. She wasn't about to tell him how it was she and her sisters didn't have the same options to consider. They could either marry or not. If they didn't marry, their choices for positions of employment were limited.

Laura knew she was one of the lucky ones, lucky to have found a living that would pay her way in life should she remain unmarried. With her commissions, she could afford to let a townhouse in a respectable part of London, employ a few servants and perhaps even a companion.

But she had never aspired to remain unmarried.

"What will be next for you, Miss Overby?"

Her attention turning to the boy by the water, Laura sighed. "Besides more paintings, I should hope a husband and a few children." She paused, thinking their conversation had become far too personal, and yet she didn't mind. It was refreshing to speak of the future with someone she didn't know well, much like the conversation she'd had with Graham in the coach as they made their way to Woodscastle. "And you? What's the next position at the bank you will aspire to, Henri?" she asked, remembering it was her turn to continue the conversation. For a moment, she hadn't realized Henry had led them away from the water and closer to the cover of trees and hedgerows.

"I hadn't given it any thought," Henry replied, although his brows furrowed.

"Not even the head of the entire bank? What are they called?"

"Presidents," Henry said, his brows still forming a wrinkle on his forehead.

"Do you wish to be the president of the bank?"

He shook his head. "I'm... I'm not sure."

"Perhaps you will discover you enjoy your position as head clerk, and you won't wish to move on to another," she suggested.

"Perhaps," he hedged.

Laura slowed her steps, and Henry turned to face her. "I am quite sure I have no sway in convincing anyone of anything, Henrí, but if I could, I would do whatever I could to see to it you succeed at achieving whatever it is you want," she said with a grin. "So, what is it you *want*?" she asked as she lifted her head to regard him.

The hood of her mantle fell back, revealing a mass of blonde curls. Given the way the sunlight reflected off her hair, it appeared much like a halo. Struck by the thought she looked like an angel, Henry stared at her for a long time before he responded.

# CHAPTER 25

## A TURTLE PREPARES FOR PURSUIT

*eanwhile, at Wellingham Imports*

Emma Wellingham made her way out of her back office and was about to exit her husband's office when she stopped. She backed up several steps and turned her head slightly to the left, her gaze taking in a painting on the wall.

A new painting.

Of herself.

"Oh!" she breathed as she clutched the ledger she was carrying to her chest.

"It's perfect there, don't you think?" Thomas asked as he rose from his desk and moved to stand next to her.

"It's rather large," Emma replied. "It didn't look this large on the easel. How long...?" she struggled to think of when it could have been hung. She had been in her office all morning reviewing ledgers.

He leaned over and kissed her on the cheek. "First thing this morning. I had Mr. Allen bring it from the townhouse since he was taking Mrs. Allen there from Woodscastle," he explained. "One of the carpenters hung it shortly after it arrived."

"Was I here?" She didn't remember hearing any pounding as she worked in the back office.

"No. You hadn't yet come up from the warehouse," Tom replied, his gaze still on the portrait. "How is our son doing down there?"

Emma allowed a sigh. "I think he would be doing better if he and Lady Harrington had..." She sighed again.

"What happened?"

Furrowing a brow, Emma replied, "It's what didn't happen. They haven't yet been together. Graham paid a call at Harrington House on Saturday, but Hannah was out. Shopping, probably, given the Weatherstone ball is tomorrow night—"

"By the way, we're going to that," Thomas murmured.

Emma's eyes widened. "We are?"

Thomas nodded, a grin youthening his features. "Weatherstone himself invited me. When I was at the club last week. He hasn't forgotten our successful delivery of his tobacco from Virginia, and now he's asking about buying shares in the company."

"I had the same query from someone else," Emma replied. "The letter was delivered with this morning's post."

"Oh? Who sent it?"

Emma paused a moment before she said, "Edward Harrington."

Thomas gave a start, his eyes darting about as he struggled to remember the names of all the Harringtons and their children.

"Hannah's boy," Emma offered. "The heir to the Mayfield earldom."

His expression brightening, Thomas said, "Well, he's

obviously got a good head on his shoulders, but then I suppose I should expect nothing less."

"We have no more shares to sell," Emma reminded him.

"About that," Thomas said as he moved to his desk. "I think I know how we can offer shares without diluting the shares we and our employees own."

Emma angled her head to one side. "You're not selling mine," she said on a huff.

"I wouldn't think of it," Thomas assured her, reminded that when he married her, she owned just over half the company's stock. "We offer new shares to fund the expansion in Boston."

Emma furrowed a brow. "Make the Boston operation its own company?"

"Exactly. Sinclair can head it up for now, as he's already doing. Graham already knows everything about it, so I won't feel as if I'm dumping everything on him when I decide to retire."

A slow grin lifted Emma's lips. "It's a brilliant idea," she said, just as a knock sounded at the door.

"Come!" Thomas called out.

The door opened to reveal their son. Although Graham seemed happy to find them together, he gingerly stepped into the office. "Mother, Father," he said as he gave his mother a peck on the cheek.

"You look as if you've lost your best friend," Emma said quietly.

"That's because I cannot find her," Graham replied on a sigh.

"You and Hannah still haven't seen one another?" Thomas asked in disbelief.

"I stopped at the Simpsons' on my way here. She was there this morning for a portrait sitting, but she had already taken her leave," he said on a sigh. "I have missed her by mere moments a number of times over the past few days." He finally allowed a wicked grin. "I'll see her tonight, though. Her son has invited me to dinner at Harrington House."

Emma and Thomas exchanged quick glances. "How fortuitous," Emma said before she told him of their plans for a stock offering for the Boston operation. "It's seems Edward Harrington is interested in investing, as is Lord Weatherstone."

Graham crossed his arms as he considered the plan. "That young man continues to bely his age," he murmured softly.

"You sounded quite impressed with him when you spoke of him yesterday," Emma commented, remembering their discussion over dinner.

"That's because I am. And not just because he's Hannah's son," Graham replied. "There's something about him..." He gave his head a shake. "Well, let's just say he's sixteen going on six-and-thirty."

"He's an heir to an earldom now," Thomas commented, "so his maturity will suit him well for that task."

"Indeed," Graham agreed.

"So, are you of the opinion Sinclair can run the Boston office if it expands even more than it already has?" Thomas asked.

Graham nodded. "Oh, yes. He's got a head for business and the connections necessary to make it work, especially now that he has recently married a gel from an influential family."

"We offer him a large number of shares—"

"But not all at once," Emma interrupted. "He gets more after every... say five years. To ensure he's vested in the company," she explained.

"All right," Graham agreed. "That means we have to keep some back."

"And the rest we sell to those who wish to invest."

"Lord Weatherstone and Edward Harrington."

"I'll get to work on the valuation," Emma said as she turned to head back to her office. "In the event Weatherstone asks about it tomorrow at the ball."

Graham gave a start. "You're going to the ball?" he asked in surprise.

"We are," Thomas replied.

"Even though I have nothing to wear," Emma called out from her office.

Thomas leaned back in his chair, his gaze on the new painting. "I think you should wear exactly what you're wearing in the painting," he called out.

Noting his father's attention was directed at the wall behind him, Graham turned and took a step back. "Well, that's certainly larger than it looked in the parlor," he said in surprise.

"That was my thought, too," Thomas agreed. He angled his head to one side. "Tell me. What did you think of Miss Overby? I understand you spent some time in her company."

"In her father's coach, yes," Graham admitted as his brows waggled. "Cousin Laura is a fine young woman. Very accomplished for her age, I think. Reminds me a bit of Edward in that regard." He hadn't even realized he used the young man's given name until he noticed his father staring at him. "What is it?"

"Nothing," Thomas said as he gave his head a shake. "But you mentioned you'll be at the ball tomorrow night."

"I will. That's where I'll be announcing my intention to marry Hannah."

"You have appropriate clothes?"

Graham nodded. "I paid a call on a tailor's shop in New Bond Street."

"Garth's?" Thomas guessed.

"Yes. Besides the trousers and topcoat, he had the perfect waistcoat. A turtle green brocade. Fit perfectly."

"Turtle green?" Thomas repeated.

A slow smile spread over Graham's face. "Indeed. And I'm wearing it tonight as well."

## CHAPTER 26

## A DISCUSSION OF UTMOST IMPORT IN THE PARK

*M*eanwhile, *back in Hyde Park*

Henry thought Laura's question and her comments leading up to it were the perfect opening for him to put voice to every concern he had been struggling with for the past month. Concerns about his new position at the bank, about his aged parents and his lack of a wife, about Hannah and her need for a husband. His nephew and the responsibilities he would face as heir to the Mayfield earldom.

The words were about to tumble forth, beginning with his thoughts on the situation at the bank, when he noticed how Laura was regarding him.

With true concern. Her queries hadn't been made in the interest of keeping up her end of the conversation. The look in her eyes was evidence of her want to know. Her want to offer answers.

Her desire.

Henry blinked. Perhaps her eyes merely reflected what he knew was in his own.

At that moment, there was only one way to discover if she truly felt for him what he had gleaned from her words.

Lowering his face to hers, he captured her lips with his own and kissed her. When she made no move other than to lean toward him and lift herself onto her toes, Henry deepened the kiss.

The faintest scent of jasmine surrounded them. She tasted of honey. When her gloved hand rested on his shoulder, as if she needed to keep herself upright lest she fall against the front of him, he wrapped an arm around her waist.

Perhaps it was because he pulled her closer, or perhaps it was because his lips left hers to travel along her jawline to her neck, but her whispered, "Henri" had him pausing, his lips still suckling her soft skin.

"Are you going to kidnap me?"

Henry jerked back, blinking to discover Laura staring at him despite the glaze of desire over her eyes. "I hadn't planned to," he whispered, wondering why she would ask such a thing. "Unless you think it necessary that I do so?"

Laura blinked several times before she lowered her feet to the ground. Then she swallowed as she stared up at him. "Of course not. Unless…" Her eyes suddenly widened. "That's what you wanted? To kiss me?" she asked in disbelief, as if she just then remembered what she had asked him.

"It's but one thing I wanted. *Want*," Henry replied, bemused when she didn't make a move to leave his hold.

"What else do you want?"

Henry sighed and glanced around them, finally spying a park bench to the west. He let go his hold on her waist but kept one of her hands on his arm as he led them to the bench. He pulled a handkerchief from his pocket and brushed away the dust from the bench before allowing her to sit. When he followed suit, he angled in her direction, one of her gloved hands held in his.

"To start with, I'd like to finally move into my own townhouse. I have one, you see, a few doors down from the one my parents own."

"What's keeping you from doing so?"

Henry sighed. "My parents are getting on in years, and with my sister having married and moved out, I..."

"Felt responsible for them," she finished for him.

"Exactly."

"What else?"

"My sister is widowed but has loved your cousin, Graham, almost since he was born."

"As he does her," Laura said, her eyes widening in delight. "He plans to propose during dinner tonight."

Henry allowed a tentative grin. "Well, this is good news," he murmured. "My nephew is in need of a father."

She nodded her understanding. "Lady Simpson says Lord Harrington is sixteen but has the demeanor of one much older."

Frowning, Henry finally nodded. "Perhaps he is more in need of a confidante than a father," he said in a quiet voice. "Although I do not believe I can be that for him, perhaps Graham Wellingham can."

"Graham is much impressed with your nephew. Said he is the son he wishes he would have had with your sister."

Henry gave a start. "You say that as if he has already met Edward."

"Oh, he has," Laura replied. "At Brooks's. They spent an evening in conversation over brandy."

His head bent as he considered her words, Henry felt a combination of relief and curiosity. For the past year, he had worried that his nephew might look to him for fatherly advice—advice Henry didn't feel qualified to render given he had never been a father himself.

The boy's grandfather, Mayfield, had never been much of a father to Charlie, but then Charlie's upraising probably wasn't any different from most sons of the *ton*.

"Thank you for telling me that," Henry said when he shook himself from his reverie.

"You're most welcome," Laura replied, an impish grin bringing delight to her eyes. Angling her head to one side, she asked, "What else do you want?"

Inhaling softly, Henry was tempted to say, "Another kiss," but instead he said, "I do want the position at the bank. Not because I have thought I could do a better job of it than Mr. Streater, of course." He shook his head to reinforce his words.

"Then why?"

The simple query had Henry realizing something he hadn't considered before. He had always thought his desire for the position of head clerk had to do with rank. With privilege. A means of rising above his father's original life in service by becoming a member of the *ton*. The new position would afford him that status as well as provide an income much higher than the one he now enjoyed. "The promotion comes with a raise in pay," he said simply.

"For which you have plans?"

"Indeed," he said. "I can afford to hire a staff for the townhouse. Have some necessary renovations done."

*Afford to take a wife.*

"So you'll be moving soon?"

He inhaled deeply. "I would, but I don't wish to live there alone."

Laura glanced down at how he had captured both of her hands in his. "Have you someone in mind you wish to live with?"

Henry lifted first one hand and then the other, bestowing

a kiss on the back of each before holding them together between his own. "You. Should you agree to be my wife," he said in a whisper. His brows suddenly furrowed. "Will I have to kidnap you, do you suppose?"

Her eyes glancing sideways, Laura allowed a brilliant smile before she said, "Are you proposing marriage?"

"I am."

"Then you needn't kidnap me," Laura said with a shake of her head. "I'll go with you. Willingly."

His lips were on hers once again, his kiss as fervent as how she returned it. Despite those who walked past them, pretending not to notice their indiscretion, they continued to kiss for several minutes. They were fairly near to laughing when their lips finally parted.

"I shall have to pay a call on your father," Henry said once he finally ended the kiss. "Will he be at your home this evening? Or... or now?" he asked as he sobered.

Laura couldn't help but giggle at hearing Henry's query. "Right now... he's probably still at Wellingham Imports. You must know he works for Graham's father."

"I am in good stead with Thomas Wellingham," Henry stated. "And Mrs. Wellingham was the midwife when my sister was born," he added, as if he thought it necessary to provide proof.

Laura furrowed a brow. "And yours, I should hope?"

Henry smirked. "I was impatient. She was too late for my arrival."

"Oh!" Laura scoffed, trying hard to hide her grin.

"Father did what he could before he fainted," Henry continued, his expression sober until he, too, grinned. "Although I have been a more patient man since, I suddenly find I am no more," he claimed. "At least, when it comes to you. If you'd prefer, I can drop you at my parents' house on my way, or—"

"I'm going with you," Laura stated. "My father will not believe you have proposed if I am not there."

"Why ever not?"

Laura inhaled softly before her gaze lowered to where he still held her hands. "He doesn't think a husband should allow his wife to spend her days painting portraits of people in their homes," she replied. "*Would* allow, I suppose I should say. You, of course, would not have such qualms." At seeing Henry's reaction—his expression slowly changing from bliss to one of consternation—she realized he agreed with her father. Laura pulled her hands from his. "I must be allowed to paint, Henrí."

"You'll have your own studio in our townhouse, of course," he said by way of a compromise.

Laura didn't miss his use of the words "our townhouse," but the thought that she wouldn't be allowed to continue her portraiture work had her leaning away from him. "That's very kind of you, Henrí, but... but I must paint people in their homes. Where they are comfortable. Where they are surrounded by their own treasures," she replied. After another moment, when she knew she hadn't changed his mind, she added, "I... I think it's best if we go back now."

Henry stared at her, his crestfallen face looking far older than when they had embarked on their outing. "Of course. I... I didn't mean to keep you away from your work for so long," he murmured. He stood and offered his arm.

"Please don't be angry," she said quietly.

"I am not," he replied, his quick pace towards the coach at odds with his words.

"Should you change your mind—"

"I won't. I cannot," Henry interrupted before he gave his head a shake and slowed his steps a fraction. "I apologize. I did not mean to sound like a petulant child, but on this matter I must agree with Mr. Overby," he murmured.

"You did not," Laura said on a sigh, her words said over the last of his. "And I am sorry that what you and I want are at odds in only that one regard."

"As am I," Henry managed.

Without sounding as hurt as he felt.

When they reached the coach, the driver barely had time to open the door before Henry handed her into it. He turned to the driver. "Take her back to the house. I'll find my own way home. Miss Overby. Thank you for a pleasant after- noon," he said as he turned, tipped his hat, and gave a bow.

Before the driver could shut the door, Laura called out, "Thank you for the walk, Mr. Simpson."

At first, Henry bristled at her use of his formal name as he set off on the path that led to the southeastern entrance of the park. Then he realized it would have been entirely improper for her to call him by his given name with the driver standing there.

After she had learned that everything he wanted was coming to fruition, Henry thought it a wonder she could think she would be allowed to continue her painting in other people's homes once they were married.

After their entirely improper kisses in broad daylight, it was a wonder she could play at being proper.

*She knows of all my wants*, he thought as he felt an ache grow in his chest. How could he still want her so much knowing she wouldn't abide his wishes?

At least no other man would marry her, for he was quite certain there wasn't a man in all of England who would allow his wife to do what she insisted she must.

Although the thought should have brought with it a sense of relief, Henry found he felt nothing of the sort.

Frustrated, he shoved his hands into his pockets and stalked off towards Park Lane.

# CHAPTER 27

# COMMISERATING WITH A SISTER

*a half-hour later, at Harrington House*
Hannah regarded her reflection in the cheval mirror in her bedchamber and allowed a sigh of satisfaction. The dark pink dinner gown she wore, a sharp contrast to the mourning clothes she had been wearing this past year, looked even brighter than it had in Suzanne's.

Her maid had done her hair in a style far more ornate than usual, as if she had been in on whatever surprise Tom and Victoria had in store for her.

Turning away from the mirror, she dared a quick glance out the window. The park was directly across the street and displayed its early spring greenery. Nursemaids with their charges in tow were making their way to their homes. Those on horseback were headed towards Rotten Row to begin another season of late afternoon parades.

A man who looked exactly like her brother plodded along the pavement taking steps no larger than her own.

Sure it was indeed her brother, Hannah opened the drapes with one hand and leaned her cheek against the glass.

Although Henry usually walked with perfect posture, holding his head high, he looked now as if he had lost his best friend.

When he was directly in front of Harrington House, she was sure he would turn and walk up to the front door. Instead, he continued walking north.

Alarmed, Hannah rushed from the room and down the two flights of stairs. Although Potter was quick to pull her mantle from a peg and hold it out for her, she waived it off as she hurried past him and out the door. "Henry!" she called out.

The bent man paused and turned around as she rushed to stand before him. "Hannah," he said, as he tipped his hat.

Oblivious to her lack of a bonnet or hat, Hannah regarded Henry with an expression of confusion. "Whatever has happened?" she asked as she struggled to catch her breath. "Is father...?" She dared not finish the query when she saw Henry's dour expression.

"He's fine, I think, although I have not been home for the past couple of hours."

"What's wrong, Henry?"

He struggled to speak, clearing his throat. "It seems I want too much."

Hannah furrowed a brow. "Come inside, Henry. We'll have a cup of tea. I have some time before I must leave for Fairmont Park."

"Ah. Your reunion dinner," Henry replied, his words making him sound peevish.

"What's that supposed to mean?"

Henry straightened, his brows furrowing to match his sister's. "Never mind."

Hannah took her brother's hand and pulled him in the direction of Harrington House. After a few steps, he came willingly, and once they were in the vestibule, Potter saw to his greatcoat and hat as Hannah ordered tea be brought to the front salon.

"Now tell me what has happened," Hannah demanded as she led him to an upholstered chair and nearly pushed him into it.

"I proposed marriage."

With absolutely no regard for her dinner gown, Hannah fell into the opposite chair. "To whom?"

"Miss Overby, of course."

Hannah glanced up at the clock on the fireplace mantel. "Laura Overby?" she asked in a quiet voice. "I... I wasn't aware you were courting her," she murmured. "Did you begin in the past... five hours?"

"I did. I was," Henry replied, his words curt.

"She turned you down?"

Henry's head jerked, as if his sister had slapped him across the face. "She accepted, actually. Turns out, we want the same things. Well, all except for her... painting."

"Oh, Henry, you didn't," Hannah whispered. She guessed where the two of them might have disagreed. "Painting is her avocation, Henry. Surely you did not expect her to give it up to become your *wife*?"

"Of course not," he countered. "I just didn't want her painting portraits in other people's homes. While I'm at the bank and unable to provide pro—"

"Oh, don't be ridiculous," Hannah chided him. "She paints portraits of people of *quality*," she added. "You've no need to be concerned that she would be in any kind of danger."

"What if she was accosted by a footman?"

Hannah blinked. Harrington House had a number of footmen whom she might have at one time wanted to accost her, but she didn't think Laura Overby would welcome such advances. "She has paint brushes," she replied. "A marked man would have a hard time escaping the butler's wrath."

"Ha ha," Henry replied, not the least bit amused.

"I was being serious," Hannah countered, annoyed by her brother's attitude. "Of all the short-sighted excuses you could come up with for not marrying the woman you have secretly pined for over the last three weeks, I cannot believe you settled on *this* one."

Henry jerked his head up, his eyes narrowing in warning. "*You* of all people have no right to lecture me about *pining* for someone."

Gasping, Hannah had her hand up, ready to slap him across the face. She suddenly lowered it. "Whatever are you talking about?"

"Whoever," he corrected. "Graham Wellingham."

Hannah frowned. "I'm fairly certain it's 'whomever,' but whatever it is, I'm quite sure..." She allowed the sentence to trail off, realizing she really didn't know what was in store for her on this night.

From Tom's invitation, she expected Graham would be present at the dinner party he was hosting at Fairmont Park. More than anyone, Tom knew of her regard for his cousin. He probably even knew of the bargain she had struck with Graham all those years ago.

"Yes, I expect you'll be wed to Graham Wellingham within the week," Henry said with derision. "Or will it be in the morning?"

"Henry!" she scolded. "You could be wed this week, too, if you weren't so *damned* stubborn."

Henry's head snapped up, as if she *had* slapped him across the face. He was about to admonish her for her curse, but she held up a staying finger, and he knew to hold his tongue.

"Don't you *dare* lecture me about cursing," she warned.

"Laura Overby is an *artist*. She is well-regarded in her profession. For you to expect her to give up her avocation as a condition of becoming your wife is an... is an *insult*."

"Insult?" he countered in disbelief. "I'll have you know, she told me her father is of the same opinion."

Hannah angled her head to one side, a sign *she* was about to insult her brother. "That does not make it right," she said in a hoarse whisper.

Henry winced. Whenever his sister spoke in whispers, she was doing so from a position of annoyance.

Impatience.

Anger.

"You are saying I am *wrong* in my concern that my wife might be accosted whilst she paints in someone's home?"

Hannah straightened and considered his question before she shook her head. "You are not wrong," she admitted in a quiet voice.

"Ha!" he managed before Hannah directed a dagger-filled look in his direction.

"A situation easily mitigated with a... a footman or... or an old crone of a maid," she stammered. "It's not an all-or-nothing scenario, Henry," she added when she saw how he settled back in his chair.

His only response was a heavy sigh.

"Do you love her?"

Henry allowed another sigh. "I feel affection for her," he acknowledged.

"Do you think about her all the time?"

He rolled his eyes. "Well, not *all* the time," he replied defensively.

"Do you worry about her?"

He inhaled softly before clearing his throat. "All the time," he whispered.

Hannah angled her head to one side and gave a huff.

"Oh, Henry. Come to some to sort of agreement and marry the poor girl. Put yourself and our mother out of your misery."

"Misery?" he repeated. "*I'm* not miserable," he insisted. He clamped his mouth shut when he noted how his sister stared at him. "At least, not all the time," he amended. He dropped his head into his hands. "It's time I move into my townhouse, Hannah. I hoped to do so with a wife who could oversee the household—"

"Oh, Henry. You can hire a good housekeeper to do that," she argued, obviously impatient with him. Then her eyes widened.

"What is it?"

"Not what, but whom," she said in a whisper. "I know *exactly* whom you should hire to be your housekeeper," she murmured. "That is, if you can get her away from Fitzsimmons Manor," she added.

"Lord Chamberlain's housekeeper?"

Hannah nodded as her attention went to the clock on the fireplace mantel. "With this extra errand, I must be going, or I will be late to Fairmont Park, and I shouldn't wish to miss *my* opportunity for a happily ever after," she added as she stood. "God knows I've been waiting a long time for it."

She was out of the salon before Henry could rise to his feet. He followed her into the vestibule. "Might I prevail upon you for a ride? I forgot how far it is to King Street," he said, a bit sheepishly.

"First, I'm taking you to Fitzsimmons Manor," Hannah replied as Potter draped her mantel over her shoulders.

"You are?"

"Yes, and with any luck, I'll be dropping you and the housekeeper at your townhouse. You'll need to arrange for her return, however."

"I'm quite sure I can manage that," Henry replied,

knowing he would need the time in the coach to come up with a suitable apology.

And to build up an appetite. He was fairly sure he was going to be eating some crow on this night.

# CHAPTER 28

# DUELING DINNERS

*A* *few minutes later, Fairmont Park, north of London*
Lady Victoria Statton Grandby regarded the dining table with a critical eye, sure something was missing. She was in the middle of counting silverware when her butler appeared on the threshold, a silver salver held in one hand.

"What is it, Clark?"

"A note was just delivered, my lady. I have reason to believe..." He paused, a pained expression replacing his usual staid features. "It has to do with this evening's dinner."

Victoria plucked the note from the salver and turned it over to study the wax seal. A '*W*' was embossed in the red wax, but there were no other markings to indicate its source.

"Is there a problem?" Tom asked from the threshold.

Glancing up from the missive, Victoria inhaled softly at the sight of her husband dressed in his finest dinner clothes. He appeared as if he had recently been shaved, and his hair was still damp. Tempted to ruffle it with her fingers, she instead held out the note in his direction. "A letter arrived. It's addressed to you," she said quietly.

Tom furrowed a brow as he reached for the note and

broke the seal. Unfolding the stationery, he quietly cursed after reading a few lines. "It seems Graham has received a dinner invitation from Edward Harrington," he murmured.

Victoria's eyes widened. "That's good, is it not?"

"For tonight," Tom replied as he continued to read the note. "What I don't understand is why it's taken so long for this to reach us," he said as he turned the letter over and read the outside. "He wrote it last Friday evening."

"Oh, dear. Are you saying he's not coming tonight?" Victoria asked in alarm, lifting her hand to her hips as she attempted to hide her disappointment.

Tom looked up and noticed his wife's fine blue dinner gown and coiffure for the first time. "I am. God, but you're rather gorgeous this evening." He stepped around the table and kissed her on the cheek.

"Bounder," she accused, even though a frisson shot through her when she remembered what they would be doing after their dinner guests took their leave. She sobered more when she considered what Tom had planned for that evening. "This was supposed to a be a reunion of two lovers, you said," she reminded him in a quiet voice. "Now it's *ruined.*"

"I know," Tom replied. "Cousin Edward has foiled our plans, it seems. I'm quite sure Graham only accepted a dinner invitation at Harrington House because he believed Hannah would be there," he murmured. "Which means Edward believed she would be there, as well. Which means..." His eyes suddenly widened.

"What?" Victoria asked in confusion.

"We'll have to see to getting Lady Harrington back to Harrington House this evening. While Graham is still there."

Victoria nodded. "Of course. But... we'll have to tell her why. So much for your surprise." Her eyes widened. "But...

what if Mr. Wellingham leaves to come here when he discovers Hannah isn't there?"

Tom winced, remembering how determined Graham had been when he was in his office. "Seems we're in a pickle," he murmured.

Clark cleared his throat, and when the two turned to stare at him, he said, "Lady Harrington's coach has just pulled into the drive. Should I... send her back to Harrington House?"

Tom and Victoria exchanged glances. "No," Victoria replied firmly.

"What?" Tom arched a brow, his confusion evident.

Victoria's fists once again went to her hips. "If Mr. Wellingham wants her that badly, he can come to her," she stated.

His eyes darted sideways, in time to catch Clark doing the same thing in his direction. Tom sighed. "Very well. We'll carry on with dinner as planned, but we're going to have an uneven number at the table until Graham shows up." He glanced over the place settings and frowned. "Was it only going to be the four of us?" he asked.

"Well, it was supposed to be eight, but..." She sighed. "Gabe and Francis haven't yet returned from their wedding trip, and I received word Lord and Lady Haddon aren't coming because, well, Juliet isn't feeling up to it."

Tom's brows lifted before a grin appeared. "So a little lord or lady is in their future?" he guessed.

"She's not yet sure," Victoria replied, as the sound of the front door opening had them moving to greet their only dinner guest.

"Vicky!" Hannah said happily as she hugged her niece by marriage. "I've been looking forward to this dinner all day," she said as Clark removed her mantel. She turned her attention on her nephew. "My, but don't you clean up nicely?" she teased. "If you wear those clothes tomorrow night at the Weatherstone ball, I'll be sure to dance with you."

"You had better," Tom countered. "They say I'm only allowed two with my wife, but I intend to cheat."

Hannah's grin remained in place until she noticed the quiet. "Am I the first to arrive?"

Tom cleared his throat. "For now," he managed. "It seems our other guests will not be joining us."

Her grin fading, Hannah blinked several times. "Has something happened?"

Victoria was quick to step up and take her arm. "Juliet is ill, so the Haddons are not coming this evening. Gabe and Francis—"

"Are in Italy," Hannah finished for her, knowing the Earl of Trenton's oldest son and his new bride would have been on the invitation list.

"Our other... *guest* seems to have mixed up his invitations. With any luck, he'll realize his mistake and join us by the time the dessert course is served." Victoria pulled Hannah toward the library.

Hannah stared at her. "*He?*"

Victoria dared a glance in her husband's direction, hoping Tom might provide an answer. She didn't want to ruin the surprise if Graham did make an appearance.

"We have someone we'd like you to meet," Tom said as he moved to the liquor cart in the library. "Actually, you were introduced a long time ago, but we thought to reacquaint the two of you." He lifted a carafe of wine. "A glass of claret?"

Hannah shook her head. "Brandy," she stated. She moved to sit on the edge of the settee and glanced up at Victoria. "So he's not coming," she murmured, disappointment apparent in her crestfallen expression.

"It seems your son invited him to dinner at Harrington House," Victoria replied, deciding she didn't wish to be part of a ruse. She sat next to Hannah and reached for one of her hands. "I understand if you'd like to return there right away, but—"

"Edward has met Graham?" Hannah asked in alarm. She turned her attention on Tom, her eyes wide with what appeared to be fright. "*How*? When? Edward hasn't said a word of it to me!"

Tom offered her the glass of brandy and gave a glass of claret to his wife. "He wanted to surprise you," he said gently, but his brows furrowed at her reaction to the news.

"Well, he's certainly done that," Hannah replied, before she took a long sip of the brandy and nearly choked. "Oh, good God, I don't know what I was thinking," she said as her face screwed up in disgust.

Doing his best to suppress a grin, Tom took the glass from her and returned to the liquor cart. "Your need for fortification, I would guess, Aunt Hannah. And as for the *how*, it seems my cousin—*cousins*," he corrected himself, "attend the same club."

Hannah fell back against the settee's cushion, a slight gasp sounding. "Brooks's," she murmured. "Edward went with Mayfield last Friday evening, after they played billiards." She sighed as she glanced over at Victoria. "But he didn't tell me."

Victoria gave a slight shrug. "Unlike most men, your son is good at keeping secrets."

Tom rolled his eyes as he gave his aunt the claret. "Here I thought I was doing rather well," he said under his breath. "Pardon me. I need to speak with Clark a moment."

Furrowing a brow as her husband left the library, Victoria said in a quiet voice, "I would not blame you if you wished to return to Harrington House. We can even join you on the ride if you'd like some company."

Hannah downed half of her claret in a few gulps. "No. I

will not allow this to spoil your dinner. *Our* dinner," she amended. "Besides, I have news about my brother."

Victoria's eyes widened. "Whatever has happened?" she asked in alarm.

Realizing her words had been misunderstood, Hannah said, "It's not a matter of life or death, but..." She shook her head.

"He's met someone."

It was Hannah's turn to give a look of alarm. "How did *you* know?"

Victoria tittered. "He's a bank clerk. He's probably the most staid man I've ever met. If something has happened that would have you remarking on it, it would have to involve a woman," she replied.

"Oh, dear. He has become rather staid," Hannah murmured.

"Have you met her?"

Hannah nodded. "As have you." She pointed up to the portrait of Tom and Victoria that hung above the fireplace.

Victoria jerked back at the same moment Tom returned to the library. "What is it?" he asked, his gaze going to the portrait.

"He is courting Miss Overby?" Victoria asked, a look of delight crossing her face.

"I leave the room for not even one moment, and I've obviously missed important gossip," Tom complained.

"They went for a ride in the park this afternoon," Hannah began, ignoring her nephew's comment, "and from what Henry said when he paid a call at Harrington House, I fear I shall not be blessed with another nephew or a niece. Ever," Hannah lamented.

"Laura Overby?" Tom asked as he took a seat across from the women. "She seems very amiable."

"She is," Hannah assured him. "I think she even likes

my brother, and Mother is certainly impressed with her. But Henry cannot abide a wife who paints portraits in people's homes, and she doesn't wish to give up on her avocation."

"Nor should she," Victoria stated. She and Tom exchanged a meaningful glance.

"I knew better than to bring up the topic," Tom said to Hannah. "Besides, I rather like that my wife has an interest in something other than shopping and gossip. Something she can do without my presence. I do require she have a groomsman nearby in case of trouble, though," he added, referring to the times Victoria spent training race horses.

"Miss Overby is making a good living on referrals alone," Victoria said after giving her husband a wink. "She doesn't require a husband, unless she wants children, of course."

Hannah sighed. "I think Henry was on the verge of tears when he told me," she murmured.

Tom leaned forward in his chair. "Uncle Henry?" he asked in surprise. "Tears? When was this?"

Hannah dared a glance at the clock on the mantel. "Not even two hours ago," she replied. "I felt terrible having to dismiss him, but I think he's made a stupid blunder, and I told him so."

"What about Miss Overby? Is she... all right?" Tom asked.

Hannah blinked as her mouth dropped open. "I have no idea. Henry put her in the coach and sent her back to my parents' townhouse whilst he went for a walk." When she noted Victoria's expression of curiosity, she added, "She started painting our family portrait this morning."

"Oh, how awkward the sittings will be," Victoria murmured.

"Indeed," Hannah said on a sigh.

Clark appeared at the door and announced dinner was

served. While Tom stood and offered his arms to both Hannah and his wife, he made eye contact with the butler.

His nod barely perceptible, Clark's eyes darted toward the front of the house. At the same time, Tom heard the sound of a horse leaving the grounds, and he gave the servant a knowing nod.

Leading the women to the dining room, Tom felt a good deal of satisfaction at having a stable full of fast horses. He doubted any of them had been used for such a mission as the one that had been dispatched on this evening. But his aunt's happiness depended on it.

As did his cousin's.

# CHAPTER 29

## SECOND CHANCES

*The hour before at the Simpson townhouse, King Street*

Laura stepped down from the Simpson town coach and hurried inside, determined to make her way to the parlor before anyone in the household could discover her presence.

On the one hand, she wanted to return to her avocation. Simply lose herself in the portrait and spend the remainder of the day painting. On the other, she thought to turn around, cross the street, and hide in the Wellingham's townhouse for the rest of the day. Perhaps pen a letter to Lady Simpson with her regrets. Apologize profusely while she explained she could not continue the commission.

For a moment, she even considered going home. Her mother would be there with a shoulder to cry on, although Laura would probably have to share it with her baby brother. Lady Overby was quite insistent about seeing to her own children's comfort, even if there was a nursemaid in the upstairs nursery.

In the end, Laura opted to paint. Her reputation was more important than a bruised heart. She could count on painting as a means of making her living for the rest of her life. Affairs of the heart were merely momentary distractions.

Her thoughts went to her parents. Two people who'd had a brief encounter years before they reconnected by chance to marry and live happy lives. Two people who loved each other and proved their devotion every day with how they behaved with one another, despite having five children.

That very behavior was *why* they had five children.

Her mother, the former Lily Harkins and illegitimate sister of the Earl of Trenton, could have married an aristocrat —she had whispered only the year before that the Marquess of Reading had proposed to her at one of Lord Weatherstone's balls. The same year she had agreed instead to marry William Overby.

How different life would be with a marquess for a father! Especially since the marquess had fathered four bastard sons, two legitimate sons, and one illegitimate daughter.

*I might not exist*, Laura thought in dismay. *I wouldn't exist*, she amended, loading a brush to continue her work on James' face.

He had kind eyes, she thought. Perceptive eyes. Eyes that had seen it all but wished to see more. No wonder he was still so spry. He had to be older than eighty!

Absorbed in her work, she was unaware when she was no longer alone. Unaware of who had joined her. Of who had taken his place behind the chair that had held Lady Harrington earlier that day.

In fact, Laura might have continued to paint for another hour or two, except Henry drew attention to his presence when he murmured, "I am thinking it would be appropriate for you to add horns and a tail to your depiction of me."

Laura froze, the paint brush less than an inch away from Henry's face on the canvas.

She hadn't even realized she had begun to paint him, his

image still fresh in her mind's eye. On the canvas, his eyes were filled with mirth and longing, his long cheeks shortened by the hint of a smile that lifted his lips and made him far more handsome than the man who currently regarded her with an expression that suggested he might be on the verge of tears.

"Mr. Simpson," she whispered. "I... I didn't hear you come in," she stammered as she stepped away from the canvas.

"Your concentration on your work is remarkable," he said as he moved from behind the chair and made his way toward her. "Which merely drives home my point about your need for protection."

About to take a step back, Laura remembered she could not—there was a chair behind her, and she didn't want to end up in it. Not with Henry advancing on her. Not with him displaying an expression she couldn't discern. "Thank you," she said as she dipped a curtsy. "And for your concern."

He bowed and reached for her hand, which forced her to give up her hold on the brush.

"Did you walk all the way here?" she asked in a whisper, her eyes wide with worry.

Sighing, he gave his head a shake and said, "My sister gave me a ride in her coach," he replied. "I just came from Harrington House. Surely you noticed how my ears are blistered from my sister's well-deserved rebuke."

Laura furrowed a brow. "Why ever would Lady Harrington scold you?"

Henry stepped closer, about to tell her why when his attention briefly darted to the painting before he did a double-take and stared at it. "Oh, my sweeting, you've captured my father perfectly," he murmured in awe. His eyes squinted as he leaned in closer and stared at himself. "And rendered me far more handsome than I deserve," he added on a sigh.

"Nonsense. I merely painted you as I remembered you in the..." Laura swallowed the rest of her comment, her head dipping as her cheeks flamed with color.

"Do you suppose being in love does that to a person? Makes them look younger? More handsome?" he amended.

Laura blinked, momentarily confused. Had she painted him in a manner more flattering because she had felt affection for him?

For she had felt affection for him. Still did.

How could she not? He had kissed her so sweetly. Held her so close and said things she had never hoped to hear from a man.

Or had she simply painted him how she remembered him from that morning, his enigmatic expression making it difficult to discern his mood?

His expression now certainly wasn't enigmatic. He was gazing at her in a manner more like the one he had displayed in the park. A manner that suggested he had completely forgotten about the words that had separated them.

Even now, his expression had her insides melting. Her heart racing. Her breath held in anticipation of what he was about to say.

Then she remembered he had asked her a question, and he was waiting for her to respond.

"I really couldn't say, sir," she murmured, struggling to keep her gaze on anything but him.

"My sister reminded me I can be a fool sometimes—"

"Surely not."

"Oh, most assuredly. Much like I was earlier today, in the park."

Laura inhaled softly, her disappointment evident. "For having kissed me?"

Henry shook his head. "Not for that, surely," he replied. "For... for what happened afterwards. For having made the comment that you would not be allowed to pursue your passion should we wed," he explained. "I was an idiot."

Laura dipped her head. "You only put words to what you believe, sir. What's important to you," she reasoned. "You cannot be faulted for having—"

"I can if it means I cannot have you," he interrupted.

Swallowing, Laura raised her eyes to find his filled with regret. Or perhaps it was sorrow. The light from the east window was no longer very good, and she had a hard time seeing them clearly. When she blinked, she realized why.

Tears had formed in her eyes and had blurred her vision.

"Oh, please do not cry, my sweeting," he whispered, his hand lifting so his thumb nearly touched her cheek. He held it there, suspended until one of the tears spilled from her lower lashes. His thumb wiped it away at the same moment his lips lowered to capture hers.

The kiss was not quick, nor was it long, but his other hand had lifted to cup her cheek as if he feared she would pull away. He used that hand now to lift her head so her gaze met his. "Please, forgive me," he said.

"For what?" she managed to say before a hiccup sounded.

"For not being more... more open to what life can be like when one has decided to marry an artist," he stammered. "For sending you away. For being... an idiot."

Laura blinked twice in an effort to keep more tears from escaping her eyes. "You still wish to marry me?"

He nodded. "I do."

"After only one day—?"

"It has been more than a fortnight, actually," he said.

Her eyes widened. "I don't recall—"

"My imagination may have filled in most of it, but our time together has most assuredly confirmed my hopes."

"Hopes?"

Angling his head first to one side and then the other, he said, "Of finding a woman who would understand what it is like to live on the fringes of Society. To be related to the *ton* but not a part of it—"

"Your promotion to head clerk ensures you will be part of the *ton*, sir," she argued.

Henry blinked and then remembered he had mentioned his impending promotion while they were in the park. "Hmm," he murmured, suddenly at a loss for words.

Laura took a deep breath and let it out slowly. "Besides the matter of finding someone who understands our mutual situation, did you have other... requirements... for a wife?"

His eyes darting to one side, Henry struggled to remember the list he had at one time assembled. "Uh, amiable, which you are," he replied. "Not too young, which you... aren't?" he half-questioned.

"I'll be one-and-twenty on my next birthday," she stated, deciding he didn't need to know that her twentieth had just occurred only the month before.

His eyes widened. "Although your beauty suggests you are younger, your manner belies your age. Huzzah!"

Laura furrowed a brow. "Thank you?"

He grinned, the first hint of humor he had displayed since arriving in the parlor. The expression youthened him considerably, and Laura felt the same sensations she had experienced when they were in the park.

Excitement. Adoration. Arousal.

"How *old* are you?" she asked.

"Six-and-thirty," he replied. "The other clerks at the bank think I am at least fifty."

Laura blinked before she thought he was teasing.

"I am not teasing," he said, even though he was doing his damnedest to suppress the grin that widened his lips and made him appear younger by another decade. "Unfortunately," he added on a sigh.

Laura grinned. "You have been a man without a wife for a very long time," she said quietly.

His brows wrinkling so his younger appearance disappeared, Henry nodded. "It will take some time," he said in a whisper. "I'll require an occasional reminder that I must be... patient," he added with a huff. Then his face seemed to fall further. "Oh, dear. I'm making a cake of this, aren't I?"

"Perhaps," she hedged, doing her best to hide her amusement. "Where would we live?"

Henry's face brightened so quickly, Laura nearly took a step back. It was as if the sun had once again come directly into the parlor from the east window, casting him in a most flattering light.

"I own a townhouse," he announced, apparently forgetting he had mentioned it earlier in the park. "I... a few doors up the street," he said as he motioned towards the north.

"You live don't there now, though."

He shook his head. "Not... yet. It was part of my inheritance, and I've kept it up. There's barely a housekeeper and a... well, let me take you there. So you can—"

"Are you bribing me, sir?" she asked as her manner sobered.

"Henrí," he said, his accent abysmal.

Laura's lips quirked. "Call me *ma cherié* and I might consider it," she dared with an arched brow.

Henry blinked. "*Ma cherié,*" he said, his French accent much better.

"Lead the way."

Offering his arm, Henry seemed to let out a breath as he escorted her down the stairs, out the front door, up the street and to the townhouse at 9 King Street. He paused a moment so she could stand before the stucco-clad brick townhouse and look up at its four stories.

Feeling a hint of pride at how the colormen had managed to make the stucco appear as if it were marble, Henry studied the black trim around all the windows and the bright blue door that stood before them. A brass door knocker in the shape of a mermaid gleamed despite the lack of direct sunlight. Two topiary trees trimmed into spirals flanked the door, and green wrought iron fencing separated the small front lawn from the pavement.

Laura tittered. Her free hand moved to cover her mouth when she giggled again.

"What is it?" he asked, his nervousness apparent.

"Now I know exactly how my mother felt when my father showed her the house he had purchased for them in Curzon Street," she said as she turned to regard him. At his questioning glance, she added, "She was giddy with delight."

Henry grinned as he pulled a key from his waistcoat pocket. "I rather like seeing you giddy. I shall have to sort what it is I must do to have you giddy on a regular basis."

Laura slapped the arm she held. "So that will be how you manage me?" she asked as he unlocked the door and opened it.

She stepped in and then to the side, her breath held as Henry moved to stand next to her. "Oh, Henry," she murmured, not bothering with the French version of his name.

Henry discovered he rather liked his name when she said it. All breathy and awestruck. He imagined her saying it as he pleasured her in the master bedchamber, and then, when he knew his manhood was imagining the same thing, he had to redirect his thinking to the townhouse lest his arousal make itself apparent in his rather tight trousers. Redirect his thoughts to what he intended to show her.

His future depended on it, for he knew at that moment he had to have her as his wife.

When had he ever felt so sure about a young woman before? When had he ever imagined an entire life with the same woman? A life with children? A lively home? A willing woman in his—or her—bed? A woman to whom he didn't have to pay for the privilege of spending a night?

"Oh, Henry, this is lovely," Laura whispered. Unlike the Simpson's townhouse, this one had its callers entering directly into the great hall. A quick glance to the left revealed a cloak room, and to the right, a small salon. Directly ahead was a modest hall table devoid of decoration, and behind it, the marble stairs curved up to the first floor.

Several doors were visible down the halls on either side of the staircase, which had her thinking there was at least a study and perhaps a dining room on the ground floor.

"Good afternoon, Mr. Simpson," a pleasant voice sounded from just beyond the stairs.

"And to you, Parker. Don't mind us. I'm taking Miss Overby on a tour," Henry said, at the same moment a house-maid appeared and dipped a curtsy.

The middle-aged woman's face brightened. "Then you've picked the perfect time of the day, sir. I finished the dustin'. Would you like me to set a fire in the parlor... or your bedchamber?"

A flush of red colored Henry's cheeks. "That won't be necessary, Parker," he replied.

Laura could barely contain her amusement, one hand lifting to cover her mouth.

He dared a glance in her direction. "I assure you, I have never brought another woman here. Other than my mother," he amended.

"You don't house your mistress here?," Laura countered, her voice sounding light despite the nature of the query.

"Never," he replied. "I... I don't actually employ one," he added, hoping the admission would help his cause.

Left speechless by the comment, Laura stared at him.

"I used to, but... I did not renew our contract, and I cannot believe you asked such a question," he replied as his brows furrowed.

No wonder those at the bank thought he was fifty.

Dipping her head, Laura said, "I did not intend to embarrass you, sir. Truly." When she noticed how his expression softened, she added, "But I will not tolerate you bedding another woman. If I'm to be your wife, you will be required to honor your vows as I will honor mine."

Henry immediately nodded. "Of course," he said, wondering if she had acquired the idea from her mother or had made the decision to marry someone honorable on her own.

"My parents have been devoted to one another since before their marriage," she explained, as if she could read his mind. "I want a marriage like theirs."

"Then you shall have it," Henry agreed. "Are there other requirements I must meet to earn your hand in marriage?"

Laura inhaled softly. "I didn't mean to sound so... demanding," she murmured.

"Far better you do so now," he replied as he angled his head. "It's only fair we know what it is we're about to do."

"What about you?" she asked. "What... what do you require?"

Henry inhaled and indicated they should head down the hall. "A happy wife," he replied as he paused before a door and opened it. "Study," he said as he allowed her to step in and look around.

"Very manly," she intoned as she noted the ebony desk and bookshelves. "I take it your mother is a happy wife?"

Henry nodded. "She is. My father does his best to see to

it she has everything she requires and most of what she wants," he said, a twinkle sparking in one eye. "He's terribly perceptive and always on the search for how to please her."

"Oh, I should have liked to marry him," Laura teased, a grin brightening her expression.

"I learned from the best," Henry said, one brow arching as he moved to the next door and opened it. "Dining room" he said, as leaned in and glanced around. "I've not once eaten in here," he added with a hint of disappointment.

"Well, we'll have to host a dinner party for our families," Laura replied as she let go of his arm and moved into the room. A dining table long enough to seat twelve stretched down the middle of the long room. There were buffets at both ends, both in need of decoration.

"I should like that very much," he agreed. "Once there's a suitable cook," he added.

"Who cooks for Mrs. Parker?"

"She takes her meals at my parent's townhouse with the servants there," he replied. He reached out a hand. "Come. There's much more to see."

Laura took his hand and allowed him to lead her further down the hall. "The kitchens are at the back, of course," he said as he pushed open the last door to reveal a kitchen that looked as if it had never had a meal prepared in it.

"I had this renovated to include all the latest in kitchen equipment," Henry said before she could ask.

"You'll be able to hire a cook from France," Laura remarked in awe as her gaze swept the room.

"Will that make you happy?" he asked.

"I should think it would make *you* happy," she countered. "And ensure you come home for dinner every night."

"If you're here, I will."

Laura stared at him a moment, knowing he spoke a vow. "I believe you," she whispered.

He pulled her towards him, his lips capturing hers in a bruising kiss meant to possess her. Meant to seal the deal they had just put voice to and ensure she would be his wife. When he finally allowed her to take a breath, he sighed. "I've more to show you," he whispered.

"At this rate, we'll never get into the attic," she teased.

# CHAPTER 30

## A DINNER GUEST IS MISSED

*M*eanwhile, at Harrington House
When Graham arrived for dinner at Harrington House at exactly seven o'clock, he was rather surprised to be greeted by Lord Edward Harrington. Before he'd even made it into the great hall, the young man intercepted him with an enthusiastic greeting in the vestibule.

"I feared you had changed your mind," Edward said as he motioned for them to head toward the central staircase.

Graham's gaze swept the great hall as Edward made the comment, his brows rising. "I wouldn't miss it," he replied. "Things here look much the same."

Edward blinked. "You've been here before?"

"Edward?" a female voice called out from the front salon.

The baron gave Graham an apologetic glance and hurried to stand before Temperance Fitzsimmons Harrington, Countess Mayfield. "Good evening, Grandmother. I have someone I'd like you to meet."

But Temperance had already directed her gaze on Graham, and a slow smile appeared before she hurried forward. "Oh, my but you've matured quite nicely since last I saw you."

"Indeed, but you haven't changed a bit, Aunt Tempy." He rolled his eyes. "Where are my manners? Lady Mayfield, it's very good to see you again," he said before giving her a deep bow.

"Oh, we'll have none of that," she scolded.

"You *know* each other?" Edward asked in surprise, as Lady Mayfield embraced Graham and then stood back to regard her distant cousin with a sigh.

"Of course," she said as she beamed in delight. "His mother is one my cousins. And you've grown so tall," she remarked.

Edward quirked a brow. "Did you know this?" he asked of his dinner guest.

Graham inhaled and was about to respond in the affirmative when Temperance gave her grandson a quelling glance. "I had Graham's company on many occasions. Usually at garden parties, when your grandfather refused to attend." She turned her attention on Graham. "You were such a good sport to be the only young man in attendance at most of those *soirées*."

"It was my pleasure," Graham said with a nod, hoping he sounded more sincere than he felt. His mother had insisted he become acquainted with her father's side of the family, given George Fitzsimmons had kept her from them when he was alive. The black sheep of the Fitzsimmons—and brother to Matthew Fitzsimmons, Viscount Chamberlain—George insisted he be allowed the liberty of making and selling men's hats. His vocation resulted in a line of popular top hats and a successful shop where Emma learned her accounting skills.

"I didn't refuse to attend those parties," Stanley, Earl of Mayfield, protested as he emerged from his study. He bussed his wife on the cheek before turning to regard Graham and

Edward. "I was merely detained with earldom business." He angled his head as Graham gave a leg. "I knew I should have recognized you this Friday past. Saw you at Brooks's."

"Good evening, my lord," Graham replied. "Yes, I was there in search of my father and instead was found by my second cousin," he added as he indicated Edward.

"You have since found your father and your mother, I hope," Temperance said as she hooked an arm into Graham's and led them toward the stairs.

"I did, indeed. I've spent the past couple of days in their company—and at the company. Much has happened since I left London to start the office in Boston."

"Does your return mean that the Boston office is no longer in operation?" Mayfield asked from behind him as they climbed the stairs.

"Not at all. My presence was required here, so I hired another clerk and turned over the Boston office to my partner, Sinclair. I expect he'll be adding more staff as the year progresses, given how many exports he'll have to see to."

"Exports?" Mayfield repeated.

"Tobacco, turpentine, pelts," Graham said as he paused to allow Temperance to go ahead of him into the parlor. He waited until both Mayfield and Edward were in before he joined them. "It's become very lucrative for Wellingham Imports."

"I don't suppose there are any company shares for sale?" Edward half-asked.

Graham marveled at the young man's interest. When he had been Edward's age, he had been more concerned about racing horses in Hyde Park with his cousins and when he might steal a kiss with Hannah.

Which had him wondering where his future wife might be.

"We'll have to discover the answer to that from my

mother," he replied. "And speaking of mothers, is Lady Harrington about?" A footman offered him a cup of coffee, and he took it with a nod, surprised by the number of servants who seemed to appear from thin air bearing various drinks and plates of nuts on salvers.

"She should be here by now," Edward replied as he dared a glance towards the parlor door.

"Oh, Lady Harrington won't be joining us this evening," Temperance said as she accepted a glass of wine from a footman who was taller than Graham. "She was invited to Fairmont Park for dinner this evening."

Graham nearly choked on his first sip of coffee while Edward did, sputtering and coughing until a footman saw to removing the cup from his hand so he could pound his own chest. Hurrying to join the boy, Graham asked, "Are you all right?"

Edward aimed an expression of pain in his direction before he said, "But, she said nothing of having dinner with Cousin Tom when I last spoke with her," he complained.

Once she was convinced Edward wasn't about to keel over from his coughing fit, Temperance took a seat in the room's only settee and said, "I was just as surprised to hear of it as you, darling. She had dinner there only a fortnight ago, which has me believing Lady Grandby has important news to share." Her eyebrows waggling in delight, she added, "Hannah has assured me she will tell me if she's allowed."

"I was invited there for dinner tonight as well," Graham murmured, realizing his note to Tom hadn't been delivered, or at least not in time to put a stop to the dinner arrangements.

His disappointment must have been apparent, for Temperance sobered. "Oh, dear. You meant to renew your acquaintance with her over dinner this evening," she said, her eyes nearly rolling in shared dismay.

"I had hoped to, yes, my lady," Graham replied. "I haven't seen Lady Harrington since I departed for the United States. Over seventeen years ago," he added, realizing he had been about Edward's age at the time.

"I feel like a prize idiot," Edward announced, which had the earl nearly choking on a walnut.

"Harrington!" Mayfield barked. "I rather doubt you've ever been an idiot in your entire seventeen-year history."

Ignoring his grandfather's assessment of him, Edward turned his attention on his grandmother. "Do you suppose if we were to send a footman to Fairmont Park, we could convince Mother to return here? At least in time for the dessert course?"

Temperance exchanged a quick glance with Mayfield, her brows furrowing until she settled her gaze on Graham. "We could," she murmured. Then she turned to Edward. "Have Potter see to it, won't you, darling?"

Edward was quick to give his grandmother a bow before he left the parlor.

Even before Temperance patted the seat next to her, intending for Graham to join her, he knew he would being summoned to her side. "My lady, I understand you are one of the editors of *The Tattler*."

Obviously not expecting the comment, Temperance said, "And if I am?"

"I have news to share and a request to make of you."

Her guarded manner disappearing, she said, "Oh, do tell, and I shall see what I can do for you."

Sure he would burn in hell, Graham took the seat next to Temperance and said, "Cousin Tom's wife is indeed expecting a child. In time for Christmas. He told me of it when I paid a call at his office this Friday past."

The countess' eyes widened in delight. "Well, it's not unexpected, but it's so good to hear a confirmation from a reliable source," she said. "Now, what is it you require of me?"

Graham had always appreciated his great aunt's forthright manner. Mayfield might have been the earl, but it was the countess' head for business and appreciation for how gossip ruled the *ton* that kept the Mayfield earldom in good stead. "A very clear notice in your newsheet regarding the unavailability of Lady Harrington for matrimony. She is already affianced."

Although he expected a violent reaction from his great aunt, he was surprised when she merely arched a brow.

"Are *you* to be her husband?"

"I am," he acknowledged.

Her eyes followed Edward as he reappeared in the parlor and was about to join them at the settee. "Yet the two of you have exchanged no correspondence since your departure from these shores," she argued.

Graham felt the heat of embarrassment color his throat and cheeks. "I did send a letter when I first arrived in Boston, but after that, I felt it would be... *inappropriate* given her marriage to Cousin Charlie." Although he had nearly used Charles Harrington's title when speaking of him, Graham decided to remind the countess he was family.

"So you are the turtle."

Graham blinked and then turned an accusing eye on Edward.

"*I* didn't tell her," Edward claimed.

"Hannah did," Temperance whispered. "A few months into her widowhood. When she was lamenting your lack of writing skills," she added pointedly.

Dipping his head, Graham said, "Guilty as charged. But she made a bargain with me, and I intend to collect."

He was about to say more, but Temperance wasn't paying any attention to him. Her gaze was on Edward, and for a moment Graham thought she might cry. "I'm so sorry, my lady. I didn't mean to offend the memory of your son," he said, thinking that might be why she looked as if she was on the verge of tears.

When Temperance returned her attention to him, she said in a quiet voice, "You will attend me in my salon before you leave this house tonight."

Graham gave a start. "My lady?"

"We have important matters to discuss. Matters that are not intended for publication in *The Tattler*."

Feeling as if he was being summoned to a trial, Graham nodded. "Yes, my lady." He would have said more, but the dinner bell sounded, and Lord Mayfield appeared to take his wife's arm. Following behind, Edward and Graham dared glances at one another.

"If it's any consolation, a footman has been dispatched to Fairmont Park," Edward whispered.

"I thank you for your quick thinking," Graham replied.

Edward allowed a shrug. "I am ever so sorry I did not secure my mother's promise that she would be here this evening. I assure you, her absence was entirely unexpected."

"As Mayfield has already said, you are not an idiot," Graham insisted.

Finally nodding, Edward said, "That means much coming from you, Cousin."

Furrowing a brow, Graham considered how to respond and finally grinned. "We're family," he replied, now wondering if they were closer than merely cousins.

## CHAPTER 31

## CONFESSIONS AND CONVICTIONS

*M eanwhile, at 9 King Street*
Laura continued her perusal of the town-house's kitchens when she heard another woman's voice come from somewhere on the ground floor. That's when she realized Henry was no longer at her side.

"Good afternoon, Mr. Simpson," an elderly woman called out as she hurried into the great hall. "I apologize. I didn't hear you knock."

"I didn't, Mrs. Harkins. Truth be told, I expected you would still be upstairs, reviewing the rooms," Henry said as Laura joined him in the great hall. "Have you decided if you'll accept the position? I realize it's not as grand a house as Lord Chamberlain's, but I value your experience as his head housekeeper."

As he expected, Beatrice Harkins' attention was no longer on him, but on the young woman who once again clung to his arm.

Laura's eyes were wide with recognition as well. "Grand-mother?" she said before she let go of Henry's arm to embrace the older woman.

"Oh, now Laura, we mustn't in front of Mr. Simpson," the housekeeper said as she patted the back of Laura's shoulder with a gnarled hand and pushed away from her granddaughter. "Whatever are *you* doing here?" she asked before her face brightened again. "Oh, a painting, perhaps?"

"I expect she'll do many here," Henry said, just as Laura turned to him, her face displaying her confusion. "I've proposed marriage, you see, and I wished to show her the house before I pay a call on her father."

"You're hiring my *grandmother* to be your housekeeper?" Laura asked in dismay.

"I thought to, yes. Actually, it was my sister's idea. Rather novel, don't you think? Since you'll be out of the house most days with your painting appointments, I expect you'll require a housekeeper who can manage the house without you," he reasoned. "Someone with a good deal of experience. Someone we can trust."

Laura blinked, her gaze falling on Beatrice Harkins' proud face. "I understand now," she said as she nodded. "And have you decided if you will? Accept the position, that is?"

Mrs. Harkins pretended to think on it a moment before she said, "But of course I will. I've been at Fitzsimmons Manor since before I was twenty, but I have a few years left in me. With a good staff, including Parker, of course, I'll manage just fine." She leaned forward and lowered her voice. "This house is far finer than Lord Chamberlain's."

Despite the compliment coming from a servant, Henry couldn't help but smile. "You'll oversee the hiring of the rest of the household maids?" he asked.

"If you'll allow it," she replied. "And the butler, too, but I rather imagine you'll want to do that."

Henry hadn't thought that far ahead, and at the moment, he only wanted to think about Laura and her reaction to the house. He was about to respond to the comment about the butler when he heard the sound of a coach pulling up. "Ah, that will be your ride back to Fitzsimmons Manor," he said to Mrs. Harkins.

"Vera good, sir. I'll turn in my notice to Lady Chamberlain and start here in a fortnight, if that's acceptable?"

Henry looked to Laura. "Will that be soon enough?" he asked quietly.

Laura shrugged. "I've no idea," she whispered.

Dipping his head, Henry offered an arm to Mrs. Harkins and led her out to the coach. Once it was on its way, he returned to Laura's side and took one of her hands in his. "Tell me what you're thinking," he encouraged.

Blinking tears from her eyes, Laura said, "It's terribly kind of you to offer her the position," she whispered. "She must be... sixty if she's a day."

"But she's well regarded in the Fitzsimmons household," Henry argued as he pulled her into his arms. "I didn't think you would cry over it," he murmured.

She sniffled. "Not over that, exactly," she whispered. She lifted her face and gave him a wan grin. "Thank you."

Henry regarded her a moment before he kissed her. When he pulled away, he said, "Now you're probably wishing I hadn't sent her away so quickly."

"Why do you say that?"

He sucked in a breath. "Laura, I want you so badly," he said in a hoarse whisper. "I have wanted you so badly these past few *weeks*," he added more loudly.

Laura gave a start at hearing the vehemence in his voice. "You mentioned that before," she said in awe. "How is it you could *want* me when we hadn't even met until... until *today?*" she asked with some surprise.

Henry lowered his forehead to hers. "I've been watching you. When you arrived on Monday mornings and departed on Saturday afternoons."

"From your bedchamber window," Laura murmured.

"Yes," he admitted. "Given your schedule, I thought you were a housemaid."

She furrowed a brow. "And yet, you still *wanted* me?"

He nodded. "Yes. I even confessed it to my sister, who seemed to find it quite amusing, and now I know why," he said with a huff. "She must have known why you were staying at the Wellingham's."

"Well, your mother did."

Henry stared at her. "My *mother*?"

"She invited me for tea, or... or she would join me for tea over there," she explained. "Before she hired me to do your family's portrait."

For a moment, Henry merely stared at Laura, a myriad of thoughts chasing their tails in his head. "She spoke of me?"

Laura nodded. "And your sister, of course. She's quite proud of you both."

"She told you the whole sordid tale, didn't she?"

Her eyes widening, Laura shook her head. "Sordid?" she repeated.

"About her and my father."

Laura blinked. "If you're referring to a duke's daughter running away to marry a butler, I hardly think that's *sordid*," she argued. "It's like a... a fairy tale."

Henry stared at her a moment as he held his breath. "It was scandalous."

"No one knew, at least not for several years," she argued. "And by then, they were landlords with a street of beautiful townhouses." She furrowed a brow. "Why does it bother you so?"

Shaking his head, Henry struggled to put into words the frustration he had felt ever since learning he was born of two worlds. How his uncle was a duke but his father had been a servant.

"Your father was not a butler when you were born," Laura reminded him. "Nor was my mother still a lady's maid when I was born."

Henry stared at her for a long time before he suddenly pulled her into an embrace so tight, she could barely breathe. "I knew there was a reason I wanted you," he whispered into her hair.

"Wanted?" she repeated.

"Want," he amended. "Tonight I will take you with me to your father and ask his permission to marry you. On the morrow, I will acquire a marriage license—"

"After your sitting," she interrupted. "And do you really need to ask my father's permission? I am nearly of age."

He swallowed the rest of his words regarding his plans for a license. "I wish to show him the courtesy," he finally managed. "Then, tomorrow night, we'll go to Lord Weatherstone's ball, where I shall kiss you in the gardens and announce our betrothal."

She gave him a nod. "Before that, will you give me a tour of the rest of this beautiful house?"

Henry's eyes darkened. "We may not make it past the third story," he warned.

"What's up there?" she asked before she blushed a bright pink. "Henrí," she scolded.

Grinning, he let her out of his hold and offered his arm. "Now, where should I start?"

Laura stared at him before a brilliant smile lit her face. "The third story?"

They laughed the entire way up the stairs.

# CHAPTER 32

# A TRUTH REVEALED

*L*ater *that night at Harrington House*

The servant who had been sent on horseback to Fairmont Park had returned the hour before with word that his message had been relayed to the butler there.

Meanwhile, a footman from Fairmont Park had arrived at Harrington House with a message that had been given to Potter. The ancient butler nodded his apparent understanding, and when Lady Mayfield was about to order the sixth course be served, he appeared at her side.

"What is it, Potter?"

The butler bent to whisper in her ear, "An invitation from Fairmont Park for Mr. Wellingham to join them for the dessert course, my lady."

Temperance's eyes widened, and she allowed a chuckle. Noting how everyone else at the table had turned their attention on her, she said, "It seems great minds think alike." She lowered her voice for her instructions to Potter. "Is the footman awaiting a response?"

"He is not. He took his leave upon delivering the invitation. A *verbal* invitation, I might add," he said with obvious derision.

"I'm quite sure the situation did not allow for the niceties, Potter," she gently scolded, wondering if Edward had managed to pen a note before sending the Harrington House footman to Fairmont Park.

"Yes, my lady." Potter managed to appear admonished.

"That will be all." She watched as Potter shuffled out of the dining room and considered the options.

The footman who had been dispatched to Fairmont Park had already returned, and he had also not waited for a response.

Temperance feared if she sent Graham on his way to Fairmont Park, Hannah might well be on her way from Fairmont Park back to Harrington House, and the two would pass one another in the night.

A possible reunion would be pushed off until the following day.

If she kept Graham at Harrington House, Hannah would return eventually—she lived there, after all—and a reunion of the two long-lost lovers would happen.

Right before her eyes.

What a dazzling first-person account it would make for *The Tattler*!

"What is it, Grandmother?" Edward asked, noting how the countess seemed to study her wine glass with an unwavering gaze.

"It seems your idea of sending a footman to relay an invitation for the dessert course was thought of by someone at Fairmont Park," she murmured.

Graham straightened. "You have word from Lady Harrington?"

"Not from her, no," Temperance replied on a sigh. "Just an invitation for you to join them for the dessert course."

When Graham looked as if he was about to launch himself from his dining chair and take his leave, she added, "But I forbid you to go."

Graham settled back in his chair. "My lady?"

"Lady Harrington will be returning here when dinner there is done. I shouldn't want you two acting like... like two ships passing in the night, never to see one another again."

His brows furrowing, Graham allowed a nod. "I see your point, my lady."

"Why, that's brilliant, my love," Mayfield said, his words slurred from too much wine.

"It is a good plan," Edward remarked, his mood having sagged over the course of the dinner. His best laid plans had failed, and he feared Graham Wellingham would want nothing to do with him after this night.

*W*hen the clock struck half-past ten o'clock and Hannah still hadn't appeared in the dining room at Harrington House, Temperance motioned for the footmen to deliver the dessert course.

"I have business with my cousin this evening," Temperance said once the sweets were delivered to the table. "Will you and Edward play billiards after dinner whilst we talk?" she asked of her husband.

Mayfield exchanged a glance with Edward. "We will indeed."

"You can join us in the billiards salon when your business is complete," Edward suggested, his attention on Graham.

"If my attentions are not directed elsewhere, then I shall," Graham replied.

"When you're finished with your port, do join me in the front salon, won't you?" Temperance requested as she rose from the table.

The three men stood in unison, and Graham gave her a nod of acknowledgement.

Although he would have preferred a game of billiards with Edward, he knew her summons was of a most serious nature.

*A half-hour later*

"My lady?" Graham asked from the threshold of the small salon at the front of the house.

"Oh, Graham, do come in and sit down," Temperance said. She held a missive in one hand, a cup of tea in the other, and she looked as if she might be about to cry.

"What is it, my lady?"

Passing the note to him, she allowed a sigh. "It seems there won't be a reunion for you on this night. Hannah has gone to her parent's townhouse to spend the night there. It seems Lady Simpson has arranged for a family portrait to be painted—"

"By Miss Overby, yes," Graham interrupted.

"Their sittings are at eight o'clock in the morning," she complained. "You know of it?"

Graham nodded. "I made the acquaintance of Miss Overby when I stopped at my parent's townhouse in search of my own parents. She is the daughter of one of our brokers at Wellingham Imports and was... boarding there whilst she painted portraits of my mother," he explained. "I think she might still reside at the townhouse while she paints the Simpsons. As for the time, I rather imagine the sittings must be that early to accommodate Henry's schedule at the bank."

Nodding her understanding, Temperance straightened on the small settee and changed the subject with her next query. "I am not blind, Graham."

Graham blinked and furrowed his brows. "I did not think that you were," he replied carefully.

"My grandson?" she clarified.

"Are you referring to Edward? Or... or one of Julia's boys?" he asked, remembering that Charlie's sister, Julia, was married to Alistair Comber and had at least a couple of children. At that moment, he appreciated how his mother's letters had included news of everyone on her side of the family.

"Edward, of course. You referred to him as your second cousin, but... is he really your son?"

His head jerked back as if he'd been slapped across the face. Graham stared at the woman he had known all his life as a great aunt. She wasn't, not really, but she was a cousin and had accepted his mother as if she were her true niece.

"Oh, dear. If he is, you didn't know," Temperance whispered, her mouth left open in wonder.

"My lady..." Graham started to say before he dipped his head. "If he is..." He paused and started again, not about to admit to anything scandalous. Temperance was involved with London's premiere gossip newspaper, after all. "I wish he was. He's an excellent young man. Well read and far older than his years would suggest." He swallowed. "May I ask why it is you would think such a thing?"

Once again, Temperance looked as if she might cry. "I learned the truth about Charlie long before he proposed to Hannah. You see, it's become my business to know of all the gossip."

"My lady?"

"I feared if he didn't marry as young as he did, word would get out, and he would be discovered. End up in Newgate or dead, even if he was the only heir to the Mayfield earldom," she went on, oblivious to Graham's growing confusion. "Silly me," she said as tears streamed down her face.

Graham was quick to offer a handkerchief. "Are you saying Cousin Charlie was a...?" He stopped and swallowed the rest of his query.

Charles Harrington had been one of the most amiable of all his cousins. A happy boy, a charming young man. He made friends with everyone. Girls flocked to him at garden parties and *soirées*.

Graham had always thought it was because Charlie was the heir to the earldom, but Hannah had professed once that she wished Charlie were her brother rather than Henry, for Henry had already begun to exhibit his serious nature, insisting on providing protection as if their father was already in the grave.

Charlie wasn't the least bit serious. Charlie was friendly and funny, engaging and enthusiastic, clever and cunning.

"It's all my fault," Temperance murmured. "I knew what he was, probably from the time he left for Eton." When Graham merely stared at her, she said, "Come now. I've worked with Patience at *The Tattler* for over twenty years. I know all about... homosexuality," she whispered. "So I encouraged his overtures with Hannah. Gave him the rings to give to her. Told him exactly what to do. Except in bed, of course, because I sorted that Mayfield would have already explained it all or... or taken him to a brothel."

Graham felt the heat of embarrassment color his face as the countess struggled to tell her story. "It was up to Hannah to agree to the match," he reasoned.

"Oh, no. I knew Lady Simpson championed you, so I appealed to her father. Did you know he was once a butler?"

Nodding, Graham said, "My father mentioned it a long time ago, when I might have complained that Hannah was beyond my means to marry."

A new round of tears escaped Temperance's eyes. "It was poorly done of me. To go to him like that. To bribe him with the opportunity for his only daughter to be a countess, and all he need do was encourage her to accept Charlie's offer."

Graham stared at Temperance, a cacophony of emotions briefly rendering him mute. "It was still her decision," he argued. His thoughts had already gone back to that night before he had left Hannah for the last time, though. To the one and only night they had spent in a bed together.

She had gifted him her virtue, he thought as a penance for her having accepted another's marriage proposal. Now, given what he was learning from his great aunt, he thought it might have been for another reason entirely.

"Charlie needed an heir," he whispered.

Temperance inhaled softly as she nodded. "He did. And I think I have you to thank for that," she whispered as one of her hands clutched his. "It's brilliant really. Of course Edward would resemble you—you're second... or third or fourth cousins," she said with a sigh.

"He... he might not be my son," Graham warned. "He could be Charlie's," he reasoned. Only Hannah would know, but even then, would she know for certain?

Drying her cheeks with the handkerchief, Temperance allowed a nod. "He could be," she agreed. "But I rather doubt it."

The clock on the mantel struck midnight, and Temperance blinked several times. "Well, I trust you and Hannah will have your reunion sometime later today," she said before she sniffled. "Perhaps in the gardens during Lord Weatherstone's ball. That would be appropriate. More marriages have resulted from trysts in those gardens than probably any other location in all of England," she claimed, a hint of amusement lighting her features.

Graham winced, deciding he wasn't going to wait *that* long. "Actually, that's where I intend for our betrothal to be announced," he said as he considered how he might arrange it. "I have every intention of finding her long before the ball. In the meantime, I will go to the billiards room and give my regards to the earl and his heir."

Temperance nodded, once again giving his hand a squeeze. "It's on the first floor, next door to the parlor," she said. "You're not terribly angry with me?"

Shaking his head, Graham said, "Of course not, my lady. Especially now that you'll do the same for me as you did for your son."

Allowing an impish grin, Temperance said, "Thank you for coming tonight."

"Thank you for dinner." He leaned over and kissed her on the cheek. "Good night, Aunt Tempy."

Graham took his leave of the salon and made his way up the stairs. Despite the revelations Temperance had divulged on this night, Graham felt a surge of self-satisfaction.

He was fairly sure he had a son. And he was determined to be a father.

## CHAPTER 33

## A DIFFERENT SORT OF DINNER

*eanwhile, at 9 King Street*

"I cannot believe this is the best I can do for our first meal together," Henry murmured as they sat before the fire he had set in the mistress suite. A supper of bread, cheese and apples was spread out on the carpet in front of them, all of it pilfered from the pantry in his parents' townhouse, and they each held a glass of wine.

"I think it's charming," Laura argued, taking a sip of her wine as she regarded the empty wall above the fireplace. Although a clock was positioned on the mantel, there were no other accoutrements, no decorations or plasterwork.

She decided a painting would be most appropriate in the spot.

They had just returned from her family's townhouse. Laura was relieved her father had agreed to meet Henry without an appointment. William Overby had offered port and a chair in his study as if he were already good friends with Henry.

Although Laura had spent all of Sunday—the day before —with her family, her siblings had greeted her with enthusiastic hugs and pleas for attention. Once they spied Henry, though, they quickly remembered their manners and quieted, the second youngest running for Lady Overby to hide behind her skirts as she held the baby boy.

With the men ensconced in the study, Lily insisted Laura join her for tea and explain how it was a man had accompanied her to their home and was now asking for permission to marry her.

Laura hadn't said anything the day before.

"I admit our courtship has been brief—"

"Has he ruined you?"

Laura's eyes widened as her mouth dropped open. "Mother, no," she replied.

"But surely he's kissed you," Lily insisted.

After a pause, Laura said, "He has kissed me. And I him. This afternoon. In the park. When he... proposed marriage." She didn't add anything about Henry's initial disapproval of her painting portraits anywhere other than in her studio. Better her mother believe her husband-to-be was supportive of her avocation.

When Lily's face brightened in delight, Laura relaxed, but only for a second. "I expect he'll want to take your virtue next."

"Mother!"

"Which will be his right. That is, if your father gives him permission. But I rather think he already has since they're still in the study. Probably enjoying a brandy."

"Did Father.... did you and Father...?" Laura clamped her mouth shut, not wanting to ask such a personal question given her youngest brother seemed to be listening to their every word.

Lily dipped her head as an impish grin appeared. "Not because of your father."

Laura blinked. "What's that supposed to mean?"

Leaning toward her daughter and lowering her voice to a whisper, Lily said, "I might have paid a call on your father at his bachelor quarters. To…" She waved her free hand in the air. "To *expedite* our betrothal."

"You didn't." Laura's mouth had dropped open and looked as if it would stay that way for some time.

"I did. I was quite insistent that we spend the night together. And if you tell any of your siblings before I do, I shall deny it and instruct your father to do so as well."

Laura closed her mouth when her baby brother grinned, as if he had known for some time that his mother had seduced his father. "I'm not going to be the one to suggest we spend the night together," she whispered, wishing her little brother wasn't staring at her with such a huge grin on his face. She felt doubly embarrassed by what they were discussing.

"You do know what to do?" Lily half-asked.

Rolling her eyes, Laura gave a sigh. "I looked at that book you insisted I read," she replied. "I must say I was not expecting color plates and illustrations," she added as her face bloomed with color.

"I thought that one rather tame. There are some from France that—"

"Mother! The baby," Laura whispered hoarsely.

Lily glanced at the babe she held and grinned at seeing his delight. "I'll be sure he reads the same book," she said in a teasing voice. "Before he has a chance to tup anyone."

"Mother!"

Ignoring her daughter's rebuke, Lily continued to grin. "I understand Mr. Simpson's townhouse is even finer than this one," she remarked.

Blinking, Laura stared at her mother in confusion. "How is it you know about Mr. Simpson's townhouse?"

Lily couldn't hide her glee. "My mother had dinner with

us. She had the Simpson coach drop her here rather than at Fitzsimmons Manor," she explained, practically giggling in delight. "She took her leave not a half-hour ago," she added in a hoarse whisper.

"She told you," Laura said with a roll of her eyes.

No wonder she and Henry had been so welcomed!

"Apparently, working for a duke's nephew is more lucrative than working for a viscount," Lily said as she continued to giggle. "Or else she's decided she would prefer answering to you rather than Lady Chamberlain."

The babe seemed to sense his mother's good mood, for he babbled and then gave her a grin that displayed his two lower teeth.

"Indeed, young man. More welcome words have not been heard in this house for a very long time," Lily said as she turned her attention to the bundle in her arms. She lifted her gaze to her daughter and said, "Mother is over the moon about taking on a new household."

Laura sighed with relief before her brows furrowed. "Won't it be awkward? Having my grandmother as my... my housekeeper?"

Lily shook her head. "She'll expect you to treat her as the servant she'll be when she's acting as housekeeper and then as a grandmother on her days off," she explained. "But do ask her advice about menus and such. She has years of experience and loves to be needed."

"I intend to take advantage of it," Laura replied. Her look of worry didn't ease, though, when her gaze settled on the door to the study. "Do you suppose Father is being difficult?"

Lily aimed her gaze on the same door at the same moment laughter emanated from beyond. "I rather doubt it. Your father has already seen to a respectable dowry for you, and Mother's assessment of Mr. Simpson was quite positive.

At this point, your father is probably regaling your betrothed with embarrassing stories from your youth."

"He wouldn't," Laura countered, her eyes wide with horror.

"Either that, or they're onto discussing business. Your father has his accounts at the Bank of England. I rather imagine the two have been acquainted in the past." Lily smiled as she lifted the babe to her shoulder. "If he is telling stories about you, be glad of it. It will give you subjects upon which you can speak between now and the day you marry. Make for a less awkward courtship."

Although Laura couldn't imagine sharing the embarrassing moments of her youth with a man who was older than she was, she understood her mother's comment. "I think Henry wishes to marry quickly," she whispered.

Lily gave a shrug. "I should hope so. He's half again as old as you, and he needs an heir."

"Mother," Laura scolded, wondering how Lily had read her mind.

The door to the study opened, and Henry and William emerged with huge grins on their faces.

Laura was lifted from her seat, her father embracing her with a quick hug and a jerk on her shoulders. "I've given your man permission to take you to wife," he said in a low voice. "I will see to the dowry on the morrow. Be sure to take *every* advantage," he added with a wink. "Your mother certainly did with me."

"Father!" she admonished him, her face pinking with her embarrassment.

"And do invite us to the wedding. I should like to be the one to give you away," he went on, ignoring her scold.

Laura's eyes brightened with tears, "Oh, Father, of course you will."

She kissed him on the cheek then. The same moment the reality of what she was about to do settled over her.

She would go with Henry to the townhouse, share a dinner with him, and then share a bed with him if that's what he intended. As her betrothed, it was his right to claim her body. Claim her virtue. Ensure no other man could lay claim to her.

Yet they hadn't even known one another an entire day.

*T*he thought should have had Laura feeling panicked. Maybe to the point of asking that they take some time to consider what it was they were doing. Take some time to think on it.

She would have, but once they were back in the Simpson carriage, one of Henry's arms wrapped around her back and her head settled against his shoulder. He explained exactly what they would do before next morning's sitting for the portrait.

"After supper, I think it best I give you some time alone before I invade your suite, though," he whispered, at the same moment the coach pulled up to his townhouse.

"But, why?"

"Give you a chance to review the house on your own. Form opinions of each of the rooms without worry of offending me," he murmured. "Besides, you might come to your senses and decide I am not the man you should marry." A moment later, an "oof" sounded when she pounded a fist against his chest.

So much for having second thoughts.

When they were once again in the townhouse and completely alone—the housemaid had retired to her chamber in the Simpson's townhouse—Henry retrieved their food from the kitchens and they climbed up the stairs to the mistress suite.

"May I inquire as to why you changed your mind?" Laura asked as she settled onto a rug in front of the fireplace and set out the food.

Henry struck a fuzee and lit the bit of kindling that had been set with a few lumps of coal in the fireplace. "Changed my mind?" he countered, his brows furrowed.

"About marrying me. About allowing me to paint," she clarified.

Henry sat with his legs stretched out before him and his back against the front of a chair. "I will admit I am used to getting my way," he replied carefully. "I suppose I thought if I refused your request to continue painting, you would capitulate and still agree to be my wife."

"I could not," she whispered.

"Oh, I know that now," he murmured. "I spent the next hour walking. Thinking. Wondering how it was I would manage to live the rest of my life without you."

Laura's eyes widened. "Mother said that my father said the very same thing to her. When he was apparently too stupid to realize she wouldn't turn him down should he propose." She paused, her eyes wide. "Her words," she quickly added.

Henry chuckled. "I don't think my sister had any sympathy for me, either," he said. "Made me realize you hadn't requested *I* change anything about myself. About what I do for my living. So I will admit she helped in changing my mind."

When he didn't say anything more, Laura angled her head to one side. "And?" she prompted.

"Your father told me the story you just told me. From his perspective."

Laura blinked. "How different was it from my mother's telling?" she asked in alarm.

Once again, Henry chuckled before he leaned over and kissed her on the corner of her mouth. "It wasn't," he whispered. "If anything, Mr. Overby was far more critical of himself than Lady Overby apparently let on."

"What did he say?"

Henry opened the bottle of wine and poured a generous amount into the crystal glasses he had found in the study. "That he could not imagine a life without Lily," he replied. "I have spent the past fortnight imagining you as my wife," he whispered. "I have spent the entire day imagining how we might live our life together. What I have not been able to do is imagine a life without you."

Tears collected in the corners of Laura's eyes, and she was quick to lean over and kiss him on the mouth. When she pulled away, she knew she had stunned him. "I do believe I have fallen in love with you, Henrí Simpson," she whispered.

Henry blinked before he swallowed. "On the one hand, I might ask what took so long, but on the other, I remember what an ass I was in the park, and I find I am grateful beyond measure you would even have such feelings for me."

"You merely put voice to your convictions," Laura argued. "I could not find fault with you for that." Her eyes drifted down to the food spread out on the carpet. "But I will admit to feeling heartbroken for the entire afternoon."

"And now?"

Laura set about pulling apart the loaf of bread and breaking chunks of cheese off the wedge. "My heart is full, but I am starving," she replied. "And I rather imagine you are as well." She handed him a piece of cheese and then the bread before she took the glass of wine he offered. "If you're expecting to make love to me this evening, then you will need your strength."

"You make it sound as if I'll have a momentous task in front of me," he teased before he sobered.

"Do you? I wouldn't know, you see, since I've never..." She paused as her cheeks turned pink. "But Father always claims he's famished in the mornings."

Henry laughed aloud before he leaned over and kissed her. "I rather imagine it will be like that for me as well."

Laura returned the kiss before dipping her head. "Was he generous? With my dowry?"

"He was," Henry replied as he nodded. "More than enough to provide a settlement for you and a half-dozen children."

Her eyes widening in alarm, Laura repeated, "A half-dozen?"

Chuckling in delight, Henry helped himself to an apple and took a huge bite. When he had finished chewing, he said, "I expect we'll both be famished every morning."

"If that is the case, then I shall require some clothes to wear on the morrow when I go to breakfast," she hinted. "My valise is over at the Wellinghams." Her brows furrowed. "They're probably wondering where I am."

"I shall fetch it on your behalf with the excuse that you have moved in here," Henry said. "I will return later tonight, after everyone has settled for the night elsewhere."

Before his departure, he showed her how to control the gas lighting in several rooms. They kissed in the vestibule and he took his leave with the promise he would return later that night.

*L*aura didn't expect Henry to stay away until half-past midnight. He had been worth the wait, though.

Rather than spend the night at the Wellingham townhouse, she instead slept in the mistress' suite in Henry's townhouse.

*Our townhouse*, he had said again when she spoke with him upon waking the next morning.

Her entire body tingled from his touch. She was sure her lips were swollen from his kisses. His promise of what he would do to her after the ball had her wishing they could simply skip the entire affair and spend the time in his townhouse.

At some point, he would have to tell his parents of their plan to marry. She half-expected he would do so over breakfast, but until then, she would simply revel in the memory of what he had done to her. In the words he had murmured as he pleasured her. In being held in his arms as he slept.

By the dim light of a candle lamp, she studied his profile and memorized his features. Considered how she might paint him. How she would feature him and in what sort of setting.

The wall above the fireplace was empty of decoration, and she now knew exactly what she wished to see there every morning.

# CHAPTER 34

# THE MORNING OF A MOMENTOUS DAY

*The following morning at the Simpson townhouse*
Laura stood before the Simpson family and regarded her subjects in an entirely new light. The mood in the parlor was different from the day before.

Henry's manner was so jovial, his mother thought him drunk. James stood especially proud, as if he knew something no one else did. Lady Simpson appeared confused, as if she suspected others knew something she did not.

And then there was Lady Harrington.

The baroness looked as if she had cried herself to sleep and then attempted to cover the puffiness with too much powder.

Apparently something had gone horribly wrong with her dinner engagement the night before—and it had something to do with Cousin Graham.

As for Laura, she could hardly hide her own smile. She was sure her face was a bright pink. Every time she made eye contact with Henry, she wanted desperately to run up to him and kiss him. No one commented on her good humor, though, as the attentions of the others had been on Lady Harrington, apparently since breakfast.

Laura couldn't think about all that now, though. She had a portrait to paint.

She faced her subjects and did her best to appear professional. "If you could just remember your positions from yesterday," she reminded them before she moved behind the canvas, made a quick note of the time, and went to work.

*T*he departure of Henry from the parlor at exactly nine o'clock in the morning had the Simpson women breaking the silence with hushed murmurs.

Laura supposed it was because Henry had kissed his mother on her cheek before making his way to her, lifting one of her hands to his lips before saying his farewell.

Earlier, he had reminded her that he would be escorting her to the Weatherstone ball. At hearing her comment that she had nothing to wear, he had said that she should pay a call at Suzanne's and have the gown put on her husband's account. When she had put voice to a protest, he merely reminded her that by the time the invoice made it to him, they would be wed.

A shopping trip was apparently in her immediate future.

Although Laura couldn't make out what Hannah was saying to Lady Simpson, she could certainly hear James when he announced, "Well, whatever he had for breakfast, I think I should like some as well."

Hannah tittered, the first sign of humor she had shown since Laura had met the woman. "I ate the same foods as he did, Father, so that cannot be the reason he is in such fine feather this morning." Her manner quickly sobered, and her forlorn expression from earlier that morning once again took its place.

Laura had thought the baroness would be happy on this morn. Happy that Graham had made his appearance at Harrington House for dinner the night before—at the invitation of her son, no less—and made his intentions to make her his wife known to all those at the dinner table.

Her glum expression suggested otherwise.

"I don't care what has him so happy, as long as it continues," Sophia said, her gaze settling on the back of the canvas, as if she could see through the material to the woman who stood beyond.

Sophia had already taken a look at the painting the night before, her curiosity piqued when Laura wasn't in residence at tea time and Henry wasn't at dinner. Her son's visage in the painting far more pleasant than his usual scowl. Sophia was fairly sure she knew exactly what—and whom—had seen to lightening his mood.

While examining the painting, Sophia had noted that other than a pencilled outline, nothing had been done with respect to Hannah. Aware Hannah's countenance had been anything but happy these past couple of days, Sophia decided Laura knew better than to attempt to paint her.

*W*hen nothing else was said, Laura bent her head from her place in front of the canvas and took a look at the remaining family, giving a start when she noted the three of them regarded her with raised eyebrows and expressions of curiosity. "Did you wish to remain in place?" she asked. "I can certainly continue my work without you should you be required elsewhere," she added, sure her face had bloomed with color. She quickly returned to standing, well aware they could only see her shoulder and arm from their vantage.

"I'm happy to remain in place for a time," Sophia offered.

She turned her gaze on her daughter. "But I rather imagine my daughter will wish to return to Harrington House. Her son is in residence this week."

At the mention of Edward, Hannah's eyes widened. She had hardly spent any time with her son since his arrival from school, although she knew he had a busy schedule—not all of it of his own planning.

The Earl of Mayfield seemed determined Edward be introduced to anyone involved in the earldom's business and learn all he could as quickly as possible. If Hannah didn't know it was because Mayfield had decided he wished to step away from his duties, she might have been concerned the earl thought his death was imminent.

Since she hadn't had dinner with him and the Mayfields the night before, she didn't know if he had decided to follow his grandfather's wishes and remain in London or if he would be returning to school the following week.

A thought that Graham would know because he had been there had her feeling regretful.

"Oh. Should we be including the young baron in this painting?" Laura asked, as she once again bent sideways to take in the tableau of the remaining Simpsons. "There is room for him between the two men," she offered.

Hannah and Sophia exchanged quick glances. "I think not," Sophia murmured, apparently intending for only Hannah to hear. "There isn't room for all my other grandchildren, and if there is the one, then all the others should be included."

"Then Gregory should be standing there," Hannah reasoned as she pointed to the space behind and between her and her mother. "Even if he is a half-brother, he is still your son."

"A capital idea," James said, despite the fact that Gregory

wasn't his son. "I'll pay a call at Grandby and Son later today. Give me a chance to see Tom and ask after my investments."

"Really, James, it's good of you to offer, but isn't my oldest still in Yorkshire?" Sophia asked.

"He's due back any day," Hannah offered. "At least, according to Edward. My son seems to know everyone's whereabouts." This last was said in a quieter voice, as if she didn't intend for anyone to hear it.

"If Edward has half the head for business Gregory has, the Mayfield earldom will be in good stead for the next century," James said with pride. "He might not be my son, but I would gladly claim him as such if I were allowed."

"Pardon me, sir, but are you referring to Mr. Gregory Grandby?" Laura asked, once again peeking around the edge of the canvas. She was delighted to see her subjects more relaxed and contented then they had been the day before. Clearly Henry's happy countenance had livened the mood that morning.

"I do, indeed, Miss Overby. Are you familiar with him?"

"Only because my father has some investments with him," she replied. "And because Mr. Grandby is married to my mother's cousin."

"Ah, yes. Christiana. For a time, she was my favorite daughter," James teased.

"That's because she was his *only* daughter," Hannah quickly put in, her eyes lit with humor.

Laura caught the expression and stared at the baroness, determined to remember every detail so that she might capture her good mood in paint.

"I believe I have been seated too long," Hannah said as she stood up. "Will you be at the Weatherstone ball this evening?" she asked of her parents.

Sophia and James exchanged glances. Although Hannah was sure they would answer the same way they did every year

—"We always say we will, but then we do not,"—James replied, "This year, we will."

From behind the canvas, Laura allowed a brilliant smile, sure Henry must have said something to his father about his intentions for this night. When she glanced around the edge of the canvas, she nearly laughed when she caught sight of Hannah's expression of shock.

"Then I shall see you there," Hannah said when she had recovered, before kissing their cheeks and taking her leave of the parlor.

A few minutes later, Laura would have discovered she was alone in the parlor, except she was far too engrossed in her painting to have noticed when the older Simpsons took their leave.

## CHAPTER 35

## FINALLY REUNITED

*ine o'clock in the morning, 300 Oxford Street*
"I am at a loss," Graham said when Tom Grandby invited him into his office and waved him to a chair.

Graham had walked the half-mile from his parents' townhouse in King Street to his cousin's office, deciding he needed the exercise and a means to clear his head. "Is she deliberately avoiding me?"

Tom shook his head. "She is not. In fact, I was under the impression she wasn't even aware you were in London until Victoria mentioned you were unable to join us last night."

Graham jerked in the chair. "What was her response?"

His cousin shrugged as he considered how to respond. "I think her initial word was a ladylike curse followed by a sort of moaning—or it could have been a groaning. With my aunt, you really cannot tell. And then she looked as if she might cry and a moment later it was all 'chin up' and queries about how married life was treating us," he explained.

Although the night before hadn't happened exactly as he explained it, it had *felt* like he described it.

A comedy of errors worthy of a play.

"So… she was sorry to have missed me?"

Tom nodded. "I think she is rather cowed, actually. I don't think she knows what to think about your return to London." At Graham's look of confusion, he added, "On the one hand, I think she's been waiting for your return her entire life, and on the other, she would just as soon wait the rest of it without ever seeing you again."

Graham rolled his eyes. "She is not *frightened* of me, I hope."

"I'm quite sure she wasn't until I described how large you are."

"Large?"

"Well, when you left London, you were all tall and gangly, and now you're taller and you have arms that look as if you could compete in a bare-knuckle match."

Snorting, Graham stared at his cousin. "I probably could," he hedged, knowing his years spent moving crates in the Boston warehouse had helped develop the muscled physique he now possessed.

"Was it awkward last night? At Harrington House?" Tom asked, curious as to why Graham hadn't spoken of his dinner with the Earl and Countess of Mayfield and their grandson, Edward.

Graham shook his head. "Surprisingly not. I'm quite sure Edward didn't explain to anyone why it was he invited me, and yet Mayfield didn't ask, and Temperance seemed happy to see me. Shocked poor Edward when she hugged me—he didn't know we are related, you see," he said with a grin.

"Temperance?" Tom repeated in surprise. "You call the countess by her given name?"

"She's always been Aunt Tempy to me, although she's really a cousin, I think," Graham replied. "Cousin to my mother's father, in fact," he added as he raised a finger to emphasize his point.

Tom grinned. "She's a good one to have on your side," he murmured. "And not only because she writes stories for that damned gossip rag."

"My thoughts exactly," Graham agreed, remembering the evening before with mixed feelings.

His night had been entirely too restless. Memories of his dinner at Harrington House had both delighted and haunted him. Who knew the Countess of Mayfield could entertain so easily with her stories? But then her avocation as the editor of *The Tattler* explained how it was she knew so much gossip about the *ton*. So many great tales. So much *on-dit*.

It was her job to know.

The private meeting with her in the salon had been almost too enlightening. From Temperance's words, he knew Hannah had remained tight-lipped about her relationship with him. She had probably been for her entire marriage, given anything she said could be considered fodder for *The Tattler*.

"Again, I am so sorry about what happened last night," Tom said on a sigh. "I sent a footman to Woodscastle—"

"I had already departed, I suppose."

"And then we sent another to Harrington House while they were apparently sending one to us," Tom went on.

"The footman gave the butler at Harrington House the invitation, but Aunt Tempy forbid me from leaving," Graham murmured.

Tom furrowed his brows, but when Graham didn't offer an explanation, he decided to withhold what Hannah had said. How she seemed determined for Graham to come to her rather than the other way around.

"I am thinking I may try again later today," Graham said

as he straightened in his chair. "At some point, I will find her. Probably run into her on the street."

"Or she'll find you," Tom suggested. "She's not hiding from you, if that's what you were thinking."

Graham nodded, his mood finally lifting a little. Given the number of times he had missed Hannah, he was beginning to think she didn't want to see him again. "I appreciate what you were trying to do. You couldn't have known her son had arranged other plans for me given my missive was delivered so late."

*My son*, he almost said, for he was quite sure Hannah's apparent reluctance to see him had nothing to do with her full schedule and everything to do with Edward.

When he finally had her where he wanted her—alone, and preferably beneath him on a comfortable bed—he would demand an explanation for why she hadn't told him about the boy.

"Will you go to Harrington House and wait for her there?" Tom asked.

Graham winced. Although dinner with the earl and his wife had been a far more pleasant experience than he had expected, he thought awaiting Hannah at that particular location wouldn't be a good idea. "I'd prefer we have it out in a neutral location," he replied, realizing his tone of voice must have made him sound almost sinister. "That is to say, in a park or a folly. Someplace where we might speak without servants eavesdropping on our every word."

*Away from prying eyes and the chance of gossip that might hurt Hannah*, he thought but didn't say out loud. At least the countess had control over what gossip was included in *The Tattler*, but that wasn't the only newsheet that featured the *on-dit* of the day.

"If I can help at all," Tom started to say.

"I will take you up on that offer should it come to requiring a third party," Graham promised. He sighed. "I think I shall take a walk back to my parents' townhouse," he murmured, thinking he might even head down to Wellingham Imports and start his new position there.

Tom arched an eyebrow. "That's not a long walk from here."

"No, it's not. Which means I'm not likely to get into any trouble," Graham said as he stood and held out his right hand.

Tom shook it and warned, "You *do* realize you've just jinxed it."

Graham chuckled as he took his leave of Grandby and Son and headed up Oxford Street towards the short connector to King Street. He hadn't even reached Swallow Lane when his gaze fell on a coach that was stopped for a pedestrian.

A glossy black Tilbury coach bearing the Mayfield crest in bright gold paint.

He recognized the driver—the man had been driving the coach in which he and Edward had ridden the night before.

Perhaps even this very equipage.

"Collins!" he called out as he moved to the edge of the curb.

The driver acknowledged him with a wave, and when he was forced to wait for a dray cart to cross from Swallow, Graham ran up to the coach. "Are you driving Lady Harrington?"

"Indeed, sir."

Graham considered what to do. He had half a mind to simply open the door and climb in, but sanity prevailed. He didn't want to start an argument in such a confined space if Hannah was trying to avoid him.

"I'll give you a five pound note to pull over on King Street," Graham offered as he held out the blunt.

His attention on the note and then on the surrounding traffic, Collins finally said, "I just came from King Street, sir. Just fetched her ladyship from an early morning appointment there."

Graham remembered that Laura Overby was painting the Simpsons' portrait. Hannah had no doubt been posing for the past hour. "Trust me when I say she won't mind returning," he claimed.

"I cannot afford to lose my position, sir," the driver argued.

"You won't. The countess is a relation of mine."

Satisfied with the response, Collins set the coach in motion and turned south onto King Street.

Hurrying across the rest of Oxford Street and very nearly crushed by a steam bus, Graham finally made it to the other side relatively unscathed. His boots would require a cleaning, but at the moment, he couldn't be bothered with such mundane thoughts.

He was finally going to have it out with Hannah. Scold her for not telling him about Edward. Admonish her for having avoided him these past few days. Punish her with kisses, because he wasn't of a mind to do anything else with her in a cramped carriage.

The Mayfield town coach came to a stuttering halt as Graham ran up to meet it. He stepped up and opened the door, ready to begin a less than gentle greeting.

He couldn't speak, though. Not when Hannah faced him, her eyes wide. "Graham," she breathed.

She launched herself into his arms, her own lifting to wrap around his shoulders as she hugged him close. Her hat, a stylish velvet and silk flower confection, was crushed into the small of his shoulder.

Graham was forced to take a step back as she collided with him, his own arms wrapping around her waist and bottom lest she bowl him over onto the pavement. "Hannah," he whispered.

The scents of sweet lemon and honeysuckle assaulted his nostrils as he held her close, his rehearsed words of rebuke flying from his brain. When he leaned back in an effort to make eye contact, he sighed when he saw there were tears streaming down her cheeks. "Oh, Hannah. There's no need to cry," he whispered.

"When you didn't come to Fairmont Park last night, I thought you were angry with me," she replied, her head once again disappearing into his chest.

"I thought the same of you," he said on a sigh. "Especially when you didn't return to Harrington House by midnight."

Hannah inhaled sharply. "I spent the night in my old room at my parents' house," she murmured. "We're having our portrait painted, you see, but I think you already know that."

Graham dared a glance at Collins, who was watching from his box with an expression of shock. "Take us to Number Three," he called out as he lifted Hannah into his arms and climbed into the coach.

"Right away, sir."

Graham settled onto one of the benches, relieved the velvet squabs were large enough for his tall frame. With Hannah firmly settled onto his lap, her head still resting on one of his shoulders, he sighed again when he felt her body shake with a sob. "It's all right, my sweeting," he murmured as he removed her hat and tossed it onto the other bench.

"I was a fool," Hannah whispered.

"I believe I had that honor," Graham argued. "I should

have stayed in England. I should have claimed you, and courted you, and married you before your come-out."

Her lower lip protruded before she said, "True."

"You should have told me about Edward."

Hannah jerked in his arms, about to put voice to a denial, but she gazed into his eyes and knew he had discovered the truth. "Perhaps," she hedged. "He does look an awful lot like you. Is that... is that how you guessed?"

Graham shook his head. "Aunt Tempy knows."

Hannah's eyes widened with fright. "No. She can't."

"She thanked me."

Blinking, Hannah gave her head a quick shake. "I never told her, and she has said *nothing* to me on the matter," she whispered.

"Apparently she is as good about keeping secrets as she is about sharing gossip," Graham murmured. "But I do wish you would have told *me*."

Hannah swallowed as she regarded him with a combination of sorrow and relief. "What would you have done?" she asked in a whisper. "If I had written that the heir to the Mayfield earldom was really your son?"

Graham furrowed a brow. "Is he? Truly?"

Nodding, Hannah sounded a long sigh. "Charlie didn't know, though. I made sure he believed Edward was his. He had no reason not to."

"Does *Edward* know?" Graham asked, wondering if the young man had known all along.

Hannah shook her head. "I'm not sure what he believes. He's too damned clever for his own good, though," she complained. She repeated her query. "If you had known, what would you have done?"

*What, indeed?*

It wasn't as if Graham could have returned to England

and claimed the boy as his own. "I would have thanked you," he murmured. "Congratulated you. Reminded you of our bargain and waited as I have done these past eighteen years to make you mine," he replied.

Hannah buried her face in his chest, her soft sobs causing her body to tremble in his hold. "And now?" she murmured, her words nearly lost in the wool fabric of his coat.

Tightening his hold on her, Graham said, "Well, I am reminding you of our bargain, because I still intend to make you mine."

The sense of relief he felt at saying the words out loud and then hearing her half-sob, half-chuckle in response had him grinning.

She sniffled and pulled her face away as the coach came to a slow stop. The slight jerk of the carriage meant Collins had stepped down from the box and was making his way to the door. "Right now?"

Graham managed to move her from his lap onto the seat next to him. "Well, in a moment or so," he replied.

The door opened, and Collins leaned in slowly, as if he feared what might be occurring inside. "We're at Number Three, my lady, sir," he said.

Graham leaned forward. "Very good, Collins. If you'd like a respite, pull into the mews—"

"Behind Number Five," Hannah interrupted. "Or..." She gazed up at Graham. "You can simply return to Harrington House."

Frowning, the coachman said, "Are you quite sure, my lady?" He noted the way his mistress stared at the large man who sat entirely too close to her and decided she must be familiar with him.

"I am," Hannah replied, never taking her eyes from Graham's.

"Very good, my lady."

He waited patiently until the two finally stood and made their way out of the coach and to the red door. When Graham opened it and the two disappeared inside, he climbed back up onto the box and drove the coach back to Harrington House.

# CHAPTER 36

## REVELATIONS

*3 King Street, London*

The excitement Hannah felt might have been due to a combination of anticipation and anxiousness, trepidation and arousal. Whatever the cause, her heart hammered in her chest as Graham led her into the Wellingham townhouse.

"Would you like tea?" he asked as he helped her with her redingote in the small vestibule.

"Tea?" she repeated in disbelief. From his words in the coach, she was expecting him to ravish her.

"Well, if you were thinking I was going to... strip you bare and have my way with you, I am not a barbarian," he whispered hoarsely.

"Oh," she sighed, sounding disappointed. "And if that's what I *was* thinking? But without the part about you being a barbarian?"

Graham arched a brow, unsure of how to respond. "I thought you might wish to become reacquainted before I ravish you."

She huffed out an impatient sigh. "I'm not getting any younger, Graham. But then if you do strip me bare in the light of day, you're going to see parts of me that do not look like they did when you last saw them," she argued, her expression fierce. "And they're becoming worse by the day."

A slow grin spread over Graham's face, forcing a dimple to appear at the base of one cheek. "You've no idea what I've been imagining every night for the past eighteen years," he murmured as he took her hand and kissed the back of it.

"I suppose it cannot be any worse than what *I've* been imagining," she whispered, her lips finally curling into a grin at the thought of him old and gray, stooped and frail. "Oh, Graham."

"No regrets, please, Hannah," he said as he led her to the kitchens. "You bore a son for whom we can both be proud."

"So... you *have* met him?"

Graham nodded as he pulled cups from a cupboard. "Had drinks with him at Brooks's Friday evening and then dinner at Harrington House last night. He's..." He sighed, not sure how to describe the young man who behaved more like a man of Graham's age.

"He's rather an old soul, don't you think?" she asked as she opened a canister and spooned some tea into a pot.

Lifting the hot kettle from the stove, Graham poured water into the pot as Hannah watched. "He's definitely older than his age would suggest," he agreed. "Very clever. So much so, Mayfield is insisting he remain in London to take over running the earldom."

Hannah paused in adding sugar to the cups. "He discussed that during dinner?" she asked in surprise.

"Oh, that and much more," Graham replied as he searched for milk.

"I don't need milk," Hannah murmured as she set the cups on a tray and added the teapot.

"Since when?" he asked as he pulled a canister of biscuits

from another cupboard, rather glad everything was still in the same place as it had been when he was younger.

She paused, her gaze briefly on Graham before she regarded their assembled tea in awe. "Probably since Edward was born," she murmured as she examined the tea tray and the matching cups, saucers, sugar-pot and creamer.

"What is it?" he asked as he placed several Dutch biscuits on a plate and added it to the tray.

Hannah grinned. "I haven't been in a kitchen in an age," she said in awe.

"I would not have guessed," he replied.

"*You* appear quite at home in one."

Graham shrugged. "Although I did have a housekeeper and a cook in Boston, I fended for myself at the office," he replied. "I am a commoner," he added in a quiet voice. His eyes narrowed. "Will that be an issue for you? I rather imagine you've grown accustomed to life as an aristocrat."

Hannah lifted the tray and said, "Not at all. You forget I have been both," she said as she headed to the parlor.

Graham followed, rather liking how her bell skirt swung back and forth as she walked ahead of him. "I haven't forgotten," he replied as he watched her place the tray on the low table and then take a seat on the velvet settee. He moved to sit next to her, his large frame forcing her to slide sideways.

"You're terribly close," she whispered, once he was settled next to her so their thighs were pressed together.

"I intend to be far closer in a few minutes," he warned with a teasing grin.

A frisson shot through Hannah. "Not in here, surely," she replied.

Graham chuckled as he leaned down and kissed her hair. "Of course not. Will you do the honors?" he asked as he indicated the tea.

Hoping her hands weren't visibly shaking, Hannah

leaned over and poured the tea. She lifted one saucer and offered it to Graham. When his fingers gripped the porcelain, they brushed against hers, and it was all she could do to not snatch her hand away.

"I'm not going to bite you," he teased.

Hannah reached for the other saucer and had barely straightened on the settee when she turned to regard him with a look of shock. "Why ever not?"

Graham blinked and stared at her before a brilliant smile appeared. "Oh, you minx. Your earlobes will be between my teeth before we've removed your gown," he warned, and then he once again kissed her hair.

"I've missed that," she whispered, her gaze on her tea as the liquid swirled in the cup.

Furrowing a brow, Graham took a short breath. "Surely Harrington nibbled your ears."

Hannah shook her head. "He did not." When she noted Graham's expression, she added, "Charlie was not very... experienced. Nor particularly amorous."

"Oh?" The word came out in two syllables, even though Temperance's words from the night before had rattled around in Graham's head for all the waking hours since. His attention went to his tea, and he drank over half the cup in one gulp.

"He did not visit me in my bedchamber very often," she said, finding it easy to speak of her late husband with the man who had been her best friend since their youth. She drank some tea and made a sound of appreciation.

"No mistress?" he asked, deciding there would have been one in name only, even though Charlie had courted Hannah in earnest. Every day and night for an entire week, bestowing her with rings for every occasion.

Rings provided by Charlie's mother.

"At first, I thought so," she said. "But one night he came

home smelling of cologne." She watched as Graham placed his empty teacup and saucer on the table and then felt his arm lift and wrap around the back of her shoulders. Settling against him with a sigh, she added, "Several nights, in fact."

"Another man's cologne?" he guessed in a whisper.

Hannah gave a start, but she finally nodded and said, "We had a guest come for dinner the first year we were married. He was well known to the Mayfields. Apparently Charlie had attended school with him since Eton," she went on, her head turned so her cheek rested against the side of his chest. "He wore that same cologne."

Glad Temperance had shared her secrets with him the night before, Graham regarded Hannah with a look of understanding. "Oh, Hannah."

"He had become my best friend—"

"But not your lover."

"I miss him for that reason," she admitted. "He had become what Henry was no longer. I loved Charlie, even though *he* never got a child on me," she added with a sigh. "He was so relieved when I told him I was with child. As if he was happy to have the responsibility done with, although I think he wanted a spare, but..." She allowed the words to trail off as she sighed again. "So Charlie was like having another brother. One with whom I got along better than I did with Henry."

Graham wondered what had happened to cause a rift between the twins, but he didn't ask about it. There were more important matters to discuss. "I am sorry for your loss," he whispered. "And more sorry I did not stay to remain your lover. Who knows? I might have gotten another child or two or three on you," he murmured against her hair. "Ensured the Mayfield line continue."

"It's not too late," she said, her voice breathy. Although she hadn't meant to tell him about Charlie this way, she was glad to have it over with. To learn that Graham might have stayed had he known the truth of her marriage. "I would dearly love another child. One that would be *your* heir. And a daughter, too."

"As many as you want," he breathed. "You'll not be able to keep me from your bed."

"*Our* bed," she murmured. She closed her eyes and allowed her head to fall back, breathing deep when she inhaled the scent of musk and man, Bay Rum and spice. She glanced up to find Graham watching her, an enigmatic grin lifting the corners of his lips.

Charlie would do that right after his ecstasy. Although he sometimes pleasured her before he took his own, he usually appeared in her bedchamber right after her maid had finished brushing her hair, claiming he had need of her.

He didn't really, but she supposed he thought he needed to say such things in order to keep up appearances.

Sometimes he asked permission. Other times he did not.

On those nights, there was no foreplay. Just a quick and frantic race to a release that would leave him replete and recharged. *I shall not be tempted by the courtesans on this night*, he would say, right before he took his leave of her bed and headed for his club.

At first, Hannah was never sure if that meant there were nights he was tempted by courtesans. Nights he might have spent in some other woman's bed.

After a time, she knew he only said it to cover the fact that he was spending his nights with another man. She thanked his discretion, for she never heard rumors about him. She supposed his mother helped in that regard. Lady Mayfield controlled what gossip was printed in *The Tattler*, after all.

Hannah sighed. "Why didn't you fight for me when Charlie was courting me?"

Wincing, Graham wanted desperately to put off such a serious discussion. "I didn't think I had to. I thought him the horse. I am the turtle, remember?"

Hannah inhaled softly as she recalled their afternoon staring at clouds. "I am truly sorry," she whispered. After a pause, she added, "When you didn't pay a call immediately upon your return to London, I thought you had changed your mind."

Graham lifted his head and captured her lips with his own, kissing her until a need for air had him settling back against the settee. "I never changed my mind."

"You must have hated me."

"Never," he replied in a soft whisper. "I simply blamed your mother."

Hannah once again turned her head to stare at him. "You hate my mother?"

His head moved on the back of the settee as he murmured, "Never. Nor your father, since I now know it was Lady Mayfield who influenced him," he said in a whisper.

"Temperance?" Hannah said in disbelief.

"She knew about Charlie. Knew he needed a wife before rumors could become his undoing. You were… friendly with Charlie, and you were available, so she saw to it he courted you in earnest."

Hannah gave a start in his arms. "Yet, you don't seem angry with *her*," she whispered.

"She did what any mother would do to protect her son," he reasoned. "I cannot blame her for that." He paused before he added, "Well, I *could*, but she's always been Aunt Tempy to me, and she's rather pleased I could provide an heir when she knew her son probably would not."

Hannah lifted her head from his shoulder. "I still can't believe she knows," she said in a whisper.

Despite the seriousness of their discussion, Graham

grinned. "She is no fool, Hannah," he said softly. "Mayfield *is*, though. Edward will be a marked improvement for the earldom when he inherits."

"That's because Mayfield no longer wants the responsibility of being an earl," Hannah said on a sigh.

"I rather imagine I might feel the same way when I reach his age. All I'll want to do is eat, drink, and make love to you."

Hannah gave a huff. "And what is it you want to do now?" she challenged.

Graham chuckled. "Eat, drink, and make love to you," he murmured with a grin. "In our bed," he added. He inhaled and then straightened on the settee, his arm guiding Hannah so he could kiss her on the lips. "I shall have to find us a suitable townhouse," he whispered. "But until then, I do have a bedchamber upstairs we can use." He grinned when she didn't put voice to a protest. "I rather doubt your gorgeous hair style will survive what I'm about to do to you."

Hannah let out a nervous giggle. "Promise?"

Graham was up and off the settee, lifting Hannah into his arms even before she knew quite what was happening.

Hannah wrapped her arms around his neck as he trudged up the stairs, angling her to be sure her slippered feet didn't hit the bannister. "I can walk," she whispered.

"You'll need your strength," Graham countered when he stepped into his bedchamber and lowered her until her feet touched the carpeted floor.

Hannah closed his bedchamber door and turned her back to him. Her gaze swept the carved wooden door and the plasterwork and silk fabric that covered the walls and ceiling.

At first, Graham didn't understand what she was about until she said, "You have to undo my buttons if you expect to undress me."

"Oh. Of course." He stepped forward and lifted his

hands to her back. He struggled with the fastenings. "I don't have much experience with undressing ladies," he murmured.

Hannah turned her head to rest her chin on her shoulder. "No mistress in Boston?" she asked, her voice light.

"No," he replied. When the bodice sagged from her front, he placed the flat of one trembling hand on her bare back and smoothed it to the side—until she pulled her arms from the sleeve. He lowered his lips to the nape of her neck and placed a kiss there, his nose tickled by the short curls that had escape her elaborate hair style.

She inhaled softly before divesting her other arm of its sleeve. "Did you... *do* you have a wife there?"

"No," he said as he helped to pull down the fashionable bell skirt of her gown. Then he offered a hand as she stepped out of it.

Hannah turned her attention to his cravat and top coat. "So, only... ladies of the evening?" she guessed, unsure if they even had such a thing in Boston.

Graham cleared his throat at the touch of her fingers sliding on his neck as she undid the knot. "Hannah, I may as well have been a monk," he murmured. "I spent my nights reliving our only one together. It's what's kept me sane. Sleepless and celibate."

Her eyes wide at hearing his words, Hannah seemed to relax as her hands moved to unwrap the silk from around his neck. "As did I," she admitted. "I rather imagine it will be very different now," she added, as she undid the buttons of his top coat and pushed it from his shoulders.

Graham took over removing it before he tossed it onto the back of a chair. "Why do you say that?"

"In the event you hadn't noticed, you're... taller. And your arms are..." She exhaled and then inhaled slowly. "*Larger*," she said, turning so he could pull the ties of her corset.

"Unfashionably so, it seems," he murmured as he plucked the corset ties.

"I didn't say that."

Undoing the ties of her petticoats, Graham paused and lowered his lips to her shoulder. He didn't kiss it, but nibbled the curved flesh as he considered her words. "But you were thinking it."

Hannah inhaled softly, finding it hard to keep up her end of the conversation. "I was actually thinking you had the physique of a pugilist."

Graham placed his hands on either side of her waist. "A bare-knuckle fighter?" He pushed the corset and petticoats down past her hips and then let gravity do the rest. He nearly groaned out loud when she shimmied and then stepped out of the puddle of silk and muslin. When she turned to face him, he said, "I will fight for you," he whispered.

"I rather doubt that will be necessary," she murmured, her fingers lifting to his chest.

"Edward seems to think you'll have a line of suitors at your door starting tomorrow."

Hannah grinned as she managed to undo every button on his waistcoat and was pulling the hem of his shirt from out of his trousers before he noticed. "Then I suppose it will be necessary for you to make your intentions known. And quickly."

Graham pushed the neckline of her chemise past one shoulder, his lips forming kiss after kiss on her heated skin. "Is this making my intentions known?" he asked as he moved his lips to her jaw.

"Quite. However, not to the line of suitors," she whispered, her breaths short. She moved her fingers lower.

"So... threaten them with a right cross, perhaps?" he asked in a teasing voice. "Or a left hook?" He wasn't oblivious to her fingers as they undid the fastenings on his trousers, especially when the last button was undone. His manhood was so engorged, it sprung forth when released from its prison and landed in her far more hospitable hand. He jerked, breaking his hold on her shoulders.

"Hannah," he breathed as he gathered up the folds of her chemise and stripped it from her body.

Aware of the lightweight fabric billowing as it made its way to the floor, Hannah giggled and then wondered if he was even aware of what he was saying. "A simple announcement is all that will be required. Tonight. At the ball."

"Then when I have recovered my ability to speak, I shall do so," he managed to get out between soft gasps and quiet curses. "After I spend the day in that bed with you."

One of her thumbs rubbed over the wet silken skin that barely contained his manhood, her fingers wrapping around the shaft and squeezing until she heard Graham's much louder gasp. "And after today? Will we share a bed, do you suppose?"

She had to inhale when his mouth came down on one of her breasts. Although nearly flat, the mounds they formed when his hands moved to cup them filled his palm. "You will hear no complaint from me about a shared bed. Especially since you'll be my wife."

His thumbs circled the rosy nipples until they puckered. When his lips took purchase, gently nipping and suckling both, Hannah sighed and slid her grasp down the length of his manhood and back up and down until she had established the rhythm she knew would bring him to ecstasy. Even now, his gentle hold on her hips and his lips on her breasts were becoming tenuous. She smiled when she heard his breaths come in short pants.

This, they had done before—although never in such an elegant bedchamber and never quite so naked. "The bed," he managed to get out, pulling himself out of her grasp.

Startled by his sudden departure from her hold, Hannah stared at him. Graham took another step back and regarded Hannah, his eyes clearing.

In the late morning light from the room's only window, her naked skin seemed to glow. He hadn't had a chance to remove her stockings or slippers—the garters were still tied around her milky white thighs—but the sight of her like this, with her nipples hard and her skin flushed and her lips swollen from his kisses, Graham was quite sure she was the most beautiful sight he could ever behold. "I am going to make you mine again," he whispered, not giving her a chance to do anything more than inhale sharply as he lifted her into his arms and moved to place her on the bed.

Hannah wasn't about to protest—the space at the top of her thighs was pulsing—she was so wet with desire, she wanted nothing more than his velvety rod to fill her.

Who but Graham would she ever allow this kind of intimacy?

Slowly, she settled into the linens, sighing as she felt their softness surround her.

Graham leaned over the bed, sprinkling her body with kisses as he moved onto the bed and then positioned himself so his legs were between hers. His kisses became longer and slower, moving toward the throbbing space. First one hand and then the other moved beneath her knees, gently lifting them so her legs bent. Using his teeth, he untied the garters on each stocking, slid a finger beneath the top edge of each and slowly moved them down the length of each leg, leaving soft kisses in their wake.

His hands moved to the inside of her thighs, stroking the tender skin until she finally relaxed and her womanhood was open to his lips and tongue.

Arching her back at the sudden sensation of his tongue invading her most private place, Hannah inhaled sharply.

Her hands grasped at the linens, holding onto the fabric as if she had to anchor herself to the bed or float away on the waves of pleasure she felt cresting deep inside.

Her moans went from soft sounds to erotic cries in only moments as Graham's tongue flicked across her womanhood over and over until the swollen bud was red and ready. When his lips captured and suckled it, Hannah cried out, her entire body breaking apart as the waves crested and crashed and carried her to ecstasy.

The sensations were so intense, she barely noticed Graham moving up her body, didn't realize his hardened manhood was seeking her slick sheath, didn't know quite what was happening until he was suddenly inside her, stretching her and filling her and leaving her and refilling her deeply with the same rhythm as the waves that were still cresting and crashing.

"I have been dreaming of this for nearly two decades," he murmured, as he briefly paused and hovered over her. His face contorted into a grimace as he climaxed, far sooner than he had planned.

Hannah inhaled deeply in an attempt to catch her breath. "All you needed to do was ask," she whispered when he slowly settled atop her, his head landing in the crook of her neck. "Had you stayed, we would have been lovers."

At hearing the words that reinforced what she had said when they were in the parlor, Graham froze. "I rather doubt I would have been allowed to bed you," he whispered hoarsely. "The chance of scandal would have been too great."

Turning so she could see his face, Hannah sighed. "So much for you being my first and only love."

Graham lifted himself onto an elbow. "You're quite serious?" He felt vulnerable. Too tired to move. Torn between relief at hearing her admission and regret at not having stayed in London.

Wrapping a hand around the back of his neck, Hannah pulled his head back down to her shoulder. "Why didn't you ask for my hand back then?" She heard his groan of defeat and felt his body relax. For a moment, she thought he had fallen asleep, so she was startled when his voiced sounded loud in her ear.

"I had to make my fortune first."

"You thought you needed a fortune to make love to me?" she countered, struggling to keep annoyance from tingeing her voice.

The bed vibrated with his chuckle. "I *needed* to make a fortune before I was going to *marry* you," he replied. "And now that I've given it some thought, I believe I would have made love to you whenever you wished."

Turning onto her side, which forced Graham to reposition his body so he was entirely on the mattress and off of her, Hannah stared at him. "Why didn't you tell me that?"

Graham's look of hurt had her wishing she could take back her words. "I thought I did," he murmured.

At that moment, with the way the light illuminated his expression of regret, Hannah was struck by how much Graham looked like Edward. For years, she had thought Edward resembled Henry. How odd that a beam of light and regretful eyes could change her mind. "Our son is quite enamored with you," she whispered, as if she was remembering something important. "I didn't realize he was referring to *you* when he mentioned his new acquaintance during breakfast on Saturday. You made quite an impression on him."

Once again, the bed vibrated with his chuckle, and Hannah watched as a smile split Graham's face.

"What is it?" she asked. "Why are you smiling?" she queried as she allowed humor to inflect her words.

"If he wasn't already recognized as an heir to an earldom,

I would gladly announce to the world that he is mine," Graham said quietly. "Good head on those shoulders, he has. Probably got that from his mother, though."

His comment faded off as his body relaxed into the bed, and Hannah knew Graham had fallen asleep. His last words thrilled her, though.

Perhaps there was hope for the two of them.

There was that bargain she had made with him, after all.

## CHAPTER 37

## BESTOWING GIFTS OF LOVE
## AND AFFECTION

*A few hours later, at 9 King Street*

The soft inhalation of breath had Laura turning from the cheval mirror in her bedchamber to discover Henry staring at her. She glanced at the clock, her eyes widening when she noted the time. Henry had just returned from the bank earlier than expected, but he had obviously paid a call at his parents' townhouse, for he was already dressed in his evening clothes. Given the slim pasteboard box he held between his hands, it appeared he had also paid a call some-where else.

Laura recognized the style of box. She had seen her father give them to her mother for special occasions—and some-times for no reason at all.

All of them had contained jewelry.

"Do you think this is acceptable?" she asked as she modeled the gown. "I just couldn't abide wearing white," she added as she indicated her ivory satin ballgown. Other than a satin ruffle around the neckline and a deep ruffle at the bottom, it was devoid of furbelows or other embellishments. A pair of ivory gloves covered her forearms and elbows.

"You're gorgeous," Henry breathed, his mouth left open. "I rather doubt anyone will even notice what you're wearing," he added as he finally moved into the room. He offered her the box, and she gingerly took it.

"Do you wish for me to open this now?"

Henry nodded. "Of course. I know it's… probably not *proper* for me to be doing this before our wedding day, but… I'm not getting any younger," he stammered.

Swallowing, Laura opened the pasteboard box and gasped. "Henry!" she exclaimed. "There must be a hundred pearls and sapphires in here."

He glanced over the string of pearls threaded with sapphires, the choker style necklace part of the parure included in the box. The jeweler hadn't mentioned how many of the small ivory pearls and bright blue stones had been included in the necklace, bracelets, ring, ear bobs, and brooch. "I was thinking you might wear a couple of the pieces tonight. Maybe one of the bracelets and the ear bobs." He reached out and plucked the ring from the center of the velvet-lined box. "And this."

"Oh, Henry," Laura said on a sigh as he gripped her hand and slipped the ring over the satin glove. "It's beautiful. And rather large."

"While I was at the bank this morning, I could think of nothing and no one but you. I suppose that means I'm falling in love with you."

"Since that moment you interrupted my painting, it has been the same for me," Laura admitted.

"Not before?" Henry managed to sound disappointed despite the quirked lip displaying his amusement.

Laura gave him a quelling glance. "Mayhap in the park, whilst you were kissing me."

"Will you marry me?"

"Of course. I already said I would."

"I don't want there to be any doubt you are to be my wife."

For a moment, Laura wondered if he thought she was having second thoughts, but then his next words had her grinning.

"Tonight was supposed to be your come-out, but I don't want any of those widowers in the market for a wife thinking for one moment you are available."

"They won't," she assured him, her gaze still on the sapphire and pearl ring that decorated her fourth finger.

"Oh, I think they might."

Laura blinked. "Why is that?"

"I'll have to allow you to dance with others," he murmured, just before he wrapped the necklace around her neck, secured the clasp, and then kissed her. "My mother just reminded me that I'll only be allowed *two* dances with you."

Giving him a mischievous grin, Laura asked, "Did you ask her to save two for you?"

"I did, actually. Father was putting in his request with her for his two dances when he was interrupted by a caller, so I took my leave." Henry lifted one of her wrists with one hand and draped one of the bracelets on it. He closed the clasp and twisted the strings of jewels until the clasp was beneath her wrist before he lowered his lips to the satin.

"Is anything... amiss?" Laura asked, curious as to why Henry made mention of a caller.

"Truth be told, I am not sure," he replied, as he threaded one of the ear bobs through her ear piercing. "Either my father will end up gaining both a son and a daughter after this night, or he will have a daughter, a son, and a black eye."

"What?!"

Henry finished applying the second ear bob before he stepped back and admired his future wife. "The sapphires bring out the blue in your eyes," he murmured. "And the pearls glow against your skin."

Laura inhaled softly. She lifted a gloved hand to the necklace, two fingers touching the pearls as she turned to see her reflection in the cheval mirror. "Oh, Henry. It's beautiful. It's all so elegant. Thank you." She moved to stand before him and kissed him. "Now, why did you mention a black eye?"

Henry stepped to the bed and sat on the edge of it, half tempted to ask her if they might skip that evening's ball and simply repeat what they had done the night before.

He had every intention of making love to Laura upon their return later that night, of staying with her the entire night so that they could once again wake up in one another's arms. If he hadn't accepted Lord Weatherstone's invitation, he would have shut the door that very moment and allowed his lust—and his growing love for her—to get the better of him.

Instead, he dipped his head and said, "Your cousin, Graham, is speaking with him now."

Laura showed her confusion as she angled her head. "Why do you think Graham will blacken your father's eye?"

Henry pulled Laura so she was forced to sit on his knee. "Despite knowing Graham's feelings—and intentions—toward my sister back when she first made her come-out, my father gave his permission to Charlie Harrington when the young baron asked him for her hand."

"Did he not like Graham?" Laura asked.

"Oh, he always liked him. But Graham wasn't an aristocrat. He was always going to be a well-to-do tradesman, though, once he had worked for his father for a few years."

"And your father—"

"A former butler—"

"Wanted his daughter to be a baroness," Laura whispered.

"A countess, actually," Henry said. "Hannah wanted to please him, of course, and although she would have preferred an offer from Graham—"

"It would have been *years* before she was his wife."

"Exactly."

"She will be after this night," Laura whispered, not making it a question. She remembered her cousin's determination to marry Hannah. The baroness had made a bargain with him, and Graham was determined she honor it.

Laura leaned her head down and kissed Henry's forehead. "I am very glad we've been spying on one another these past few weeks," she murmured.

"Oh?" Henry replied, an arm wrapping around her waist to pull her closer. "And why is that?"

"We've saved ourselves months, or... or weeks of courtship—"

"*Days*, you mean," Henry interrupted with a quirked lip. "Remember, I'm not getting any younger."

Laura glanced back at the clock on the mantel. "Speaking of the time, might we have enough of it to...?" Her words were cut off when Henry took her lips with his.

He was determined to spend what time they had before the coach arrived kissing one another.

# CHAPTER 38

## ASKING PERMISSION BEGETS
## AN APOLOGY

*M*eanwhile, at 5 Kingly Street

Dressed in his evening clothes, James Simpson stood in his study with his head angled back and his chin aimed in Graham Wellingham's direction. He lifted a finger to it and said, "It's your right, son. Do your worst."

Graham backed up a step—they had just entered the study not a moment before—and said, "I'm not going to hit you, sir."

James furrowed a bushy brow. "Why ever not? I admit it. I am the reason Hannah married Harrington," he claimed. "And I am very sorry."

"I know," Graham replied with a shrug. "Lady Mayfield told me the whole sordid story last night."

His head jerking back, James regarded the younger man with a look of confusion. "Is it to be a duel then? Pistols at dawn?"

Graham's eyes widened in shock. "Of course not. I'm a terrible shot, and I rather think you are, too," he replied. "Besides, Hannah would never forgive me if I shot you." A grin touched his lips, and soon it had spread into a full smile.

"I've merely come to ask you again for permission to make her my wife."

James visibly relaxed, his own expression turning to one of amusement. "Well, you already have it. I suggest you make good on it this time, and as soon as you can manage."

"Oh?" Graham replied, concern suddenly evident on his face. "Why do you say it like that?"

Scoffing, James asked, "Do you have any idea how much money has been wagered on my daughter's choice of a husband?"

Graham's eyes darted sideways. "No, but I rather doubt any of it's been placed on *me*."

Clamping his mouth shut, James pretended innocence until Graham's eyes rounded. "How much did you wager?"

James gave a shrug. "Not as much as your son," he whispered conspiratorially. "He obviously knew a sure bet when he saw it."

Staring at his future father-in-law with a look of shock, Graham finally gave a chuckle. "Well, then I suppose it would be good of me to fulfill my end of the bargain." He paused a moment to shake his head. "He is a clever boy."

"Indeed," James said. "Now off with you. My gorgeous wife is no doubt wondering why I'm not already in the vestibule," he added as he waved to the door.

"Yes, sir," Graham said as he bowed. Before he passed over the threshold, he turned and said, "It's not too late for you to add to your wager."

He disappeared beyond the door as James sounded a hearty laugh.

# CHAPTER 39

# A NIGHT AT THE BALL

*ord Weatherstone's mansion, Park Lane, Mayfair*

On what the *ton* considered the second day of the Season of 1839, a line of town coaches converged on the location of the mansion that had hosted the first ball of the Season for more than a half-century.

The gardens behind the house had hosted hundreds of first kisses, scandalous liaisons witnessed by the statue of Cupid, and any number of marriage proposals.

Inside the house, several heirs had been conceived on the library's long leather-covered sofa or in the alcoves carved out of the grand hall that led to the ballroom at the back of the house.

Lord Weatherstone's annual fête was already underway when the newer Simpson town coach pulled up carrying Lady and Mr. James Simpson. They stepped down and made their way to the front door as Sophia remarked on Henry's whereabouts. "I rather expected he would ride with us," she said with some worry.

"He'll be along shortly," James said. "In the older town coach."

Suspicious—her husband's behavior had bordered on the giddy ever since that morning's sitting—Sophia asked, "What do you know?"

James grinned and gave a shrug. "We're about to find out," he replied as he allowed a footman to take his greatcoat, hat, and cane. Sophia slipped out of her mantle as another footman saw to her, and then the two were in the receiving line. In the distance, Sophia could hear the announcer calling out names as guests appeared at the top of the stairs that led down to the ballroom floor.

The next announcement had her exchanging a quick glance with her husband when the clear baritone called out, "Mr. and Mrs. Thomas Wellingham."

"I didn't realize they would be here tonight," Sophia said with some excitement.

"Weatherstone is an investor in Wellingham Imports," James explained. "He has been rather impressed by their ability to transport his tobacco from one of the colonies," he added as he studied a pair of Greek statues in one of the alcoves.

"Hannah should be here somewhere," Sophia said as she glanced around. "I suppose there have already been bets placed as to how many suitors she will have this Season," she remarked after they had greeted their hosts and were near the top of the stairs.

"Probably," James agreed. "My club's betting book has the total at eight as of last night. But it won't matter. Not after this ball."

Sophia blinked as she regarded her grinning husband with a look of shock. "I would have thought the number much higher," she murmured.

"That's just the betting book at *my* club, my sweet. It's no doubt double that at White's."

Her eyes wide at hearing his claim, Sophia gasped. As a

result, she was unprepared when the announcer called out their names. James had them moving down the stairs, almost too fast for Sophia to keep up.

"What's the hurry?" she asked, as she angled her head toward him.

"No hurry, my sweet," he replied, his face breaking into a smile as several of Sophia's family members as well as the Wellinghams converged on them with greetings near the base of the stairs. Their animated discussions nearly had them missing the announcement of the next couple.

"The Lady Victoria Grandby and Mr. Thomas Grandby."

Sophia inhaled as she watched her grandson descend the steps with his bride, and she was forced to brush away a tear with a gloved hand. "Oh, she is a vision," she murmured in awe.

Victoria, garbed in a violet gown featuring a metallic threaded overskirt, looked every bit the duke's daughter she was. Her regal bearing was matched by Tom, until he spotted the Simpsons. His face broke out into a huge grin, and the effect was lost.

"This is a surprise," he said as he took his grandmother's hand in his and kissed the back of it while at the same time James performed the courtesy with Victoria.

"We always say we'll come—"

"But this year there is a reason to," Tom interrupted. "Uncle Henry didn't tell a soul, it seems. You must be so happy. And I expect by now my aunt has agreed to her bargain."

Sophia blinked. "What ever are you talking about?"

The announcer straightened and called out, "Mr. Henry Simpson and his betrothed, Miss Laura Overby."

A hush fell over their immediate party when Sophia and James turned to watch as their son made his way down the steps. His black evening clothes were highlighted by an ivory waistcoat trimmed in gold threads.

Dressed in a simple gown of ivory satin with matching gloves, Laura clung to his arm, a pleasant expression pasted on her face. Her curly hair had been threaded with ivory ribbons, and under the gaslights of the chandeliers, it appeared as if it was made of gold. Pearls and sapphires decorated her neck and wrist.

"Well, this is unexpected," Emma said in awe.

Thomas angled his head so only Emma could hear his response. "Almost as unexpected as my finding a rather scandalous painting of you hanging in my bedchamber this evening."

Emma did her best to suppress a smile, but a blush colored her face. "As long as it doesn't end up hanging in your office." She turned her attention back to the stairs and watched as Laura and Henry made their slow descent.

"I feared Miss Overby would look as if she were about to faint," James said gleefully. "But Henry's the one who actually appears a bit peaked."

"You *knew*?" Sophia asked, her mouth dropping open.

"Well, I'm not *blind*," James replied. "A bit deaf is all."

Sophia gave him a quelling glance before she hurried to the bottom of the stairs. The couple was about to make their way in her direction when Henry stopped short. "Mother," he said as he gave a bow and Laura dipped a curtsy.

"You might have told me," she scolded gently. "I looked ever the fool in front of my nephews a moment ago," she added before she pulled Laura into an embrace. "But I forgive you. Such a pleasant surprise."

"Thank you, my lady," Laura replied, her gaze briefly darting up the stairs before she returned her attention to those gathered around her. She acknowledged Emma with a nod as Thomas took her hand to his lips. "It's so good to see you again. And for allowing me to continue to stay at your townhouse."

"We've been at Woodscastle these past few days," Emma replied. "I do hope you haven't felt as if we abandoned you."

Laura blushed, and not only because of the rising heat in the ballroom. "Not at all. My newest commission has kept me quite... involved," she added as she jerked her head in Henry's direction. Her gaze once again darted to the stairs. "I must say, I am relieved I made it this far without stumbling."

"The stairs are intimidating, but..." Sophia's words faded as her attention went to the next couple standing at the top of the stairs.

To the young man who stood with them.

"The Right Honorable Lord Harrington, the Right Honorable Hannah, the Lady Harrington, and her betrothed, Mr. Graham Wellingham," the announcer intoned.

The noise in the ballroom died down after a few seconds as the collective attentions of those closest to the stairs were directed to the newcomers. The musicians, having come to the end of a piece, stopped playing. As if in ripples, the remaining attendees ceased their conversations and stared at the descending baroness who was flanked by her son and a very tall man. Another moment passed before murmurs of surprise rode as if on a wave through the crowd and the music and conversations once again resumed in a far more lively manner.

The cluster of family members at the bottom of the stairs stared as Edward, Hannah, and Graham were forced to stop and stand on the last step.

"I see you found my aunt," Tom said with a nod as he shook Graham's hand."

"A few moments after I left your office this morning,"

Graham replied with a broad grin as Tom took Hannah's gloved hand to his lips.

"You look happy," Victoria said to Hannah as she leaned forward to kiss her on the cheek. "And *loved*," she added as one of her elegant eyebrows arched.

Hannah nodded. "I am. Is it that obvious?" she asked in a whisper as she lifted a hand to her reddened cheek. She would have used both hands, but one was gripped by Graham, and the gentle tug had her glancing toward her mother.

Victoria giggled and stepped back with Tom to allow the three to take the last step down before other well-wishers hurried forward.

"Good evening, Lady Simpson," Graham said to Sophia, his hand reaching for hers.

Sophia stared first at him and then at Edward before her gaze settled on Hannah. Her expression betrayed the myriad thoughts she was experiencing at the moment, but she didn't put voice to any of them.

"Good evening, Mother," Hannah said on a sigh.

Edward stepped forward and kissed his grandmother on the cheek. "Grandmother, you look as lovely as ever," he murmured. "It is a good surprise, is it not?"

Sophia turned to him and nodded. "Oh, the very best," she whispered. "Both of my twins betrothed on the same day?" Her eyes once again lifted to Graham's. "I suppose you already spoke with Mr. Simpson," she half-asked, realizing why it was James seemed so pleased with himself this evening.

"This afternoon, yes, my lady," Graham acknowledged. "He gave his permission." He didn't add anything about the apology his future father-in-law had offered for his part in seeing to it Hannah married another. Although he knew he would always hold a slight grudge, he understood James Simpson's motivations and Temperance's part in the plan.

Now that he had discovered he was a parent, he could understand why they had done what they had thought was right.

"Not that you required my permission yet again," James said with a huff. "I seem to recall having had the same conversation with you a few decades ago. I think you were eleven or twelve at the time."

Graham dipped his head. "True. I do seem to have the reputation of a turtle, though."

"Not in all respects, I rather imagine," Sophia murmured, her gaze falling on Edward. A slow smile lifted her lips before she chuckled.

"Mother," Hannah scolded gently, even as Edward seemed to beam with delight.

"I shall like having another father," Edward said as he glanced up at Graham. "Especially one who sees value in my returning to school to resume my studies. At least for this year."

"So... you won't remain in London for the rest of the Season?" Hannah asked, expecting Mayfield would have had his way in that regard.

"I struck a compromise with Grandfather last night," Edward explained. "I finish this year of studies and return to London in June to learn all I can about running the earldom. If he still wishes to step aside, then he must nominate me for a writ of acceleration. If I'm to act as the Earl of Mayfield, then I shall have a seat in the House of Lords."

Graham and Hannah exchanged quick glances, both rather proud at hearing the young man's pronouncement. "And if Mayfield decides he wants to remain the earl he is?" Graham prompted.

"Then I shall head to Oxford and graduate as originally planned."

Before he could say another word, the announcer called out, "The Right Honorable the Earl of Mayfield and the Right Honorable the Countess of Mayfield."

"Speaking of the devil," Graham murmured under his breath.

"Do they know?" Sophia asked of Hannah.

She nodded as she watched her in-laws descend the stairs. "I told them a few minutes before Graham came for me this evening."

"How did they take it?"

A grin of embarrassment appeared as Hannah recalled finding the two about to head into the library, apparently to wait for their coach to be brought 'round. She knew exactly how they intended to pass the time, and given the countess' high color, she realized her announcement hadn't affected their clandestine affair one iota.

"They weren't a bit surprised," Hannah commented. "Almost as if they'd been expecting it."

"Would Edward have had anything to do with that?" Sophia asked gently.

Hannah's grin was impish. "It seems my old soul-of-a-son has been making arrangements behind my back for some time," she admitted. "May God bless him."

"You and Graham will be the subjects of the featured article in the next *The Tattler*," Sophia warned.

"Oh, I'm counting on it," Hannah whispered. "The next issue is releasing tomorrow. Mayfield claims there are *twenty* names mentioned for possible suitors in the betting books at Brooks's. I shouldn't wish to turn away so many callers over the next few days."

"I shall be at your side for every one of them," Graham

said from somewhere behind Hannah, his hand still holding hers.

"Ah, here is the happy couple now," Stanley, Earl of Mayfield, said in a loud voice when he and Temperance joined their group.

Curtsies were performed and heads were bent in acknowledgement of the earl and countess.

"And a happy mother, I hope?" Temperance asked in a quiet voice as she greeted Sophia.

"I am. Relieved, as well." Sophia motioned for Laura to join her and introduced the artist to Temperance. "Miss Overby is in the process of painting our family portrait," Sophia explained. "But now that there will be a new son and a new daughter..." She allowed the sentence to trail off.

"I shall be starting another in a few days," Laura finished for her, glad when she felt Henry's hand tighten briefly on hers, as if he agreed with what needed to happen.

"Does that mean you can start ours after that?" Temperance asked.

Laura was about to respond when Henry said, "A week after that. I should like to take my wife on a quick wedding trip." He didn't add that he would take his bride on a much longer trip to Derbyshire once the timing of his promotion was settled.

The countess pushed out her lower lip in a pretend pout and said, "Agreed." She would have continued her conversation with Sophia, but Mayfield offered his arm. "Come, my sweeting. Time we take a tour of the gardens."

Temperance blushed. "Already?"

"I'm not getting any younger," Mayfield groused as he led them away.

"Man has a point," James said as he offered his arm to his wife. "Will you join me?"

Sophia blinked and did her best to suppress a giggle as she was escorted out the French doors to the gardens beyond.

Thomas Wellingham watched the older couples take their leave and turned to Emma to say, "I'm not getting younger, either."

"Speak for yourself," she said before aiming a wink in her son's direction. "Lead the way."

Edward glanced at the remaining three couples. "I'm off to find some refreshment and a young lady to dance with," he announced before he gave them a bow and stepped away.

Tom offered his arm to Victoria. "May I have this dance?"

She nodded, and the two disappeared into the crowd.

Left to regard one another with looks of embarrassment, Graham and Hannah and Henry and Laura said nothing as they all made their way to the gardens.

They weren't getting any younger, either.

## EPILOGUE

*S*<br>*even months later, Cherrywood in Derbyshire*
A light morning fog slowly lifted as the sun escaped the horizon, its autumn light casting the hills of Derbyshire in a green unlike anything Laura had seen before. She quickly mixed pigments to match, but was awestruck when the sky changed from its gray dawn to a peach and purple-streaked vista.

Selecting a larger brush, she quickly mixed the colors and set about capturing the effect on her large canvas, knowing she only had minutes before those colors would be replaced with light blues and the dark clouds that threatened from the west.

On most days of her honeymoon, she couldn't begin to paint until the afternoons, her husband keeping her abed until well after ten o'clock. By the time they ate breakfast and saw to dressing for the day, the sun would be well past the zenith.

This morning, an incessant pounding in her mid-section had her giving up the bed well before dawn. Given her pregnancy, she no longer sat on a stool on the lawn but rather stood while she worked to perfect her landscape painting techniques.

"You've such an eye for these colors," Henry said as he approached from behind and wrapped his arms around her middle. He kissed the nape of her neck before settling his chin on her shoulder. "It will look lovely in the parlor," he murmured. "Above the fireplace."

His comment was rewarded with a quickening beneath his hands. When he jerked and let out a sound of surprise, Laura had to pull her brush away from the canvas lest a streak of pink end up in the hillside she had painted the afternoon before.

"What was that?" he asked, stepping back.

Giggling, Laura dropped her brush into a glass of turpentine and turned to regard her husband. Despite the slight chill in the air, he wore only a silk banyan and bedroom slippers, and from his unruly hair, she knew he had just left their bed. "*That* was your son. Or, at least it had better be, or our daughter will be very unladylike. He, or she, or... *they* were the reason I awoke so early."

Henry gingerly placed a hand on her rounded belly. "So, it wasn't my snoring?" he murmured before his eyes rounded. "Did you say *they?*"

"I did. Either that, or I'm having a baby with more than two feet," Laura complained, her expression turning to one of worry.

"Twins," Henry said in an awe-filled whisper. "Well, I suppose I shouldn't be surprised." He pulled her into a hug. "Oh, my sweeting. No wonder your poor feet cause you such pain at night."

Laura relaxed in his hold, rather liking how Henry could show his affections out in the open like this. Back in London, he saved his most ardent attentions for when they were alone in their bedchambers. With the nearest village a half-mile away and not another house closer, Cherrywood offered privacy as well as the comfort of a country house.

She supposed they could be seen by a servant should one be standing near a window. Or by the sheep that dotted the hillside that was now glowing with the rays of the rising sun. As if by magic, the gray-green hills brightened to a lighter green and the sky transformed to a blue.

Letting out a sound of disappointment at seeing the streaks of peach and purple disappear from the sky, Laura turned and kissed Henry on the cheek.

"What is it?" he asked, tightening his hold on her.

"I would have thought landscapes easier to paint because the subjects don't move," she replied. "But I've discovered they're far harder. The light is always changing, as are the colors. I've decided I prefer painting people." She would resume her portraiture work after their return to London. Henry's promotion had been publicly announced a fortnight ago, and he would take his place as head clerk in another fortnight. In the meantime, they were enjoying their delayed honeymoon at the Burroughs' country estate.

"The work you've done so far is beautiful," he assured her. "You will finish it, won't you?"

She nodded. "Another time. Maybe later today."

"And in the meantime?"

Laura used the flat of one hand to spread open the top of his banyan. "There's a particular subject I'd like to continue studying."

"Oh?"

"For the painting that's to hang above my headboard in the mistress suite."

Henry blinked and then glanced down as her hand

continued spreading the silk from his chest and then from one shoulder. "Me?" he guessed, remembering the painting she had done of him that now hung above the fireplace mantel in her bedchamber.

Having been asleep for the times she had sketched him, he hadn't even been aware he had been modeling for the painting that depicted him half-covered by bed clothes whilst half-awake, his gaze aimed at the viewer.

"Mmm."

He kissed her forehead. "I rather like being studied," he murmured, remembering how she would smooth her fingers over his skin with the claim that she was learning its texture. "So much more fun than posing."

She arched a brow. "Then we'll have to move to a more comfortable location," she suggested, urging him toward the house.

"Can I study you, too?" he asked as he offered his arm. "You're so much more interesting than numbers."

"I'm counting on it," she replied. "No pun intended," she added when she saw his grin of delight.

*M*eanwhile, at the townhouse of Lady and Mr. Wellingham, 10 Kingly Street

"Twins?" Hannah cried out as her hands went to her belly. "Are you quite sure?"

Dr. Regan nodded, pulling his odd instrument from his ear. The other end of the flared tube had been pressed against Lady Wellingham's bare midsection.

"Quite." He had learned much of his medical knowledge from his father, a physician who had seen to soldiers in the Napoleonic Wars and was later a doctor to a duke in Sussex. "I do not know why you express such surprise, my lady. You yourself were a twin, were you not?"

Hannah frowned at the physician. "I am *still* a twin, but what has that got to do with it?"

"Twins tend to run in families, my lady."

Hannah's eyes widened, her thoughts going to her new sister by marriage. When she'd last seen Laura, she had thought her pregnancy even more evident than her own, which had led her to believe her brother had bedded his wife well before their wedding night.

Perhaps she was merely larger because she was also carrying two babies instead of just one. "Oh, dear," Hannah murmured with worry.

"What is it?"

"My brother's wife could be carrying twins as well. She's rather... rotund already," she said as she waved a hand in a circle over her own belly.

Dr. Regan furrowed a brow. "Mr. Simpson's wife is not a patient of mine, so I cannot say for sure."

"But it's possible?"

He nodded. "Indeed."

Hannah sighed. "Then I suppose we shall wallow in pity together as our feet swell along with our bellies," she lamented. Edward might have been born seventeen years ago, but she still remembered the ravages of pregnancy on her body.

Frowning, Dr. Regan said, "Or you could prevail upon your husband to rub your feet every night."

Hannah blinked. "What's this?"

Dr. Regan shrugged. "Whilst at dinner, you might mention the need to have a footman rub your feet at night. My other patients find it remarkable that their husbands are quick to take on the duty instead of allowing a servant to do so."

A grin appeared, and Hannah admonished the doctor. "But thank you for the suggestion," she added, thinking of what it would be like to have Graham gripping her tiny feet between his large hands.

On second thought, she decided the physician had a good point.

*W*hen Graham was performing those very ministrations later that night, he asked what she had done about her feet during her pregnancy with Edward.

"As I recall, I didn't suffer overmuch," she replied, her hands held atop her rounded belly. "Not like now." She allowed a moan of satisfaction when he rubbed a particularly sore spot, his warm hands chasing away the autumn chill.

"I suppose it's far more noticeable when you're carrying more than one babe," he reasoned.

Hannah blinked. "How do you know that?"

Graham gave her a quelling glance. "I have my arm wrapped around them whilst we sleep," he reminded her, rather glad she still allowed him to spoon his body around hers so her back was against his chest and his knees were tucked behind hers. He gave up his hold on her foot and held out the arm. With his other hand, he pointed to the inside of his elbow, then his forearm, his wrist, and then the palm of his hand. "There are more than two feet in there."

Hannah giggled. "According to Dr. Regan, there are. Edward will be over the moon when I tell him."

A knock sounded at their bedchamber door.

"Come," Hannah called out, thinking it was her lady's maid.

The door opened, but only a fraction. Edward peeked around the edge. "I promise, I wasn't eavesdropping. I just came to tell you I'm off to Brooks's. But, I couldn't help but overhear... tell me what?" their son asked. His eyes widened when he saw his father holding one of his mother's feet.

"Your mother isn't carrying a four-legged child," Graham stated as he managed to keep a straight face.

Edward blinked and then gave a huff. "Oh, you mean because she's having twins?" he countered.

Both Hannah and Graham stared at their son. "How did you know?"

He shrugged as he stepped farther into the room and closed the door. "You're rather large already," he replied, his gaze going to his mother. "Almost as large as Aunt Laura."

"Edward," Graham scolded.

"It's all right," Hannah murmured. "I rather imagine she's having twins as well." She patted the bed next to where she lounged. "Come in for a moment so I can tell you how proud I am of you."

Edward lifted a knee and settled on the edge of the bed. "I am glad to hear it, especially since this situation means I won't be going to Oxford," he replied.

"I do hope you don't regret having to take a seat in Parliament so soon," Graham said. The baron's writ of acceleration had been accepted, and Edward was due to take his grandfather's place in the House of Lords the following week. "You're having to take on a lot of responsibility at a very young age."

"I don't think I will regret it," Edward replied as he watched his father rub his mother's foot. "Besides, you were working when you were seventeen, were you not?"

Graham nodded. "I was twelve when Mother taught me how to enter numbers in a ledger and fifteen when I started working in the warehouse," he acknowledged.

"My taking on the earldom does mean I will have to spend some time at Harrington House," Edward said. "All the papers for the earldom are in the study there, you see," he explained. "But I plan to spend my nights here, at least until I'm older."

"I'm so glad to hear it," Hannah said with a huge grin. "With the Mayfields having left on holiday, I feared you would choose to live there."

Prior to the Mayfields' departure for the Continent, the earl announced he would be spending most of the time eating, drinking, and tupping his wife. Meanwhile, Temperance had quietly resigned from her position at *The Tattler*, claiming it was time Patience Comber find a younger assistant.

Despite her every effort to learn the identity of the new gossip maven who might replace Temperance, Hannah had no idea who the Countess of Aimsley had tapped for the duty. Given she would be spending the next couple of months in confinement, Hannah decided the timing could not have been better to be out of Society.

"I thought about it, but..." Edward allowed the sentence to trail off.

"What is it?" Hannah asked as she pushed her other foot towards Graham. "This one now, please."

"I'm soon going to be an older brother. I'd like to be here, since I've never had siblings before."

Hannah exchanged a glance with Graham.

"I'm an only child," Graham said. "And you didn't have any younger siblings," he said to Hannah. "We've no idea what these babes will mean for you," he added as he turned his gaze back on his son.

"There's no need to worry about me," Edward replied. "I intend to be an excellent brother. I'll play with the boy and provide protection for my sister."

"You'll make an excellent lord, as well," Hannah remarked. "I don't think I've ever seen you so determined about anything."

Edward placed one of his hands over hers and gave it a shake. "Thank you, Mother. And thank you for the information about the babes. This helps my odds immensely."

"Odds?" Graham repeated, his brows furrowing as he ceased rubbing Hannah's foot. "How so?"

"In the betting book at Brooks's. Right now, the money is on a boy, but there's no mention of twins. I can put money on a boy and a girl and win no matter what," he said proudly.

Graham regarded his son with a smirk. "What if she has two boys? Or two girls?"

Edward's face fell. "Oh," he said on a heavy sigh. "Can that happen?"

"Perhaps it would be better if you didn't gamble at all," Graham murmured. "Your siblings ever find out you bet against them and you may discover there's no such thing as brotherly love."

Hannah tittered when Graham drew a fingertip down the middle of her instep, her foot jerking in his hold.

"Point taken, Father," Edward replied. He leaned closer and asked in a whisper, "Is what you're doing there some sort of... of foreplay?"

Graham struggled to keep a straight face. "Why, yes, son, yes, it is," he replied.

A blush covering his neck and cheeks, Edward announced, "I'm off," as he quickly took his leave of the bedchamber.

Hannah watched him go, her eyes widening. "What did he ask you?"

Graham had already given up his hold on her foot. He was kissing her belly and then one of her breasts through the fabric of her night rail before he whispered, "He asked if it was time for me to make love to you."

Hannah gasped. "He didn't!"

"Ah, but it is," Graham murmured before he took her lips with his and kissed her. "I have to teach those two not to kick their mother," he added before he resumed his lovemaking.

The following morning, he awoke with a rather sore arm.

# AUTHOR'S NOTES

The early life of the Simpsons and the Wellinghams are included in the books, The Promise of a Gentleman and The Pride of a Gentleman, both included in The Cousins of the Aristocracy: Boxed Set. The story of how the Earl and Countess of Mayfield acquired *The Tattler* can be found in The Gossip of an Earl. The Desire of a Lady, Lady Lily's tall tales of her experiences with aristocratic suitors, includes how she and William Overby finally achieve their happily-ever-after.

Family charts for the characters in the various Aristocracy series can be found at https://www.lindaraesande.com/familycharts.html.

*King Street*

Up until 1918, King Street intersected with Oxford Street near where Swallow Passage is today. In 1819 its northern section was replaced by Regent Street. The remaining southern section of King Street is now known as Kingly Street, and the buildings that made up the set of townhouses the Simpsons owned are mostly still in existence, their lower floors a variety of shops, restaurants, and nightclubs.

*Portraits*

Until photography was perfected, painted portraits were the means by which the titled, the rich, and the middle class had their images captured on canvas. Couples were frequently painted shortly after their weddings and families upon the occasion of a boy's breeching or other important event. The older portraits in a house or castle were usually hung in a portrait gallery—a wide hall along which generations of family members could be viewed at one time—while newer paintings might be hung above fireplaces or in a salon where callers could see them.

Portraits were also painted as miniatures, which required a steady hand and tiny brushes. They could be worn as brooches or as pendants or carried in a pocket in addition to finding homes on fireplace mantels or parlor tables. These popular paintings were frequently reproduced as prints for use in book illustrations or cards.

Joshua Reynolds, the first president of the Royal Academy and principal painter to George III, was a master of gestures and poses while Thomas Gainsborough was a natural painter. George Romney practiced the classicized style and John Hoppner was considered truthful. Probably due to his own family of five children, Hoppner was good at capturing childish traits in his subjects.

Reynolds was succeeded as the royal artist by Thomas Lawrence, a painter who specialized in vivid, romantic images characterized by flawless, exuberant handling.

*Parures*

Wives of aristocrats frequently owned complete *parures*, or matching sets of jewelry that included earrings, a ring, a necklace of either long or short length, a brooch and two bracelets. A matching diadem or tiara and a jeweled belt were also worn with evening wear. The stylish or tasteful never wore the complete set at the same time as the "less-is-more" attitude was adopted during the Regency era (a marked contrast to the Georgian era before it).

# ABOUT THE AUTHOR

A self-described nerd and student of history, Linda Rae spent many years as a published technical writer specializing in 3D graphics workstations, software and 3D animation (her movie credits include SHREK and SHREK 2). Getting lost in the rabbit holes of research has resulted in historical romances set in the Regency-era as well as Ancient Greece.

A fan of action-adventure movies, she can frequently be found at the local cinema. Although she no longer has any tropical fish, she follows the San Jose Sharks and makes her home in Cody, Wyoming.

*For more information:*
www.lindaraesande.com
*Sign up for Linda Rae's newsletter:*
Regency Romance with a Twist
*Follow Linda Rae's blog:*
Regency Romance with a Twist